SAVING
Evangeline

NANCEE CAIN

D1712132

OMNIFIC PUBLISHING
LOS ANGELES

Omnific Publishing
1901 Avenue of the Stars, 2nd floor
Los Angeles, CA 90067
www.omnificpublishing.com

First Omnific eBook edition, May 2015
First Omnific trade paperback edition, May 2015

The characters and events in this book are fictitious.
Any similarity to real persons, living or dead,
is coincidental and not intended by the author.

Library of Congress Cataloguing-in-Publication Data

Cain, Nancee.
   Saving Evangeline / Nancee Cain – 1st ed.
   ISBN: 978-1-623422-02-8
   1. Supernatural Romance — Fiction. 2. Angels — Fiction.
   3. Suicide — Fiction. 4. Forbidden Romance — Fiction. I. Title

10 9 8 7 6 5 4 3 2 1

Cover Design by Micha Stone and Amy Brokaw
Interior Book Design by Coreen Montagna

Printed in the United States of America

To my parents,
who have always encouraged me to pursue my dreams,
and to my dear friend, Jill Odom,
who pointed me in the right direction.

Chapter One

"This is the third time this century we've had this conversation, Remiel."

I watch as the Boss hits the golf ball with a perfect swing and aces the hole. He grins widely and does a fist pump into the air. The odds of an amateur acing that par three shot is probably twelve thousand, five hundred to one, a pro maybe twenty-five hundred to one. But when you're *Him* it happens every time. And every damn — er — darn time He acts surprised.

That's my problem. *Everything here is so predictably perfect.*

He turns to me and I gulp, knowing He's just read my mind. The frown on His face is like witnessing an eclipse of the sun. "Thank you for correcting your language. Now, where were we?"

I take a minute, trying to decide if He's using the royal We, or if he means Him and me. Opting on *us,* I kick at a pebble and mumble, "This is the third time this century I've met with You in regard to my shenanigans." *Shenanigan* is His word, not mine. I sigh and wait for the inevitable *talk.* I concentrate on the ground, gritting my teeth with frustration and trying my best not to roll my eyes. I don't seek trouble on purpose. It's drawn to me like a magnet.

Okay, so maybe that's a lie. I may *occasionally* try to shake things up around here just to break the monotony. The last time I was in trouble, He asked me if I'd changed my name to Legion. I didn't think it was that funny, but everyone else did, especially that old windbag, Peter. Which is precisely why I played that innocent little prank on the old goat.

The Boss nudges my wing with His golf club. "Ah, yes. You know how Peter cherishes those keys. There's no need to test one's free will in paradise. I don't know why you like to torment him by hiding them. And there's nothing wrong with the word shenanigan. It's a lovely word. I like the way it rolls off the tongue. Nice catch on the eye rolling, by the way. You know I find it disrespectful."

"Yes, Sir." *He always knows.*

"Why, Remiel?" His voice is calm and even, not irritating and whiny like Peter's.

"Why what, Sir?" I wish He'd just get on with the punishment and skip the lecture. Oops, not punishment. They aren't called punishments *here.* They're *learning lessons.*

"Why do you insist on going rook?" He leans on the golf club, waiting for my answer.

"Excuse me?" *What the fuck is going rook?* "I'm not sure I understand what you mean, Sir."

"Watch your language, Remiel."

It sucks when your Boss is an om-omni…Dang, I never can keep those "omni" words straight. *Know-it-all.*

He sighs and the trees rustle with the impact. "The word is omniscient, but know-it-all is fine as long as you say it, or think it with respect." His face lights up and I blink from the brilliance, wishing I'd worn my sunglasses. "I need to brush up on modern slang. I'll add it to My to-do-list." Like a kid with a new toy, He whips out His phone and taps in the reminder. It's not that He needs a phone *or* a reminder. He just loves gadgets. He's often said the twenty-first century would be His favorite of all times if people would just set aside their petty quarrels and actually talk to one another. It's His opinion there's no reason *not* to, it's the age of communication, after all.

Putting the phone away, His gaze sweeps over the golf greens. The sigh this time is deeper, causing a rumble of thunder that lets me know He's tired of my stall tactics. "Now back to the issue at hand. Why do you insist on bucking the system, Remiel?"

Ah! He meant going rogue, not rook. I bite the inside of my lip to keep from laughing. "I'm bored," I blurt out. He stares at me and one bushy eyebrow rises. I tag on a hasty, "Sir."

"You're bored?"

I nod, warming to the subject. "Everything is just too perfect around here. It's monotonous. The humans have it made. They get to experience so much more with their free will. I think we should be allowed more than one weekend off every forty or fifty years—"

He holds up His hand. "Enough. Need I remind you, that you get in trouble every time you're away? Hell-raising is never productive, dear boy. Didn't you learn anything from Lucifer?"

I can't contain my sigh of frustration. *He just doesn't get it.*

The Boss pulls on His lower lip and narrows His eyes. "I suppose you think it would be more fun putting out *fires* down below?"

I swallow and back up a step. "Er, well, not *too* far below, Sir. Just say, on Earth." I press my lips together determined to keep my mouth shut before I get in even more trouble. If I'm not careful, I'm liable to be stuck being Peter's lackey forever. My last *learning lesson* occurred after my weekend of excess at Woodstock during the "Summer of Love." I've been manning the registration desk at the Pearly Gates ever since. Talk about a mind-numbing, lobotomizing job. Giving the same old mundane welcome speech to the newcomers is like being a stewardess reviewing airline safety. No one listens or cares.

He clears His throat pulling my attention back to Him. "Using the terms mind-numbing and lobotomizing together is redundant." The twinkle in His eyes make my feathers stand on edge. "I think I have the perfect job for you. Maybe you won't find it too *boring…*"

Oh shi—shoot. This isn't going to be good.

I land on my ass with a thud. I'm in Hell. No, it's too humid to be Hell. Standing, I dust off my pants, careful not to rustle my feathers, which must be concealed when on Earth.

My eyes damn near pop out of my head when I realize what I'm wearing. Dark pants, a clerical shirt, stiff uncomfortable white collar, a rosary in my pocket and a shiny cross on my chest. Aghast, I look toward heaven and glare. "Not funny, Sir."

A gentle breeze rustles the trees in answer. Other than the moon and a dim light from a bridge to my left, it's eerily dark out here. A glance at my watch reveals it's ten o'clock and I'm in the middle of nowhere dressed like a priest. He really should get over my weekend at Woodstock. "Ever hear of forgiveness, Sir?" I mutter under my breath.

Again, a gust whips the trees, reminding me He's aware of everything that's going on and is not amused. My attitude is what always gets me in trouble. Confused, I try to figure out why I'm here in the guise of a priest. I'm sure He and Peter are enjoying a good laugh over this.

Running a finger under the tight collar, I stomp toward the vehicle parked ten feet from me. Muttering one of Luc's favorite words, I open the car door and find keys with a St. Christopher key chain dangling in the ignition. I kind of wish he'd given me back the VW camper I had at Woodstock—the one with peace signs on it. That van saw some good times. Rummaging through the glove box, I find the Florida registration for the car and insurance papers listing Remiel Blackson as the owner. Blackson? Really? I couldn't be Remiel Goodson? A cell phone on the seat rings with the theme from *Charlie's Angels*. It's the Boss's favorite television show from the seventies.

It's passcode protected and takes me three tries to figure out He'd programmed it with *6666*. I get the not-so-subliminal message. I guess even He couldn't get past the four-digit requirement. My tech-savvy Boss has texted my assignment which I read as I exit the car.

You are Father Remiel Blackson,
a Roman Catholic priest on sabbatical.
Save Evangeline Lourdes Salvatore.
PS: Smoking is bad for you,
and don't drink and drive.

Roman Catholic? That means celibate, the spoilsport. I look around in disbelief. I'm on a deserted road in south Florida. How the heck am I supposed to find this Evangeline Salvatore? He hasn't given me any info and I'm not omni—whatever. I'm not a know-it-all. "All due respect, Sir," I add quickly.

Google, of course, it's the twenty-first century answer for everything. I'm excited to get to use the new technology I've been following from Boringville. Thunder rumbles in the distance. *Heaven*, I meant heaven. I type her name into the search engine on the phone and find a few sensationalist articles about her involvement in a tragic wreck that killed a man. It even has her address for home and work. She's a hair stylist, and the name of her salon is The Curl Up 'n Dye. The Boss is right; modern technology is amazing.

I'm about to leave when I notice a lone figure on the bridge. Dark, tangled hair spirals down her back, and her clothes hang loosely on her frame. As I watch, she marches back and forth talking to herself, looking like a wild, sleek panther ready to attack at any moment. Occasionally, she wipes her cheeks and then clenches her fists, but she continues pacing like a caged animal.

The girl stops and peers over the side of the bridge. Swinging one leg over the railing, she freezes. A feeling of dread overcomes me. *Holy shit!* I race toward her in a full-blown panic. I know in my gut it's her and it is my job to stop her.

"Don't do it," a deep male voice commands.

A whisper of a breeze caresses my cheek. With a frustrated sigh, I lower my foot and drag my gaze from the murky, dark water that beckons me with its siren's song. Glaring at the unwelcome intruder, I dash the tears from my cheeks. He stands in the shadow, and all I can make out is that he's tall with broad shoulders. Striding toward me, hands in his pockets, he starts whistling. The thought occurs to me I should be scared and run, but it's as if I'm glued to the spot. As he comes into the light, I see he's a priest. But he doesn't look like any priest I've ever known. This guy is Hollywood gorgeous. Under the dim light, he appears almost incandescent and his emerald eyes seem lit from within. Their intensity burns a hole into my paper-thin bravado, which slips away and disappears like ashes in the wind.

Dammit, I'd just worked up the courage to follow through with my plan to leave this nightmare behind, and this stranger has interrupted, dragging me back to my personal hell on earth.

Feeling naked and vulnerable under his steadfast scrutiny, I cross my arms in front of my chest, desperately trying to contain the welling anxiety building within me. A black mass flutters behind him, and I blink to clear my eyes. *Please, not again, not now.* My mother and the doctor's dire warnings about not taking my medication taunt my tortured mind.

Clutching my head with my hands, I scream to scare my demons away. Sometimes this technique worked when I was in the hospital. More times, than not, it just got me a nice mind-numbing cocktail of drugs, that would leave me nauseated and dizzy for days.

"No, no, no." I march away from the stranger, pacing back and forth, feeling trapped. These hallucinations are part of the reason why I'm here. Now my resolve to end them, once and for all, is shaken. With a trembling hand, I rake my fingers through my snarled hair. Yuck. *When did I last bathe?* My greasy hair feels like tangled string. I must look like a crazy woman.

Laughter layered with a tinge of overwrought hysteria bubbles from deep within me at this last thought. Surely an out-of-control, wild woman will scare this guy away. It usually does. Most folks never look me in the eye. It's like they're afraid my insanity is either contagious or a superpower I can use to slay them.

"Feel better?" His voice isn't patronizing. I'm used to Father Asswipe handing out condescension like communion wafers. This priest asked a simple question, and strangely, I find I *do* feel a little better. He approaches me like I'm a rabid animal, his movements slow and deliberate.

There was a time—not so long ago—when the white collar under his chin would have soothed me. I was raised a good Catholic girl, but we all know the road to hell is paved with good intentions. My descent to non-repentant sinner isn't my mother's fault. I accept full responsibility for fucking up my own life.

Tonight, the sight of the starched white collar does the opposite. It pisses me off as lingering guilt from my upbringing hangs suspended between us like a bridge between saint and sinner. I pull my clenched hands to my waist, preparing for the lecture and platitudes on the sanctity of life. I've heard it over and over throughout the years from my mother, Father Ashton, Sunday school teachers, social workers, psychiatrists, and even the damn cop who arrested me the last time I tried to kill myself.

I'd swallowed the entire damn medicine cabinet and somehow, thanks to my "hearty constitution," made it to the street in front of our house where I was found staggering, oblivious to my surroundings and out of touch with reality. The shrink told me I'd been in the process of being arrested for disorderly conduct when my mom dashed out of the house screaming and crying about what I'd done.

Instead, they rushed me to the hospital to have my stomach pumped. Lesson learned? Plan your suicide. Don't do it on an impulse when your mom is home.

He sighs. "I'm going to say it one more time. Don't do it."

"Don't do what?" I sneer. The nerve of this priest presuming — however correct his supposition is — to know my motives.

"Don't jump." His warm baritone voice fills the air with something akin to the energy felt before a lightning storm. The hairs on my arms stand up.

"What makes you think I'm going to jump, *Father?*" I make no attempt to hide my derision, hoping my rudeness will make him turn around and leave. It worked like a charm with my mother. I've managed to push her clear across the country.

"Let me rephrase. *Please* don't jump. I can't swim," he confesses with a small smile. "Do you want to have to explain my death as well as your own?" His eyes crinkle and seem to dance with amusement, which serves to light the match to my short fuse. The wind picks up and ruffles his hair, causing the natural highlights to dance against his dark brown hair. The ends curl appealingly on the back of his neck and one lock falls on his forehead. It's a bit long for a priest, but the beautician and woman in me wouldn't change a thing. He's beautiful.

"Since I don't believe in God, or the hereafter, no explanations would be necessary. You're boring me, so just leave me the hell alone, and go do your good deeds elsewhere."

His answering bark of laughter triggers my anxiety, and a wall of paranoia flies up around me. *Is he laughing at me?* I square my shoulders and utilize my menacing crazy stare. "What's so funny?"

"I haven't been accused of doing *good deeds* in a long damn time." A rumble of thunder rolls in the distance, and a strong blast of air shakes the trees, signaling a storm is brewing.

"I would think that's your business." I raise one eyebrow, looking pointedly at his collar and the silver cross glinting on his chest. The cross and priest garb are incongruent with his drop-dead gorgeous looks and mild profanity. Of course, the only priest I know personally is old Father Ashton. The ancient priest has to be at least seventy-five and has disgusting nose hairs and bad breath.

He runs a finger along the inside of the collar as if it's too tight. My mind wonders what it would be like to have his fingers run along my body. I shake my head to rid it of the ridiculous image. Maybe I'm sicker than they say I am.

He frowns. "Ah, yes…*this*. It is a bit ironic." He cut his eyes toward the sky with what could only be described as a look of annoyance before settling his curious gaze back on me. His wide, easy smile adds to his attractiveness. "Come on, let's go. You can buy me a drink."

"Excuse me?" My mouth falls open. *Buy him a drink?*

"Vow of poverty, Crazy Girl." His arms sweep out in a self-deprecating manner. "So to thank me, you can buy me a drink."

"I'm not crazy, and what do I have to thank you for?"

He raises one eyebrow and smirks. I huff with annoyance.

"Okay so I'm crazy, whatever. What do I have to thank you for?"

"Why, for saving your miserable, worthless life, of course." He throws an arm around my shoulders as if he's my damn *BFF* and guides me toward the end of the bridge. Strangely, my anxiety—my constant companion for two years—begins to crumble under his casual embrace. This in itself is terrifying. I don't know how to function anymore except in full-blown panic mode.

"What makes you think my life is miserable and worthless?" I shrug away from him, annoyed he's verbalized the obvious. My life *is* miserable and worthless. To be precise, it's downright pathetic.

"Why were you about to jump?" He pats his pockets and frowns. "Hey, you got a cigarette?"

"Ew." I wrinkle my nose with disgust. "No, I don't smoke. It's a nasty habit."

A grin spreads across his face. He's much too handsome to be a cleric with those angular cheekbones and strong, clean-shaven jaw. I bet he has a huge cult following of unsatisfied, female parishioners who love to go into great detail about their non-existent, fantasy-filled sex lives in the confessional. Hell, I'd like to do him in the confessional…

"Not nearly as nasty as Sister Winifred's habit, but that's another story. We all have our vices, don't we? Tell me, Evangeline Lourdes Salvatore, what's yours?"

"I go by Evie—" I stop short and cross my arms in front of my chest, narrowing my eyes. "Wait—how do you know my name?"

"It's my business to know. So what are your vices? Tell me all about them, and if they're really good and juicy, in minute detail, please." Chuckling, he grabs my hand and leads me toward the end of the bridge. I sputter with indignation, sounding like the dying desk fan that sits on my station at the salon. *Former station,* I quit yesterday.

"Your business? I'm none of your business! What kind of sick bastard are you?" I pull away from him again, and my pulse pounds in my ears as the bitter taste of fear floods my mouth. A shiver of apprehension creeps over my body. Trying to be discreet, I take a step back.

It's late and I'm alone on a deserted road in rural Florida with a handsome stranger who knows my name. This is the stuff of low-budget horror movies. *They're out to get me again.* I squelch the thought as my survival instinct kicks into super-drive. Which is kind of bizarre, since just moments ago I wanted to die.

"Leave me alone." I'm not sure if I'm speaking to him or the voices in my head. *Don't panic, this isn't a movie. Don't turn your back to him.* Trying to act nonchalant, I scan the ground searching for anything to use as a weapon. Dammit, I left my purse with pepper spray in it at the edge of the bridge.

"Take the frightened gazelle look down a notch. I'm not going to hurt you." He shoves his hands in his pockets and continues down the bridge — humming of all things — Led Zeppelin's "Stairway to Heaven."

"So says every sociopath in every slasher movie ever made," I grumble. But, for some strange reason, I believe him. Maybe it's the collar. I'm following him like he's the damn Pied Piper of Hamlin.

"Evangeline, if I'd wanted to *hurt* you, I would have done so already. I'm here to *save* you."

My unladylike snort would make my mother twinge. "Seriously. Tell me how you know my name, Father…?" *Please don't say you've heard the gossip.*

"Blackson. Remiel Blackson. But, you can call me Remi. Like I said, it's my business to know. Aren't you a parishioner of Our Lady of Perpetual Chaos?"

This time I laugh at his corruption of our parish church name and the absurdity of his statement. A parishioner? *As if.* "I haven't been to church in a long time, Father. I attend St. Mattress on the Springs. Everyone knows I'm a sinner of the worst kind." I'm not bragging. It's a well-known fact. Ask anyone in the godforsaken town where I've lived my entire twenty-one years. If you can call it living; maybe existed would be a better word.

"Oh, good!" He yanks his hands from his pockets and rubs them together in the worst over-acted imitation of a stage villain I've ever seen. I bite my lip to keep from smiling. "The *worst* kind of sinner is my favorite. You might even say it's my specialty. So, come on, evil Evie, tell me the worst thing you've ever done. Consider the confessional booth open and in business. I promise to go light on penance and heavy on absolution." He nudges my shoulder as we walk toward the end of the bridge.

"I c-can't." For some peculiar reason, even though everyone in the entire damn county knows why I'm a horrible person, I don't want this priest to know — not yet. He'll find out soon enough if he listens to the gossip. I'm notorious, and my reputation is widespread.

"Fine. But if it makes you feel better, I've probably done far worse myself."

I roll my eyes in a childish manner. "Yeah, right. Like what, drink a little too much of the sacramental wine? Trust me, whatever you've done can't compare." Laced with a mixture of shame and anger, my voice sounds bitter even to my own ears. Before I realize it, we're standing next to his car, and I notice he's picked up my purse on the way.

"Evangeline, sins aren't a game of one-upmanship. They're mistakes, and I've made plenty of them. I haven't always been a priest, you know." He opens the car door for me. As I slip past him into the car, the nostalgic scent of fresh cut pine boughs and cinnamon assaults my senses. Damn if he doesn't smell like Christmas in August. He shuts the door, and I reach over and switch the ignition so I can roll down the window and turn on the interior light.

Turning back to face him I ask, "Now what?" My voice trembles a little, which pisses me off. Why is this priest affecting me so?

Remi leans down and peers at me, his clasped hands resting on the open window. A hint of a smile flickers across his face. I like the laugh lines that crinkle by his mesmerizing eyes. He looks to be just a few years older than I am. I realize I haven't been around anyone close to my age since Jack. Lately, it's been my lot in life to attract older men. The worst was old Mr. Locke who couldn't get it up and ended up crying on my chest all night. What's wrong with me? I'm thinking about sex? *This man is a priest.*

"Isn't this where you're supposed to scoot over and drive off in my car, continuously looking behind you while I crash in through the windshield or sunroof?" he teases.

Stunned, I don't know how to react. No one has teased me in a long time. Most people ignore me or walk around me on pins and needles, waiting for either my head to spin around, or for me to vomit pea soup. Or, like old Mr. Locke, men use me for their own pleasure, thinking my reputation gives them license to take advantage of me. *What if he isn't teasing?*

Jesus, what the hell? I bite my lip, realizing my foolishness. I'm sitting in a complete stranger's car. Even if he does wear a priest's collar, it's no reason to blindly trust him. And yet, I don't feel compelled to get out of the car and run. He just isn't scary. *Most sociopath murderers probably aren't, you idiot. Ever hear of Ted Bundy?* I look out the windshield into the dark nothingness of my surroundings. We're miles from civilization.

Who is this priest? I don't remember hearing any town gossip about old Father Asswipe retiring. Where the hell is he from, and how did he get here? It took me hours to walk here. I chose this place because of its remoteness, and I never heard his car drive up. *Maybe he flew here.* I squeeze my eyes shut, shoving the ridiculous thought aside. *Dumb ass, you were busy concentrating on ending it.* He had to have driven up. My breathing saws erratically and blood pounds in my ears as my thoughts scatter like confetti in the wind.

He reaches a hand in the window and strokes my hair, the way I used to pet our cat, Duchess. It's soothing and comforting. "It's okay. I know you're scared," he murmurs. My breathing eases, and my heart quits hammering. A sense of warmth and peace surrounds me. I give in to this strange new feeling, tired of my lifelong struggle to keep my thoughts coherent.

Sucking in a shallow breath, I draw my gaze to his. Flames seem to spark and flare in the depths of his pupils. When I was a little girl I would lie in the backyard staring at the clouds in the blue sky and talk to the angels. At the time, my mother complained about my overactive imagination. I've always maintained it was real, despite the professionals labeling it as a symptom of my *disease*. The feeling of comfort from back then is the one that comes over me now. I blink and the flames disappear. I must be more exhausted than I realized. What do I have to lose by trusting him?

As a matter of fact, he might be doing me a favor. I think suicide is a mortal sin, which would embarrass my mom. If I'm murdered, I could have a full Catholic funeral without the guilt, and she can accept any condolences without the humiliation. *And dead is dead, after all.*

I swallow my fear and take a deep breath as I gaze at the cross dangling from his chest. It sways gently back and forth, and I wonder if a religious magician is hypnotizing me. "If you kill me, will you at least promise to make it quick and easy, with minimal pain?" My question is only half-kidding.

He reaches in the car and tips my chin up so he can look into my eyes. "I don't believe I could cause you any more pain than what you're already dealing with, do you?" The scent of Christmas infiltrates the car, and again, I have the peaceful sensation of staring at the sky and talking to the celestial host. I attempt to swallow the lump in the back of my throat, but it won't go away. All I can do is shrug my shoulders in a combination of pretend indifference and defeat. I realize it isn't him I'm scared to trust. It's me. I don't know how to deal with kindness.

"You're overwrought and tired. I'm going to drive you home, okay?"

"Okay," I whisper.

He's right. My nerves are shot, my battery drained, and my limbs feel like lead. All I want to do is curl up and sleep. And yet, I'm afraid of the nightmares that have plagued me for two years. I never sleep until exhaustion sets in, and then only in two-hour stretches, at the most. The last time I slept was two nights ago.

He walks around to the driver's side and eases into the car, snapping off the interior light. With the darkness, a lost, empty feeling engulfs me. He's taking me home. In my mind, I'm already dead. My house is my tomb. As if sensing my reluctance and fear, Remi turns and pulls me into his arms, holding me tight. Beneath the drab clerical shirt he's all hard muscle and his presence is one of quiet strength. I feel safe for the first time in what seems forever—encompassed in his dark wings. I squeeze my eyes tighter and my finger traces the outline of the cross he wears. *Arms, not wings.* I pull away embarrassed by my whimsical musings.

He smiles as he fastens his seatbelt. "Buckle up, Crazy Girl. If we have an accident, you don't want to die because you weren't wearing your seatbelt, do you?"

My heart sinks into my stomach, and I clench my fists in my lap. *He does know.* Father Asswipe must have given him an earful, or it could have been anyone else for that matter. I'm more than famous. I'm *infamous.* I frown and search his face by the dim light on the dashboard, looking for condemnation, horror, or mocking cruelty, but find none. His lips curl in to a sly smirk. I smack his arm as his warm laughter fills the car. "Nobody likes a smart ass, Father."

"Sure they do. Everyone likes me. And please, call me Remi."

He pulls out to the main road and flips on the radio. Thank God, it isn't a country station. Casting me a sideways glance and an easy grin, he opens the sunroof. I find myself smiling in return and feeling strangely carefree being in the company of someone who doesn't seem to give a damn about my past. I can't remember the last time I've felt this way. Feeling impulsive and reckless, I unbuckle my seatbelt and stand in my seat, squeezing through the sunroof to inhale the heavy, humid night air.

Storm clouds are gathering in the distance, but overhead it's clear and millions of stars twinkle like glitter on black velvet. There's no traffic on the deserted back road, and I squeal with delight when Remi kicks the speed up and cuts off the headlights. We're submerged in darkness, the road lit only by the illumination of the moon. For a brief moment I'm frightened. *Is being scared shitless becoming some sort of warped addiction?* On the radio, Pearl Jam wails "Given to Fly," and Remi cranks it up full blast as we fly down the road at a breakneck speed.

"Spread your wings and give in to the moment," he shouts, followed by a loud rebel yell as he pumps the air with his fist, sounding like a teenager on a joyride instead of a priest saving a crazy girl. His laughter is like a bright light in a dark cavern and fills the empty hole where my soul should exist. I look down at him and find myself grinning. His hair is a disheveled mess, and his pure ecstasy at living in the moment is intoxicating. I want to drink in his bliss. My hair blows behind me in chaotic disarray and goose bumps appear on my arms, but whether from the cold air, or fear, I don't know, or care. In this moment, I'm liberated from the nightmare that is now my life. I throw my head back, shut my eyes, and hold out my arms. It's both terrifying and thrilling.

I'm flying.

I'm free.

I'm alive.

Chapter Two

As we near the town where I've lived all my life and hoped to never see again, Remi flips on the headlights and slows to the speed limit. My moment of freedom is gone. My shoulders sag as the harsh reality of my life settles back onto my shoulders. I lower myself into the car and buckle my seatbelt, my limbs heavy, making my movements clumsy. He's taking me home. I swallow back my tears of frustration and clench my fists in my lap. He wouldn't understand. No one does.

He pulls in to the parking lot of a convenience store on the outskirts of town and parks the car. "Do you mind picking up a pack of smokes and maybe a six-pack of beer for me?"

"Because you *saved* my life, right?"

"You got it, Crazy Girl." He winks at me as he pulls money out of his wallet and hands it to me.

My mouth goes dry. No, he did *not* just wink at me; it's my mind playing tricks again, dammit. He's a priest, for God's sake.

"I thought you said you took a vow of poverty?"

"Well, I may have told a little white lie on that one. I'm not a monk." Thunder rolls in the distance and clouds have moved in, obscuring the moon and stars. "Please? People get weirded out by the collar. They forget priests are *humans*, too."

With a huff of annoyance, I slam out of the car to do his bidding, unable to explain this power he seems to have over me. Although, why am I surprised? Since Jack's death I've allowed men to have power over me on any number of occasions, and this is the least of them.

I throw open the door and storm into the store. The meth-head clerk behind the counter doesn't bother to look up from his porn as I slam a six-pack of beer on the counter, grab a lighter, a chocolate bar, and a dashboard hula-girl. When he doesn't acknowledge my presence, I hop on the counter and reach, snatching a pack of cigarettes.

I catch a glimpse of my warped reflection in the mirror used to prevent shoplifting, and I'm glad Ms. Fake Tits of August has the guy's undivided attention. I look like an escapee from a mental institute with my wide eyes and tangled mess of hair. I snicker over the irony. The clerk rings me up without looking up from his titty magazine. Grabbing my shit, I race out of there before he notices me.

I toss Remi the cigarettes and lighter before sticking the hula girl on the dash next to Our Lady of Guadalupe.

He smiles and flicks her hip so she sways. Giving the lighter a funny look, he tosses it in the console as he drives out of the parking lot. Without even asking for my address he pulls up to my home, confirming my suspicions. This time I'm not fucking crazy. *He knows.*

Remi parks the car and opens the pack of cigarettes. "Do you mind? It's been forever since I indulged." He offers me one.

I decline with a shake of my head, wrinkling my nose with distaste. "Oh no, go right ahead. I want to die, anyway, remember?"

He shakes his head and chuckles as he rolls down the window. Cupping his hand around the cigarette, he stops and glances over at me, looking momentarily confused. I hand him the lighter.

"Thanks." He lights his cigarette, taking a slow draw. Leaning his head back, he closes his eyes and exhales a perfect smoke ring. His moan of pleasure, resonates like something a priest shouldn't have experienced. Well, not recently anyway—after all, he said he hasn't always been a priest. I squeeze my thighs together and try to think about something besides those perfect lips on my skin. If there is a hell, I'm pretty damn sure I just sealed my fate with my fucked up thoughts.

"God, I've missed this," he murmurs. Thunder rumbles over us and I look out the window. The air is heavy with the impending rain and the leaves on the giant palm trees sway back and forth, dancing in the wind. A typical summer storm in southern Florida, they're common this time of year. He exits the car while I remain frozen in my seat, not wanting to enter my house. I don't want to be here. I certainly don't want him to be here. And yet, I don't want to be alone. Maybe the crazy docs have misdiagnosed me. I must be fucking bipolar, not schizo.

My car door opens. "Come on, Crazy Girl." He holds his hand out to me, and I stare dumbly at it as if it's a life raft in the ocean of my self-pity. Have I always been this pathetic? Yeah, probably so. It's hard to remember life before Jack. I grab his hand and step out of the car. *If he lets go I'll fall into the abyss of my depression and slowly suffocate.* It's how I've been living for the past two years. Dying one minute at a time, a slow, painful death. I can't go on like this. It hurts too damn much.

"Well, thanks for saving my life. I guess it's just another normal day in the exciting life of a clergyman," I quip, not looking at him. He drops my hand, and I pick my disappointment up off the pavement and dust it off, shoving it back into the recess of my mind. I'll handle it later, when I get the courage once again to end it all. I shuffle my way toward the house with slow, plodding steps. I never thought I'd be back here. I guess I'll have to switch to plan B — after I come up with a plan B, that is.

The strange sound of a large bird flapping its wings makes me spin on my heels to face Remi. He stands there smoking his cigarette, holding the beer, and looking at me with a thoughtful frown, his head cocked to the side. A soft breeze rustles the leaves of the trees behind us. *It was just the wind in the trees.*

I suck in a steadying breath and throw open the front door. Remi moves behind me and I hear him clucking his tongue against his teeth behind me.

Turning, I glare at him. "What?"

The wind from the impending storm blows my hair into my face and he reaches out and tucks it behind my ear. At his touch, goose bumps pop out on my skin, and a burning fire of intense need courses through my veins. I cross my arms in front of my chest and glare at him, angered by my body's response. Although I've had a lot of sex in the last two years, I haven't felt a longing need like this since Jack. *And for a priest?* I guess I *am* the immoral woman Father Asswipe has always suspected me of being. Maybe I should go confess my wicked thoughts regarding Father Blackson, to prove him right. No, he'd probably suffer a stroke and his dying thought would be *I knew it.* I'll be damned if I prove him right. Plus, I don't need another death on my conscience, unless it's my own.

"What are you doing?" I'm not sure if I'm asking him or myself.

"Making sure you get inside okay. You need to lock your doors, Evangeline. Leaving them unlocked is insanely stupid."

His uncanny knack for calling a spade a spade while still showing concern for my safety makes me snicker. "Yeah, it'd be a shame if some bad guy was inside waiting to kill me."

He chuckles and his eyes crinkle with amusement. "Exactly. I'd hate for all my hard work earlier to have been for nothing." Remi places a warm, firm hand on my lower back and guides me through the door. Once again, his touch sends a jolt of electricity straight down to where it shouldn't go. An image of those hands exploring my body as his lips taste mine makes me turn away with shame. I have to stop; the man is a priest, for fuck's sake. Even I'm not that depraved. *Or am I?*

He snaps on the light and I look around and sigh. It's pretty damn depressing in its emptiness. Over the past two days, I've cleaned out a lot of what I own and either tossed it or dumped it at the local charity. Because I can't stay focused and tend to do things half-assed, I didn't quite finish getting rid of everything. Tonight's suicide attempt is another poorly planned misstep. I'm still here. *Note to self: Get fucking organized, and get rid of everything.*

At least the place is spotless, since I didn't want my mom to have to clean after I'm gone. Mama's been through enough just having me as her daughter. I'm an embarrassment to her, and she hasn't been able to handle the shame I've brought upon the family name. She moved as far across the country as she could just to get away from the gossip.

"Nice place, if a bit Spartan." Remi closes the door behind us, placing the beer on the coffee table. Watching me, he sinks on to the couch.

What the hell? "Okay, I'm in my house." I do a twirl with my arms wide open like I'm Julie Fucking Andrews in *The Sound of Music.* "No bogeyman here. You can leave now."

"There's no need to be rude, Evangeline. There's a storm brewing outside. I'll wait until it's over. Sit down and relax. Want a beer?" He picks one up, twists the top, and holds it out to me.

"I'm not supposed to drink with my medication," I answer primly, sitting next to him.

He raises a skeptical eyebrow and chuckles. "And I'm sure you take your medication *just as prescribed.*"

Was that sarcasm in Father Blackson's voice? *Why, yes, it was.* I grab the beer from him and mumble, "I thought we already established the fact no one likes a smart ass."

Laughing, he opens his own beer, and taps his bottle to mine. "Spoken like a true smart ass. It takes one to know one." I hide my smile by chugging my beer as thunder rumbles through the air. My eyes narrow as he settles back on the couch, propping his long legs on the coffee table as if he plans to stay for a while. His nose wrinkles and he sniffs the air. "Do you need me to take out your garbage?" His eyes sparkle and his full lips curl into a winsome smile as his gaze slowly peruses me from head to toe, making me fidget. I realize I'm wrapping a tendril of my hair around my finger over and over, a sure sign of my nervousness.

"No, there is no garbage." I frown trying to figure out his motive. *Is this some sort of trick question?* The half a beer I just chugged has made my stomach queasy and my head spin. I haven't eaten since… hell, I can't remember when I last ate. I try to think as I look around at the sad, bare room. I took the garbage out when I hauled some of my stuff to the dump this morning…I look down at my filthy T-shirt and jeans and heat creeps up from my chest, making my cheeks flame with humiliation. *It's me.* I refuse to look at him, not wanting to see him laughing at me. People are always whispering about me and laughing. My heart races so fast I feel like I'm running a marathon and my chest hurts.

"You need to leave, Father." Abruptly, I stand. That unsettling feeling of agitation looms over me, threatening to swing me back once again toward my paranoid psychosis.

He stands, but instead of leaving, he marches into the kitchen. I follow, watching him with suspicion as he opens and closes my bare cupboards and the empty refrigerator. He finds one almost empty jar of mustard, a half a stick of margarine and a package of cheap brownie mix that's probably out of date. Most of my dishes are at the thrift store.

Fury marks his face when he spins around to face me. My eyes damn near pop out of my head, and I back up as dark wings expand behind him. I blink and they're gone, making me question if this is real or not.

"When did you last eat? Where is your shit? You really were serious about killing yourself, weren't you?" Another crack of thunder rattles the windowpane, but it's nothing compared to how his outburst has unnerved me.

Did he just say "shit"? Is my mind playing tricks on me again? For a moment, all I can concentrate on his use of a mild profanity. The vision of those raven-like wings spreading is too damn scary to think about right now. I swallow, unsure of how to respond to this side of the priest. He looks like a dark, avenging angel. I squeeze my eyes shut and tremble, backing away, holding my hand out as if to hold him at bay.

"Go away!" I beat the side of my head to make the unwanted apparition leave. This isn't my typical hallucination, and for the first time, I regret quitting my meds cold turkey. Sinking to the floor, I hide my face in my knees as I cower at his feet, shivering with fear. I'm tired of fighting this inner turmoil, yet some primal instinct for survival makes me struggle to keep from succumbing to the relief total insanity would provide.

Sucking in air like a drowning victim, I don't resist when strong, supportive hands pull me to my feet. I curl into his chest, clutching the front of his shirt. My trembling ceases, and I trace my finger repeatedly over the cross on his chest. Calm, soothing energy flows through the hand stroking my hair.

"It's okay, Evangeline. Calm, down. You're just overexcited and exhausted. I'm here to help you." His soft-spoken voice acts better than any anti-anxiety pill I've ever been prescribed.

His reassurance soothes like a gentle ocean wave floating me toward the shore. But, my neurosis acts like an undertow pulling me back toward the depth of my insanity, and the shore remains just out of my reach. Frustrated, I bury my face in his shirt and my knees buckle under the weight of my depression and the disappointment in my failed plan to end the inexhaustible pain. I'm so damn tired of this roller coaster of emotions. Maybe the doctors are right and it's better to be numb and on an even keel with the powerful medications. Better to never feel again.

He sweeps me off my feet and I'm too exhausted to protest as he carries me to the bathroom, plopping me on the counter. It's almost like having an out of body experience as I watch him start the bathwater, adding a generous amount of my favorite bubble bath. When the tub is full and steam covers the mirror, he places a washcloth and towel on the closed seat of the commode and cuts off the water.

Standing before me, he cups my cheek in his hand. I turn my face a fraction so that my lips brush his palm. "Evangeline."

I straighten and stare at the cross on his chest, afraid for him to see into my eyes. Eyes are the windows to the soul, and I don't want this priest, who has offered me kindness, to see I don't have one. I can't take the rejection.

"I think you can handle it from here. But I want to hear you making noise. Splash, sing, swear, I don't care. If I don't hear noise, I'm coming back in to check on you. Do you understand?"

I nod and he pats me on the cheek like I'm a two-year-old and moves toward the door. He's going to leave me. A sense of loss and desperation explodes in my chest like a bomb, but I don't dare hope he'll stay. I steal a glance at him from under my lashes, and my breath hitches at the concern in his piercing eyes.

"Noise, Evangeline. Lots of noise. I'll be in the other room."

He isn't leaving. Relief floods through me. "Yes, *Father.*"

Without thinking, I peel my nasty T-shirt over my head. His eyes widen and the color drains from his face before he quickly closes the door behind him. I should be ashamed of myself, but it was kind of nice seeing the good Father flustered. He's right; he is human, after all. I toss my stinking clothes on the floor and sink into the tub of bubbles with a grateful sigh. It feels like heaven. Leaning my head back, I soak for a moment, letting the tension in my body slip into the fragrant bubbles.

A sharp rap on the door, makes me smile and I begin to sing — off-key as usual — the old Bobby Darin song about taking a bath. The laughter from the other side of the door lets me know he approves. I don't know all the words, so make some up as I go along and repeat the chorus over and over. I scrub my body, even shaving my legs. It takes three washes and rinses to get my hair to squeak. By the time I finish, I'm exhausted and unable to find the energy to climb out of the tub. I close my eyes for just a moment, gathering my strength.

I sink to the floor outside the bathroom and chuckle, listening to Evangeline butcher the lyrics to "Splish Splash." I'm fairly certain the original song didn't say anything about rubbin' a nub. And the mental image that invokes makes me have to adjust my pants to ease the growing tension. Even filthy and stinking to high heaven, Evangeline Lourdes Salvatore is drop-dead gorgeous. I snicker at the unintended pun and thunder cracks overhead. Sometimes He doesn't get my sense of humor. Or maybe He does, and that's the problem. She's going to look beautiful once she's bathed, but I have to remember I'm here to do a job, and I better do it. Saving Evie sure beats checking in the righteous back home.

I rub my face with the heels of my palms, exhausted. Although she has some crazy ideas, has pulled some stupid stunts, and is possibly depressed, Evie isn't insane. She has what people used to call *the sight.* She's extremely sensitive to her surroundings, which means I'm going to have to work harder to not reveal who I am and my true nature. This will be difficult. I'm attracted to her like no other which makes it difficult not to reveal my true self. It's like a male peacock preening in front of his girl. Not to mention impulsivity and carelessness go hand in hand with me.

Loving corny detective shows from the seventies and film noir, the Boss always insists a job be *top secret* when saving some poor soul. Personally, I think it would be a helluva lot easier to just say, "Yo, you're not 5150," or cray-cray, or whatever the current term for batshit crazy is. Why can't we just tell folks they're in touch with more than the tangible? A bold streak of lightning follows the thunder this time. *Better not push my luck.*

Pulling a cigarette from the pack, I light it so I can think and plan. One of the benefits to being back on earth is the ability to smoke, and pre-rolled cigs are incredible. On a rare weekend off during the Summer of Love I'd discovered them and pot from a lovely free-spirited blonde. Of course, that goody-two-shoes Raphael narced on me, like He didn't already know. The Boss hadn't been happy about the cigarettes, being a health nut, but tolerated it. Illicit drugs and sex aren't allowed on weekends off so that was a different story. We're expected to act with *the dignity befitting an emissary of Him.* Using the argument it's a "natural herb" hadn't flown, because I got high and danced around Woodstock with my beautiful wings exposed. Heck, no one even noticed with all the acid being dropped around me. I tried citing free will for the sex, but that went over like lead wings. He hates excuses, and looking back, I should have just owned up to my mistakes. That's when I got sentenced to the "learning lesson" and forced into being Peter's bitch. The old codger is stuffier than the Boss and much more demanding. I've had multiple offers to move south with my fallen brother, Luc, but I hate hot weather. Thunder rumbles hard enough to shake the windows and I mumble an apology.

Let's see, the last time I was here for any length of time was during the Great Plague to save Sister Winifred, the grumpiest old nun I've ever met. It took a couple of months and was a smelly, disgusting task since bathing wasn't high on her list of priorities. This job should be a piece of cake in comparison. Evangeline's a lot prettier and, despite her suicidal ideation, not nearly as morose. I just have to get through her muddled head that life here on earth is a lot more fun than the alternative. After all, she could be stuck checking coats at the Pearly Gates for centuries.

I'm just not sure how to go about it. I think she took a step in the right direction when she pretended to fly in the car. I felt the weight lift momentarily from her slender shoulders. The girl carries more damn baggage than Paris Hilton on a trip to Monte Carlo.

Evie looked like an angel with her long, dark hair blowing behind her, head thrown back, and her arms spread wide as we flew down the road. I was tempted to Chitty-chitty-bang-bang the car, but that would have been crossing the line. I have to appear "normal," whatever that's supposed to be, and somehow identify her pain and figure out a way to extinguish it.

I can do it. At least she isn't boring.

Nope. She's anything but boring.

Chapter Three

"*Evie, you'd test the patience of a saint. Stop playing around, this yard work has to be done.*"

"*Sorry,*" *I reply with a smug grin, looking at Daddy with wide, pleading eyes. I'm lying, and we both know it. I hate yard work, and I've been stalling, wanting him to play with me instead. Daddy's gone a lot with his job as a truck driver, so when he's home, I'll do anything to get his attention.*

Daddy smiles and shakes his head. "*You'll be the death of me yet, young lady.*" *He starts the chainsaw…*

"Evangeline, wake up!"

"No," I whimper, squeezing my eyes harder and swatting at the hand on my shoulder.

The warm hand shakes me, again. "Come on, Crazy Girl, you need to get out of the tub. This isn't fair. I didn't sign on for this kind of temptation. I'm only *human* remember," Remi murmurs, his voice laced with frustration.

My eyes snap open, and I struggle to sit up, covering my nakedness as best as I can with my hands and knees. The bubbles are gone. The water is cold. And my skin burns with embarrassment. A rumble of thunder and crack of lightning splits the air and we're plunged into darkness.

"Thank God," he mutters followed by a grunt. I figure he must've run into the counter. Remi swears under his breath, and wind hits the side of the house, whistling with intensity. "Do you have a flashlight anywhere?"

"Get out," I croak. I'm thankful the power failure has spared me further humiliation. "I have a candle in here, but you have to get out."

"It's pitch black. I can't see anything," he argues.

"You've already seen everything, now get out!" Awkwardness gives way to something else. Desire surges through my body making me acutely aware of him as a good-looking man. This is so wrong.

"I'm trying. Get your panties out of a wad. Oh wait, you're not wearing any."

I screech my indignation, making him laugh as he stumbles into the hallway. Once he's gone, I lunge out of the tub and grab my comfy, terrycloth robe from the back of the bathroom door. As I knot the belt, I hear Remi trip in the other room.

"Jumping Jehoshaphat!"

I guess it wasn't technically swearing and it makes me giggle. Serves him right. Fumbling in the dark, I manage to find the candle and matches in the bathroom drawer. By the wavering candlelight, I comb the tangles out of my wet hair into some semblance of order. Only rest will erase the lavender circles of fatigue under my eyes, and I know that isn't going to happen. I would rather do without sleep than exist in the zombie-like state provided by my meds.

Easing down the hall to my bedroom, I find some clean underwear, a pair of yoga pants, and a tank top. I hear Remi on the phone in the kitchen reporting the power outage, as if I'll need electricity in the future.

My plans haven't changed. They've just been altered by the priest's interference. Annoyed, I trudge to the living area where I find him slumped on the couch, his hands covering his handsome face. He looks up, and my heart damn near stops beating. The candle shakes in my hand until he reaches up and takes it from me, placing it on the coffee table. I can't tear my eyes from his. I see my own haunting pain and torment reflected there.

A primitive, gut-wrenching strand of shared misery connects us in some intangible, mystical manner. It wraps its tentacles around my heart and constricts its hold to the point of pain. I clutch my chest, attempting to draw in a breath, but can't. *How is he able to breathe?* To me, it feels like we're suffocating together, as if on some level, we've become one. My pain is now his. Never have I experienced such empathy or such a deep bond with another person, not even with Jack. Unmitigated grief crashes over me like a tsunami. The room spins, and it feels like a vacuum of sorrow and death has just sucked the life force out of me.

He springs to his feet and handling me like a fragile vase, he lowers me to the couch, easing my head between my knees. "Breathe, Evangeline. Nice deep breaths."

It's a struggle, but I manage to suck in an agonizing, shallow gulp of air.

"There you go. Again, and deeper this time," he commands in an authoritative voice.

When my breathing quits sounding like a winded asthmatic, I curl into a fetal position on the couch with my head in his lap. I quit my meds in order to feel, but now I wish I was numb. After what I just experienced, I don't think I have the strength.

"I'm so sorry, Crazy Girl." He strokes my hair and rubs my back until my tense muscles relax under his tender ministrations. "I feel your pain."

"Are you okay?" I manage to croak as I sit up. I'm pretty damn sure he meant he literally feels my pain, and I'm having trouble comprehending how this could be true. My hand trembles when I push my hair out of my face, hooking it behind my ear. I look everywhere but into his eyes, terrified of what I might see.

"I'm fine. You're hungry, tired, and depressed. One of those is about to be relieved."

The doorbell rings, and my heart jumps to my throat. "No one comes to see me," I whisper, staring at the front door. Since Jack's death, the men I've been with have never entered my home, even after my mother moved. I guess they were too afraid my affliction would rub off on them. Instead, they would take me to a cheap motel, or use me in a car if they were in a hurry. The doorbell rings a second time, but I'm too stunned by the interruption to make a move to answer it.

"Here's a shocking thought. Maybe they're here for *me*. Believe it or not, the world doesn't revolve around *you*." He answers the door and the welcome smell of fresh, hot pizza drifts through the room.

"Thanks for delivering in this weather. You want to come in and wait out the storm with us and have some pizza?" Remi offers the delivery boy.

The color blanches from the boy's face, and he shifts from foot to foot, biting his lip. He glances my way without looking me directly in the face, despite the fact I've known him forever. His older sister is my age and used to be my best friend.

"Nah, Father, she's uh, you know, uh…Nope, I'm good. Thanks." He casts one last look of terror in my direction, and I hiss at him for the fun of it. Shoving the money in his pocket, he almost trips over his own feet in his haste to get away. He's always been an obnoxious brat.

Remi shakes his head and grins. "Gee, I bet you're real popular at Halloween. Tell me, were you voted Miss Congeniality in high school?" There he goes, teasing me again, throwing me off balance. I kind of like it.

As he walks toward me with the pizza, his eyes seem to sparkle in the candlelight. A bright aura of yellow surrounds him, almost as if he's lit from within, making him appear luminous. I close my eyes for a moment and when I open them, Remi's digging in the pizza box. Saliva pools in my mouth, and my stomach growls in a most unladylike manner.

"Eat, you'll feel better."

I glare at him. "You sound like my mother. She thinks food is the answer to all of life's problems." I frown as he takes a slice and bites into it. "Aren't you supposed to ask a blessing, or something, *Father?*"

"Uh, oh, um, right. Let's see." He ponders for a moment and bows his head. "Like fo shiz, this piz is the biz. Thanks, big Wiz." He makes a quick sign of the cross, and winks at me as he takes another bite of pizza.

Shocked and amused at the same time, I close my gaping mouth. "That had to be the worst blessing, *ever*, Father Gangsta." I shake my head, giggling as I take a slice and bite into it. The hot pizza leaves a string of cheese dangling on my chin. I pull it in with my tongue, humming my appreciation. I can't remember when a delivery pizza ever tasted this good. I miss my Daddy's homemade pizza. The sauce alone would take him all day to make.

"Why, thank you. I like to think I'm unique." His mesmerizing eyes flicker.

Unique doesn't begin to describe the handsome Father Blackson as he licks a drop of pizza sauce off his bottom lip. I want to lick the sauce off and see what his lips taste like. I pause with my slice of pizza mid-air, forcing myself to concentrate on his cross and not that perfect mouth, or the fire that seems to light his eyes.

"You're sure not like any priest I've ever known."

Raising his eyebrows, he smiles. "Known a lot of priests, have you?"

I can't tell if he's making fun of me or being serious. "Just a few visiting fill-ins for Father Asswipe."

Remi chokes on his pizza and I can tell he's trying not to laugh. "Father *Asswipe?*"

"Father Ashton. He's a pontificating, self-righteous jerk and older than dirt." The ancient priest christened me, gave me my first communion, and dragged me kicking and screaming through confirmation. Or, if I keep fucking up my suicide attempts he'll be the one to perform an exorcism. If I do succeed, he'll probably be the one to preside over my funeral, unless given a choice. I'm not exactly his favorite person. It occurs to me that I'm not even sure if suicides are still banned from being buried in consecrated ground. *Do I care?* Not really.

"Father Ashton is a man of God, Evangeline," Remi chides. I drag my gaze to his face where a hint of a smile lurks on those kissable lips.

I bet they taste divine. I shake my head to clear the thought. "Uh huh. Have you met him? Or worse, suffered through one of his homilies?"

Remi chuckles and shakes his head. "If you think his suck, you should hear some of the—" A boom of thunder drowns out his voice.

"I guess you're going to be working with him? Are you a curate or something?"

He pauses for the briefest of seconds and a faint frown creases his brow before he answers. "I guess you could say 'or something.'"

I watch as he carefully wipes his mouth. I wish I were that napkin. Why am I having this reaction to him? Am I so starved for human kindness that I'm engaging in what the shrinks call transference? The little self-esteem I have left dissipates into nothingness. I have sunk to a new level of pathetic.

Remi sits back on the couch and motions with his hand toward the pack of cigarettes on the coffee table. He has long elegant fingers, like a concert pianist. "Do you mind?"

"You know, I could die of second hand smoke," I grumble, handing them to him.

He pauses, raising one eyebrow. "Worried about dying, are you?"

I punch him in the leg, hiding my smile with a curtain of hair. "Well, maybe not any time in the next hour or so," I admit, realizing it's the truth. Now that I've bathed and my belly is full, all I really want to do is curl up and sleep.

He sighs and pushes the cigarettes away. "Since I don't want you to die, I'll refrain from smoking." He casts one last longing look at the cigarettes before returning my gaze.

"You'd do that for me?" My incredulous voice sounds husky with sleep, or is it something else?

He looks away for a second and shifts a little on the couch. "Of course. I'd do anything for you."

"Anything?"

He nods and more forbidden thoughts produce images worthy of a porn film, making me fidget. I wrap my arms around my legs, resting my cheek on my knees, and stare at him, trying to figure out his angle. When was the last time anyone was nice to me, or wanted to do something for me that didn't require sex, a lecture, an argument or medication? His unwavering gaze meets mine, as if he in turn is searching for an answer to something I can't explain. For some reason, I can't look away. It's like we know each other, yet we know nothing about each other.

"Stay with me?" I whisper.

"Stay with you?" Flames flicker in his eyes again, and I wrap my knees tighter. Will I ever learn to think before speaking?

I bury my face on my knees and mumble, "Never mind. It was stupid of me to ask. And I really don't mind you smoking."

"I'll stay."

His agreement shocks me and I look up. It's unexpected, and immediately I regret asking something so career damaging of him. "No, that's okay. I shouldn't have asked, I know it wouldn't look good. People will talk, and it's a small town full of small-minded gossips."

"What do you care? You're planning to leave this world, remember?"

My mouth drops as I stare at him. I have no idea how to deal with his teasing. He stretches his arms across the back of the couch and props one foot on his knee. Leaning on his elbow with his chin propped on his thumb, he covers his devilish smile with the finger I regularly use to flip off people. His eyebrow rises as he waits for my answer.

"Aren't you supposed to be talking me out of this and lecturing me on the sins of suicide?" I splutter. Indignation rises, bursting like a geyser. I leap to my feet clenching my fists. "Just what kind of man of God are you? How dare you be so callous about my life? Don't you care I could spend all of eternity in hell?"

"Should I?"

"What?" I screech, full of righteous anger.

"So, Crazy Girl, are you saying you don't want to die and that you believe in a hereafter?"

"I want to die someday and yes, I mean no..." I stomp my foot with frustration. "I don't know about the hereafter. And I'm pretty damn sure calling me 'crazy girl' isn't good for my mental health."

"Would you prefer I call you Bonkers Babe? It's a given we're all going to die someday. Do you or don't you want to die right now?"

Yes. No. Maybe. I rub my eyes like a tired two-year-old and confess softly, "I don't know."

He flashes his mega-watt smile, and I swear the room seems to brighten despite the power outage. "I think that's a definite improvement. And yes, I *do* care. Now go to bed, Evangeline. I'll be out here on the couch, and I'll even pray for your immortal soul. But be warned, I'm a very light sleeper, so if you plan to off yourself in the middle of the night, I'll know it and stop you." Remi rises to his feet, grabs the candle and with a gentle hand guides me down the hallway.

"Brush your teeth like a good girl." He has the nerve to swat my bottom as he shoves me into the bathroom.

"I'm anything but a good girl," I mutter, squirting the toothpaste on my toothbrush and glaring at him in the mirror. "And you're not my mother."

"Bad girls are my favorites. They make confession more interesting and fun. I'll hear yours with your nightly prayers, if you'd like." With a smug look, he leaves to give me some privacy. As I brush my teeth, I ponder this strange priest's impudence. No one has ever called me out on my bullshit like this. Even the specialists engaging in "reality" therapy were impersonal and professional when dealing with me. I

31

spit, rinse, and reluctantly smile. This is more than a physical attraction. I *like* Father Blackson.

I turn the corner outside of the bathroom and run into his chest. Startled, I let out a scream, dropping the candle. Once again we're plunged into darkness.

"Shh, Evie. It's just me, not the bogeyman."

We both stoop to pick up the candle and crack our heads together.

"Ouch, dammit. You have a hard head." I stand and rub my sore forehead as I hear him fumbling for the candle on the floor.

"Me? You're the stubbornest girl I've ever met."

I laugh. "That's not what I meant, and you know it. Is stubbornest even a word?"

His warm hand grabs my ankle making me jump and squeal again. I hold my breath wishing his hand would roam further up my leg, but he removes it. "Ah, there it is." He lights the candle, yet I'm pretty damn sure the matches were still in the bathroom. Then I remember he has a lighter. *Or is it still on the coffee table?*

Before I can think too much about it, he's grabbing my hand and pulling me toward my bedroom. My heart starts pounding, but I can't say why. Is it fear of sleep, or the fact I'm inexplicably drawn to this guy? I see his collar and sigh. Remi stops short, and I run in to his muscular back. I want to wrap my arms around him and beg him to not make me go to bed. Not alone. Not with my nightmares.

"Why the sigh?" He turns and brushes the hair out of my eyes, the backs of his fingers grazing along my jaw. When I glance up at his eyes, they flicker with a reflection of the candle flame. *Surely it was a reflection…*

"I'm just exhausted." *And confused. And scared.*

"I told you I'd stay. You have nothing to fear."

If only that were true.

I'm afraid of my dreams.

I'm afraid to live.

I'm afraid to die.

I'm afraid of being alone.

But Remi is here—a stranger, a priest, and dare I hope, a friend? He takes my hand and leads me to my bed. I pull down the cover and turning my back to him, do the girl-maneuver of slipping my bra off through the sleeves of my shirt. Without any electricity, the hiss of Remi's inhalation seems to echo in the stillness of the room. I dive under my covers, too embarrassed to tell him I'm afraid of the dark. However, my body doesn't seem to have any qualms about betraying me, and my lower lip trembles.

"G-Good night, Father."

His hand reaches toward me and I hold my breath as he makes the sign of the cross on my forehead. Cupping my cheek, he smiles and my fear evaporates, at least for the moment. "Sweet dreams, Evangeline. You are God's child and in His care tonight and always."

Unbidden, a single tear slips down my cheek, but before I can wipe it away, he does so with his thumb. "No nightmares tonight. I forbid it." His eyes crinkle and he taps my nose with his index finger before leaving my room. A lingering sense of peace and the smell of Christmas remain in his wake as I snuggle in my bed. The lit candle remains on my bedside table, as if he knew of my fear of the dark. When I hear him trip in the hallway and the resulting muttered oath, I giggle softly into my pillow. The rain continues with less fury as I drift off to sleep.

Chapter Four

Once I'm sure Evangeline is asleep, I open the front door, light a much-needed cigarette and lean on the doorjamb, exhausted. I've forgotten the feeling. We don't tire back home. The rain has slacked off to a drizzle, leaving the air muggy and hot. Nothing compares to the stifling summer heat of south Florida. The oppressive humidity practically robs you of the ability to breathe. Even Luc hates it, preferring dryer heat.

Standing in the doorframe, I pause and listen for any sound from Evie's room, but the house remains quiet. Drawing on the cigarette, I work on figuring my next move. First on the list, I have to move the car. No need to add fuel to the rampant gossip in this small town, especially if Evie decides to stay here after I save her crazy ass.

Finishing the smoke, I check the trunk and find a suitcase. I can only imagine what's in it. Itchy black shirts, dull black pants and god awful stiff collars. Thunder rumbles and I roll my eyes. "I know, I know. Job requirement. Sorry, Sir."

I haul it to the front porch and drive the car around the block, parking it on the street. It's a middle-class neighborhood and appears to be pretty safe. Besides, I have the best protection around. He'll look after us, He always does. How bizarre is it that Evie doesn't own a car? How does she get around? If I lived on earth I'd have to own a car. Driving fast is almost as much fun as flying.

Jogging back to her house, I can't seem to come up with a plan to save her. I've never dealt with anyone like her before. I guess I'll just have to wing it. Snickering at my own joke, I grab the suitcase and tiptoe into the house. It's a relief to discover some jeans and T-shirts, not just the Doomsday garb. He must not be too mad at me. Not wanting to risk waking her up with a shower, I quickly change into a pair of sleep pants and settle on the lumpy couch with my legs dangling off the armrest. With my hands crossed behind my head, I stare at the ceiling, thinking about the sad girl in the next room.

"What do you expect me to do, Evie? What the fuck am I supposed to do? She's pregnant. I can't leave her! Not now."

"But what about me? You told me you love me. You told me you weren't even sleeping with her. You said your marriage was over. I don't understand. How can it be your baby, Jack? How? And, don't even think about lying to me. I want to hear it from your lips. I want to hear how you betrayed not only me, but her, too."

I slap him hard and the car swerves. Screams mingle with the sound of metal bending and glass shattering...

A hand brushes the hair off my sweat-drenched face.

"Evangeline."

I refuse to open my eyes, not wanting to face the emptiness. I just want him to hold me.

"Jack?" I whisper. As soon as his name leaves my mouth, I know it isn't Jack. He never calls me by my full name. The bed shifts as someone stands and a frightening loneliness covers me like a thick shroud. Am I once again in bed with some nameless guy who picked me up at a bar?

Listening, I hear the snap of a light switch and the sound of running water. Peeking from under my lashes, I see Remi standing at the sink. He's discarded the clerical garb and looks disheveled in black sleep pants hanging low on his carved hipbones. The muscles in his forearms flex as he hangs his head, gripping the sides of the counter. Each deep breath he draws forces his abs to constrict into perfect sculpted planes. For once, I'm thankful to be home, and it's Remi that's here. I hate those awkward goodbyes where I can't remember a name. But, the men always remember me. I'm the party girl who'll do anything, the girl you can fuck and leave. The girl who doesn't matter.

In a moment he returns to my bedside and proceeds to wash my face as he whispers reassuring nonsense. I fight the urge to wrap my arms around his waist and hold him tight. I want to believe him when he says everything will be okay. It's been way too long since anyone has given a damn about me, and I'm not quite sure how to process it. I've learned to avoid the pain of abandonment by tucking away my need to connect to another human being except on a superficial level.

"You promised me no nightmares." My accusing look doesn't faze him as I worm my way to sit up and glare at him. My reasoning sounds silly and childish even to my own ears. There's no way another person can govern your dreams or thoughts, unless they hypnotize you, or perform a lobotomy.

He runs a hand through his golden brown hair making it even more of a tousled mess. "Were you sleeping? Or remembering?"

"Go to hell." It's a knee-jerk reaction to lash out and I regret doing so immediately.

A brief flicker of anger followed by concern, registers in his eyes. It's as if he's staring straight through me, deep into the hollow place where my soul should reside. With a heavy sigh he stands and looks down at me with a slight furrow in his brow. Guilt assails me. He's been nothing but kind to me and doesn't deserve my uncaffeinated snarky attitude.

"Sorry." I fidget under his scrutiny, as I stare at the happy trail dipping into his sleep pants. "I'm not a morning person."

"No kidding. Look, you need to learn how to deal with this shit. It will help ease the nightmares and visions." The early morning light filtering in through the curtain makes the room soft with a diffuse pink light. Covering my face with my hands, I sigh. He's right. The memory of the wreck that took Jack from me haunts my nightmares. It was my fault. The weight of my culpability makes my shoulders sag.

"You have to let this go, Evie."

"I can't." *If I let go, I'll lose Jack forever.*

"Why not?"

"Just leave it alone, Father. I'm not a good person." I don't feel like explaining, knowing he will be like everyone else and not believe me, chalking up my visions to my supposed mental illness. I scramble from the bed and run into the bathroom, slamming the door. I stare at my reflection in the mirror as I brush my teeth. I no longer recognize the girl who stands before me. I used to care about how I looked. It was an advertisement for my job as a beautician. Since Jack's death, I just haven't given a damn and it shows in my lank hair and gaunt cheeks.

I open the door to find Remi standing there with his arms outstretched on the doorjamb. The cross dangles over a perfectly contoured chest with just the right amount of hair. The man could grace the cover of *GQ*. The scent of fresh cut pine boughs and cinnamon combined with the beauty of his fit body are an assault on my senses and leave me feeling off kilter.

He groans and runs his hands through his hair, staring at the ceiling for a moment. "My, my, you certainly seem proud of the fact you're not a good person. As a matter of fact, you wear it like a Girl Scout badge of honor. Would you like a pinning ceremony or something? We could call it the *World's Most Pathetic Little Girl* badge. You've worked hard for it. You've earned it."

My mouth drops open. "How dare you speak to me like that?" Furious, I shove at his hard chest, but he doesn't budge. Fire appears to flicker in the depth of his imperturbable gaze as a lazy, slow smile spreads across his face.

"Why don't you do something about it instead of wallowing in your self-pity?"

"Move," I grind out, pushing again at him.

"Make me."

I knee him and he isn't fast enough to deflect the entire blow. He doubles over, grimacing, allowing me to slip past him.

"You don't fight fair, do you?" he gasps, struggling to stand upright by gripping the doorframe.

Even though the power is back on, the house darkens ominously and I hear the sound of ruffled feathers. A blast of air fills the hallway, blowing my hair in my face. Terrified, I run toward my mother's room, but the door slams shut before I reach it.

There's no one here but us, and when I turn to face him, I see the flames in his eyes and dark wings expanding behind him. Ducking, I cover my head like I'm in a disaster drill from elementary school. *This can't be real.* Terrified, I cower, squeezing my eyes tight.

"Stand up," he roars, his voice filling the hallway like the blast of a jet engine.

I don't want to disobey, but I'm too scared to move. I peek between my fingers to stare at bare male feet in front of me. Slowly, I raise my head to find Remi glaring at me with his hands on his hips. There are no dark feathers and his eyes have no flames leaping from them. He's just a man. A disgruntled man, for sure, after what I just did to him, but just a man. A breeze through an open window in the other room must have slammed my door shut. Wait, why would I have a window open in August? I don't remember opening a window with the power outage, but maybe Remi did.

I lash out in anger to hide my confusion. "You deserved it. You're an asshole, Father Blackson." I leap to my feet and flounce into the kitchen to start some coffee, only to remember I have no groceries. Dammit. I wasn't supposed to be here today and it's this meddlesome priest's fault. I stare out the window, lost. Now what?

Remi enters the kitchen a few minutes later dressed in his clericals minus the collar, and collapses into a chair. Leaning on the table, he covers his face, rubbing his eyes and mutters, "I'm truly in hell; what did I do to deserve this?"

"You can leave. I'm not keeping you here." *Please don't leave me.*

"If I leave to go find some breakfast for us, will you behave until I get back? Or do I need to take you with me like a bratty child?" He looks up and his penetrating gaze makes me squirm.

"Um, sure?"

He glowers and points at me like he's a high school principal. "I mean it, Evangeline. Promise me you won't harm yourself at least until I get back."

I'd laugh if he weren't so damn serious.

"Okay, I'll wait to off myself until you return. Want to help me? I promise not to tell on you."

"At the risk of getting into deep trouble, if you keep up with your smart ass answers, I'll consider it."

For the first time this morning, we both smile.

He stands and fumbles with fastening his collar. Growling with frustration, he runs a hand through his hair and storms around the kitchen muttering under his breath about Woodstock. I like his hair like that, delightfully disheveled in a just-rolled-out-of-bed way. However, his rumpled appearance, accented by his unshaven jaw, tousled hair and wrinkled clothes will cause talk in this gossip-infested, backwoods town. Of course, his car being in front of my house all night has probably already started the nasty rumor mill. Like I need more scandal. But he doesn't deserve it.

"Give me your shirt." I hold out my hand.

"E-Excuse me?" His head snaps up and his Adam's apple bobbles. He's flustered. The tiny, spiteful part of me smirks with satisfaction at having the upper hand for a change.

"I'll iron your shirt for you." I motion with my head toward the old-fashioned, drop-down ironing board on the back of the pantry door.

Remi's heated gaze never leaves mine as he tosses the collar on the table and slowly unbuttons the shirt, one agonizing button, at a time. His inherent grace makes him move like a male stripper, teasing and taunting. It's my turn to be ill at ease as he shrugs out of it. Sexual desire surges through me like a wave crashing on the beach at high tide.

My mouth feels as dry as the Sahara. I want to run my nails over that beautiful chest, as heat infuses every inch of my body. An overwhelming need to connect in a primal way permeates my loneliness. Closing my eyes, I imagine his bare skin slick with sweat and the sound of his heavy breathing of desire in my ear…

Remi sucks in a deep, audible breath and my eyes flash open. *That sounded eerily similar to my imaginings.* In the stormy depth of his turbulent green eyes I see my need reflected there. Residual shame from my upbringing pulls my gaze to the cross on his bare chest, and my cheeks flame with embarrassment over my inappropriate thoughts. He holds the shirt out to me on two fingers and I take it, careful not to make contact.

I remember, too late, I got rid of my iron. "Never mind, I don't have an iron." I hold his shirt back to him, but his eyes are closed and his lips are moving silently—no doubt, praying for my immortal, wicked soul.

I now know my true punishment for being mouthy and an ingrate. It isn't the job of saving this squirrelly girl from killing herself. It's being forced to be celibate in the presence of overwhelming temptation. Evangeline Lourdes Salvatore is the embodiment of every male sexual fantasy carried out alone in the dark, throughout the history of man. She is quite simply, sex incarnate.

Writers could wax poetic about her looks and would stumble on their descriptions. Musicians could attempt to capture her beauty in song, and it would sound like a discordant tune in comparison. Painters could try to replicate her body on canvas, but it would never capture her true beauty, or the inherent sweetness of her soul.

She has the longest, blackest lashes I've ever seen, framing her bewitching dark eyes. Even the purple smudges underneath them, the result of her exhausting so-called illness, can't detract from their magnetic pull.

I bet her lips are petal soft. Being full, they appear to be in a permanent pout since she rarely smiles. I want to nibble and tug on that lower lip she worries with her teeth when she's fighting her inner demons. Her glorious hair is a riot of tangled curls that I long to run my hands through as I bury myself deep inside of her. I don't dare linger on the memory of her naked in the bathtub…If circumstances were different, and I was human, I'd forsake my priestly duties and fall to my knees begging her to let me worship her soft, curvaceous body.

But nooooo, none of this is allowed for *Father* Remiel Blackson.

After handing her my shirt to be ironed, I close my eyes and curse my fate, conceding defeat. He's proven His point. I'm damned to hell, after all.

Luc, the lucky bastard, doesn't know how easy he got off, merely being sentenced to ruling over the damned as the Prince of Darkness. Because right now I'd do just about anything it takes to get off.

Chapter Five

Remi is leaving to go on a search and destroy mission for something edible for breakfast.

I peer at the empty driveway and then back at him. "Where's your car?"

He doesn't make eye contact with me. "I, uh, moved it around the corner after you fell asleep."

I wonder if he moved it to protect his reputation or mine. I feel like a housewife on an old sitcom and find myself imagining what his lips would feel like if he were to kiss me good-bye.

"Behave," he calls out as he rounds the corner with his long, easy gait. I jump, praying he isn't a mind reader and is just admonishing me in a general sort of way. Although it's a bright, sunny day, now that he's gone it feels like the sun is hiding behind thick cloud cover.

Reluctantly, I go back inside, regretting my decision to stay home and wait for him. I don't want the dark thoughts to take over again. Remi has shown me a slight sliver of hope in my gloomy world. I need to stay busy until he gets back.

Since the power is back on, I march into the kitchen and yank the cupboard door open, finding the out-of-date brownie mix. Reading the back of the package, the only ingredient needed is water. I'm not even sure why it was in the cupboard. I don't cook and Mama would die of shame before she'd use a mix. Is it safe to eat since it's expired? Perfect! *Death by chocolate.* My dark humor makes me snicker. I have to remember to tell Remi. That sick bastard will think it's funny, too.

As I wait on the oven to heat, I grease the pan with the half stick of butter and find myself humming the song from the wild ride last night. I long to feel the wind in my hair again and relive that feeling of freedom. Maybe the answer to my suicide quest would be to cliff dive to my death. Where can I find cliffs in south Florida? Or perhaps, I don't really want to die at the moment? The thought makes me pause. Is it because things are less depressing in daylight, or because of a certain irritating, yet kind priest?

I check the oven and it's stone cold. Crap, this is just my luck. The pilot light must be out. I can't even remember the last time I cooked anything that wasn't heated in the microwave. Scrounging through several mostly empty drawers, I find a box of matches. Now I just have to figure out how to light the damn thing. Kneeling before the oven, I stick my head inside, without a clue what I'm looking for.

"Holy Mary, Mother of God!" Remi shouts from behind me. That rustling feather sound envelops the room, and although it's dark inside the oven, the light in the room behind me seems to dim as well.

Startled, I bang my head hard enough to bring tears to my eyes. Two strong hands grasp me by my waist and jerk me unceremoniously to my feet. I shrug out of his grasp and rub the growing knot on the back of my head.

"Ouch, what the hell are you doing? That hurt, asshole." Tears spill down my cheeks.

Remi grabs me by the shoulders and shakes me until my teeth clatter. I'm about to snidely ask if he's ever heard of shaken baby syndrome, but the look of fury on his face makes me hold my tongue. The vein on his forehead has popped out, accenting his red face, and his eyes seem to simmer with fury. I hope he doesn't have a stroke since I'm not current on my CPR certification. *Or is that just for heart attacks?* I can't remember. I wipe at the tears streaming down my face.

"Don't you *dare* pull the crying card on me. I wasn't even gone that long, for Pete's sake. I trusted you. You *promised* me you wouldn't hurt yourself. You can't do this to me, do you hear me?" he shouts.

"I'm pretty sure the next-door neighbors 'hear' you, Father," I yell back. Instead of letting me explain, he's jumped to the conclusion I was trying to kill myself. And for once, I'm innocent, dammit.

"I won't allow you to die on my watch." He lets go of me and starts pacing. "Why? Why do you keep trying to kill yourself? You're young and beautiful, with a full life ahead of you. Dammit, Evangeline, life is good. You need to get your head out of your own proverbial ass and grab life by the balls."

"Oh that's Biblical." I snort and cross my arms in front of my chest. "And priests shouldn't swear." The pain from the knot on my head has receded somewhat, leaving me pissed.

Stopping in his tirade, he glares at me and points his index finger in my direction. "I happen to be a huge fan of Mark Twain who said, 'Under certain circumstances, *profanity* provides a relief denied even to prayer.' Old Mark was absolutely correct. Plus, I'll have you know, there happen to be over one hundred and thirty passages that mention the word *ass* in the Bible."

"Prove it." I'm not about to give up, *no sirree*. Besides, getting Father Blackson riled is the most fun I've had in ages. I wonder just how many of his buttons I can manage to push.

"What?" He runs a hand through his disheveled hair, making it even sexier than before.

I shrug and examine my nails. "I don't believe you. Do you really expect me to believe the word *ass* occurs that many times in the Bible? And why would anyone know this obscure fact?"

"Everyone knows this fact. You can look it up on the Internet."

"You can also look up porn," I mutter. "It doesn't mean that's what real naked women look like."

"Really? Tell me more. What's your favorite site? Are you a porn connoisseur? Do we need to add this to your list of sins for confession? And don't forget, I know what naked women look like."

I'm sure my cheeks are now the color of a hooker's lipstick as I remember him waking me in the bathtub. In an attempt to hide my embarrassment, I roll my eyes. "I'm not convinced you have your facts straight." Picking my purse up off the table, I dig through empty gum wrappers, broken hair clips, and old grocery lists, looking for my phone.

Glancing at the three missed calls, I choose to ignore the voice mail from my mother and go straight to *Google*. I type in my query. *Sonofabitch, he's right.* I bite my lower lip and glance over at him.

He's standing with his arms crossed in front of chest. One eyebrow lifts and a smug smile spreads across his face.

Grudgingly, I admit, "Okay, so you were right. You're the seminarian, not me." Only my stupid tongue makes a Freudian slip and I pronounce it *semen*-arian. My cheeks feel sunburned.

He snorts and laughs. "Uh, is that a new term for a porn star? The word is *semi*narian and technically, I'm *not* either one."

I throw up my hands. "Whatever, I don't think the Bible using the word ass in the context of a donkey counts as swearing, though."

"An ass is an ass," he retorts with a chuckle.

"We're going to argue semantics?"

"Don't you mean *semen*-antics?" He laughs, a full, deep sexy laugh that makes my toes curl.

I smack him on the arm. "You're never going to let me live that down, are you? You won't even listen to me before jumping to conclusions, you *ass*."

The amusement leaves his face and he frowns, taking a deep breath. He leans against the counter, tilting his head. "I'm listening." His intimidating look doesn't scare me. I'm beginning to think my instinct is right. He really is a nice guy.

"I wasn't trying to kill myself."

"This time."

He knows me well. "The pilot light's out." I point to the pathetic pan of uncooked brownies sitting on the counter. "You've watched too many old movies. This is a new oven. I'm sure it has safety features. I don't even know if you can kill yourself that way anymore."

"You weren't…" Remi points to the oven and then the brownies and a grin breaks out across his face. "You really weren't trying to pull a Sylvia Plath?" He throws his head back and chuckles.

I shake my head no, wondering who Sylvia Plath was, maybe an old girlfriend? I push the tinge of jealousy away; I have no right to this feeling.

"Sorry, I thought…I mean…I walk in and see your *ass* up in the air and your head stuck in the oven. Naturally, I *ass*umed—"

"Well you know what they say when one *ass*umes…"

His carefree laugh is contagious, and I'm startled by the sound of my accompanying guffaws. When was the last time I laughed this loud and this hard?

"You really thought I was going kill myself that way? Don't you think I've done my homework? It would be easier to die of carbon monoxide poisoning in a garage. Unfortunately, I don't have a car or a garage. Not to mention, my track record on suicide attempts is pretty pathetic. Don't lose any money by betting on my success." I sigh and pretend to pout just a bit.

"Hmm." He scratches his scruffy chin. "I guess I need to brush up on suicide methods so I can stay one step ahead of you. I suppose I can do an Internet search…"

"Smart ass," I reply with snicker before frowning with despair at the coffee spilled across the floor. I place the back of my hand to my forehead and melodramatically sigh. "Dear God, this is a travesty. Life without coffee isn't worth living." I'm only half kidding. I really needed that caffeine.

Remi laughs. "You're nuts, you know that, right?"

"So they say."

I mop up the mess while Remi quickly handles lighting the pilot light. I rub my eyes and pinch the bridge of my nose to stave off the absurd idea he just started it with his fingertips. A quick glance at the counter confirms the matches are still there. *No!* He must have retrieved one from the box while I was cleaning up the mess. I slide the pan of brownies in the oven, and we sit to eat our biscuits with water instead of coffee. This time he gives a respectful, but quick, blessing over the food.

Curiosity makes me ask, "So what will you be doing at the church?"

"Um, well, I'm not working with the church. I'm on a special assignment."

"What, like a secret agent priest? Instead of CIA or FBI are you SAP?" I tease, causing him to raise his eyebrows as a surprised smile lights up his face.

"Did Miss Sourpuss just make another joke?"

I mutter the phrase *du jour*, "Smart ass." But, I hide my pleased smirk by looking away.

"It's something like that. What are your plans for the day? Aside from contemplating death, of course."

This time I laugh outright. "Oh I dunno, maybe murdering a certain priest?"

He snickers. "Excellent." His eyes crinkle and that devilish smile prepares me for more teasing. "From what I've heard about Father Ashton's homilies, you'd be doing the parish a service."

"You know I wasn't talking about *him*, Father." I giggle like a young girl and cover my mouth, startled by my own reaction. It feels surprisingly good.

We finish the meal in a companionable silence. As we sit there, his fingers trail back and forth over the pack of cigarettes on the table. I imagine those long fingers caressing my skin and my breathing hitches. I don't wear makeup any more, but even if I did, I wouldn't need any blush around Remi.

"In all seriousness, Evangeline, what are your plans?"

I hop up from my seat to hide my embarrassment over my wandering thoughts. After searching through my almost bare cupboards, I find an ashtray hidden in the back and wipe the dust off with a dishtowel. The ashtray reminds me of my daddy sitting at this very table and smoking after a meal. I can almost hear the sound of his lighter flicking and snapping shut, and smell the acrid tobacco. He always said the after-meal cigarette was his second favorite, and Mama would blush, telling him to hush. As an adult, I can now surmise what his favorite cigarette was, and it makes me wonder what this priest's favorite would be...

Reigning in my thoughts, I slide the ashtray to him across the table before sitting and retrieving my napkin from the floor. "Oh, I dunno, maybe I'll die today..." His sharp intake of breath and that bristled sound of flapping feathers has me pulling up sharply from under the table. I continue with a smirk, "Of second-hand smoke."

He laughs and with an exaggerated sigh, stuffs the cigarettes back in his pocket, and leans back in his chair. "Not on my watch, you don't, but I'm pretty sure that would take years." A beep from my phone indicates another voice mail. "Don't you need to get that? It could be your job or something."

"I quit my job. I wasn't planning on being here, remember?" I grab the phone with annoyance. It's my mother again, calling to check on me. She couldn't handle living in the same town as her lunatic daughter, so instead, she phones at least six times a day. Like her phone calls don't drive me nuts.

I listen to the two voice mails and frown. Something isn't right. Mama's voice usually sounds strained with a touch of forced cheerfulness as she tiptoes around my mental health, or lack thereof. Today, her voice sounds sad and small as she inquires whether I'm taking my meds and keeping my appointments with the head peeper. The hair on the back of my neck stands on end as I push redial and wait, glancing across the table at Remi. The intensity of his gaze forces me to look away as I chew on my lower lip waiting for Mama to answer the phone. I wrap and unwrap a curl around my finger, my leg bouncing with nervous energy.

"Hello?" My mother's voice sounds weak and a little breathless, as if she ran to grab the phone.

"Hi, Mama."

"Evie, how are you? Are you taking your medications and seeing Dr. Knowles?"

I look across the table at Remi and lie through my teeth. "Sure. Everything's great. How are you?"

An uncomfortable silence ensues followed by an almost inaudible sob. My back straightens, and I clench my fist. "Mama? What's wrong?"

"I shouldn't burden you with this. Not with your *condition…*"

Mama always refers to my mental state as my *problem, condition,* or *issue.* Personally, I wish she'd just call it like it is and tell me I'm fucking looney tunes. Why is mental illness still taboo to talk about?

"I-I'm scared, honey. I've been having some chest pain. The doctor wants to schedule me for some tests. He says I may need stents or surgery."

My world tilts off its axis and overwhelming guilt engulfs me. Sure, we argue, and she drives me nuts with her worrying, but I love her. This is my fault. My mother has been a good mom, despite her inability to deal with my *issues.* It isn't her fault I'm on the fast track to hell. *I can't bear the thought of losing her, too.*

I take a deep breath to steady my voice. "I'll be there as soon as I can. When are you having the tests done?"

"I'll schedule it for next week. To give you time to get here. I can send you a little money."

"No! No, I don't need your money." She's spent most of her life savings on my 'problems' and her move to Seattle. "But, Mama, don't risk your health, if you need it sooner…" *Shit, I don't have any money, either.* I'll have to take the bus, or I'll beg, borrow, steal or sell my body. I'll do anything to get to my mother. The thought of losing my mom fills me with such inexplicable fear, I'm afraid I'm about to implode.

"I'll be okay, Evie. I don't want you to stress about this, you know how stress exacerbates your problems."

Tears stream unchecked down my face. "Please don't worry about *me*. Concentrate on you for a change. I love you, Mama…" My voices breaks and I repeat, "I love you."

"I know you do. I can't help but worry about you, that's what mamas do." Her voice sounds hoarse with emotion. "I miss you and love you, too. Call me when you have your travel plans arranged."

I hang up the phone and can't move, still stunned by the news. For weeks I've selfishly contemplated death. *My death.* Never once have I thought about anything happening to my mom.

"Are you okay? What's going on? Talk to me." Remi leans forward and captures both of my hands in his, and I clutch them like a lifeline.

Please don't let me go. Still numb from the revelation of my mother's illness, I stare at him. Present in body only, my mind races over the things I have to do to get to my mom as soon as possible.

Frowning, he looks up, sniffing the air. "Is that your soul burning?"

The smell of burnt brownies permeates the air, followed by smoke pouring from the closed oven door. Remi springs to his feet and turns off the oven. Using a dishtowel, he pulls out the pan of charred brownies. The smoke alarm screeches its ear-piercing signal, breaking through my inertia. I catapult to the top of the table to remove the battery while Remi opens the back door to let the smoke out. His strong hands grip my waist as he helps me down. I know it's wrong, but I enjoy the feel of sliding down his hard body. He tugs me by the hand to the back step for some fresh air where we sit in silence, staring at the backyard.

Needing his strength, I take his hand in mine but immediately regret showing my weakness. Trying to fake him off, I pretend to study his hand, rubbing a finger over his smooth palm. "I'm glad you didn't burn yourself."

"I'm fine. Want to talk about whatever your mom said?"

Putting down my guard, I allow myself to take comfort in his presence. "She's sick." Wrapping my arms around my legs, I pull my knees to my chest and watch the row of industrious ants marching across the concrete. Do ants ever feel overwhelmed with life? Or, are they like most people, too busy just surviving to notice that life is just a series of small steps toward death?

"How bad?" He helps an ant that's struggling to get up the step and places it back in line. My heart softens even more toward this man.

"I don't know. It's her heart." I swallow the lump lodged in my throat. "I guess I broke it..." Blinking away my tears, I look out at the rose bushes my mother used to tend with loving care. Weeds have overtaken the beds, and the bushes are long and straggly. Mama would be saddened by the way I've neglected them. My father gave some of those bushes to her. In a trance-like state I walk over to the rose bed and begin pulling the weeds that are choking the life out of the poor, neglected flowers. The analogy isn't lost on me. I'm a weed and my mother is a dying rose. Weeds don't die, beautiful flowers do.

Remi squats down beside me. "You need to make plans. Weeding this garden isn't going to get you to your mother." Standing, he pulls me to my feet, and I melt against him, closing my eyes as his hand strokes my hair. His presence reassures me as he enfolds me in his wings. Once again I feel safe and cared for... *Wings? What. The. Fuck?*

My eyes fly open and my heart pounds in my ears as I back away, staring at the priest. He stands before me in his black clericals, the cross on his chest glinting in the sunlight. His sun-kissed brown hair shimmers like a halo, yet he's a man. I close my eyes and clench my fists, digging my nails into the palms of my hands as I suck in a deep breath, steadying my overwrought nerves. I have to keep my shit together. My mother needs me.

Using my breathing exercises, I force myself to calm the fuck down. "I guess I need to pack and get to the bus station. How much do you think a ticket to Seattle will cost?"

"You're not riding a bus. It isn't safe." He folds his arms over his chest and pulls on that damn sexy lower lip.

"I can't afford to fly, I don't own a car, and I have no idea where the nearest train station is. So what do you suggest? Teleportation? Riding an ass?"

His upper lip quirks and his eyes seem to sparkle, as if he knows an inside joke. "Uh no, I don't think that's legit. I'll drive you."

"But you're a priest."

He chuckles. "Um, last time I checked, it's the twenty-first century, priests can drive. Plus, I'm on sabbatical. I have nothing but time, and I have a car. You won't literally have to ride my ass, although I'm sure you'll do it figuratively. Now go pack. I'll take you to your mother."

I'm not sure whether to be scandalized or grateful. I shove the naughty thought of riding his ass to the back of my dirty mind to save for later. We'll be in a car, *alone,* for days. "What about your reputation? You're a *priest* and I'm a home-wrecking whore. Ask anyone in this town."

"I really object to the way you speak about yourself, Evangeline. Don't do it again." Pulling a cigarette out of his pocket, he looks sexy as hell with it dangling from those kissable, but off-limits lips. Except for the white collar and cross, he could pose for a goddamned poster for the tobacco industry. He cups the cigarette and lights it, but I don't hear the flick of a lighter. "As for my reputation, we're leaving this town, so what does it matter? I have other clothes. I'll wear jeans and a T-shirt."

"Is that allowed?"

"Evangeline, go pack. We don't have time to waste."

"I don't think I have enough money, I'll pay you back somehow, someday…" *Shit, how?*

"I'm not worried about it. We'll manage. Now go." He nods toward the house, and I decide he's right. My mother needs me. I don't have time to argue with his more than generous offer.

"Thank you," I whisper, moved by his kindness. Without thinking, I embrace him in a quick hug, causing him to stumble a bit. I'm not sure who is more surprised by my action. I pull away before it can become awkward and run back in the house to pack. The lingering feeling of our bodies pressed against each other, and the memory of his warm baritone voice saying he hadn't always been a priest teases me. A warm, tingly sensation creeps across my skin at the thought of being alone with him on the road, and I bite my lip with anticipation.

Stop! He's taken vows. Can there be a safer travel companion? *Yeah, you keep telling yourself that, Evie. Denial, it's not just a river in Egypt.* I throw a few clothes, some toiletries, a ring my Daddy had given my mother, and a locket from Jack into my suitcase. As I brush my teeth, I glance in the mirror and freeze. Spitting out the toothpaste and rinsing, I look again at my reflection.

The pulse at the base of my neck visibly pounds and my breath hitches, strangling in the back of my throat. My hand trembles like an alcoholic in DTs as I reach into my hair and pluck out a single black feather. Clutching it to my chest, I sink to my knees staring at it. For years I've been told I'm mentally ill, but I never truly *believed* it deep down in my heart.

I've always thought I was smarter than the professionals who claimed to know what's wrong with me. I thought I'd been playing them. I'm not crazy. I only play crazy. But now, I'm not so sure. I open my hand and stare at the soft, black feather. All the dire warnings about stopping my medications cold turkey now haunt me. I'm used to the so-called visual and auditory hallucinations. But this is beyond anything I've ever experienced. I've never *felt* them before. This is as real as I am. *Or is it?*

Chapter Six

"Evangeline? Are you okay?" A sharp rap on the door follows the query.

Cold terror courses through my veins and I clench the feather tightly in my fist. Remi knocks again. Pulling my knees to my chest, I wrap my arms around my legs and hide my face, squeezing my eyes shut as I hold my fists over my ears. If I can't see or hear, maybe whatever this is will go away.

The door opens and a hand strokes my hair. It's tempting to give in to the kindness, but I keep my eyes shut and hands over my ears.

"Everything will be okay. Come on, sweetness, let's go."

Ignore it. It will go away. I rock and begin to hum to drown out the sound of his muffled voice. *Not real, not real, not real...*

Warm, strong hands lift me from the bathroom floor pulling my hands away from my ears. Startled by his touch, I look at him. "Oh for heaven's sake, Evangeline, snap out of it. We don't have time for your whack-a-doodle-do shtick." His hair ruffles off his forehead with his deep breath and his fingers drum the countertop.

I shake my head over and over. *Not real, not real, not real...*

"Stop it!" His baritone roar echoes in the small bathroom and scares me shitless. If he *is* real, I'm in serious trouble. And just what is he?

My throat constricts and the words come out in a hoarse gasp. "Go away."

"Look at me." The concern in his voice sounds comforting, not scary. I grasp his solid biceps and cautiously peer up at him. Remi. Not a monster. Underneath my hands I feel skin, muscle and bones, there are no black feathers sprouting from his back. "You're real, aren't you?" I whisper, squeezing his biceps harder. My fear subsides, as his serene presence washes over my frazzled nerves.

"I'm a real smart ass at times, remember?" He grins, placing me on the counter and with his index finger forces my chin up. "And so are you. Look at me."

I couldn't have disobeyed even if I wanted to.

"You've been under a tremendous amount of stress and you don't sleep. The mind is a powerful thing. Whatever you think you saw or heard, it's due to exhaustion. Now grab your things and finish packing. I'm going to take a quick shower and we'll be ready to hit the road to get to your mom's. Okay?"

Almost believing him, I nod and hop off the counter hugging him tight. Just to reassure myself, I search his back, running my hands up and down his shirt. All I find is a man's back. I'm not sure whether to be relieved, or terrified that my mind is slipping further down the fast track to being a total whack job. Prying himself from beneath my hands, he maneuvers me away from the bathroom door and shuts it.

I hear the shower and my mind replays him taking off his shirt. There had been no wings. I look around for the black feather I'd held in my hands.

It's gone.

Or perhaps it was never there.

What a morning. My heart damn near stopped when I found Evie's cute butt up in the air and her head stuffed inside the oven. How was I supposed to know gas stoves have safety features on them now? I'm sure He had quite a chuckle over my panic attack.

I groan at the memory of her sensuous body sliding down mine when I helped her off the table during the burnt brownie fiasco.

Everything about her unsettles me, and it's causing me to be more careless than usual. I've had to stop myself at least six times from blurting the truth to her, the latest being when I found her cowering in the bathroom, afraid of me.

I flush the feather I retrieved from the floor, sweating like a sinner in hell. I can't read thoughts—not like He can—but I'm good at reading body language. It comes from playing cards with the best. Matthias is a downright cutthroat poker player and even Peter plays a mean game of Go Fish. By correcting the situation and stealing back my lost feather I've just nailed the coffin shut on what Evie thinks is her tenuous grasp on sanity. Guilt eats at my conscience, but I had to do it. I have my instructions to not reveal my true nature, and disobedience isn't an option. Not unless I wanted to be Peter's bitch for the rest of this century, or go shovel coal for Luc.

Dammit. I shuck off my clothes and step into the shower. I know I'm in way over my head and should ask for help, but hey, although angelic I'm still a man. I don't need no stinking directions. I can figure this out on my own. Deep in my heart, I know this is no longer just a job. The fact is, I care about her and don't want her to get hurt. My growing feelings are wrong and doomed from the get go, but when I'm with her, it's like she's the missing piece to my puzzle.

Frustrated, I pound my fist on the wall of the shower. I have to put aside my feelings and do what's best for her, not what I want. I take a deep breath, resolving to do the right thing. This is my job, after all. I don't really have a choice.

And now we're going to be enclosed together in a small car for at least fifty hours driving time, plus nights together. What have I gotten myself into? I'm the one that wanted to do this on my own. Time to start formulating a fucking plan. I turn off the shower, and after toweling dry, dress in jeans and an old T-shirt with that dumb looking Godspell clown on it. I guess twenty-first century references to Him are rare on T-shirts. I check my wallet, knowing I don't have enough cash to pay for two rooms, food and gas. I'm pretty sure Evie doesn't either. I take out my phone and zip a quick text to the Boss. Maybe He can wire me some money or something. Do they even wire money anymore?

To my surprise, in a less than a minute, I have a response.

Not my problem. You might consider obtaining a real job. Please be more careful around Evangeline and watch your language.

Great. After my last *job* as the check-in clerk at the Pearly Gates I'm qualified to do what? Be a Walmart greeter? Since I plan to wear my jeans, T-shirt and boots, I skip shaving. It makes me feel more like me and not Father Blackson. Although when I think about it, wearing the collar would probably be a safer option when dealing with this tempting human.

Next time I see him, I'm going to ask Adam if Eve's full name is Evangeline.

In his priestly garb, Father Blackson appears almost angelic. But nothing has prepared me for his panty-dropping appearance in a faded red *Godspell* T-shirt, jeans and scruffy jaw. My mouth goes a little dry, and I almost wish he'd put the collar back on, as it provides — albeit not much of one — a visual barrier to his innate sex appeal. He closes the trunk and opens the car door for me. I remember Daddy doing that for Mama. He stands there until I buckle my seatbelt.

Slamming the door shut, he walks around and eases into the driver's seat, slipping on a pair of sunglasses. As he drives down the street where I've lived my entire life, relief spreads through my heavy limbs. It's as if the tremendous weight of my reputation is being lifted from my shoulders and kicked to the curb as we drive away.

I'm leaving.

A smile plays on the corner of my lips, and impulsively I roll down the window, flipping off the town that has branded me a whore. Feeling a little giddy and foolish, my cheeks burn a bit when Remi laughs at me. Maybe Mama was right, perhaps I should have moved with her to Washington instead of remaining here thumbing my nose at the gossipers. Then again, we probably would have killed each other by now. We love each other, but we don't necessarily like one another.

I once again stare appreciatively at the handsome man sitting next to me. "You're such a waste. No man who fills out jeans and a T-shirt like you do should be celibate." I cover my mouth with my hand, and my eyes widen with horror. *Holy crap, I just said that out loud.* As usual, I have no filter between my brain and mouth.

His eyebrows lift above his sunglasses and he chuckles. "Why, thank you. I could say the same about you, too."

"What?"

"You're beautiful, and if you'd get rid of this warped need to punish yourself, you could be happy. It's a shame you're not with some great guy planning the wedding of the century. You know, the All-American dream of a happy home with the requisite white picket fence, a dog and two or three kids."

I snort. "I'm no prize and men don't marry home-wreckers like me. They just fuck me and cast me aside; ask anyone in this godforsaken, gossipy town, especially *the wives*." I shrug. "Which is fine, I mean, I don't need anybody. And I've *never* wanted the white picket fence or the kids." I rub my stomach where the scars remain. Kids will never be an option for me. My mother told me the doctors tried their best, but glass from the windshield sliced and diced me like a filet on a butcher's block. It's probably for the best; I have enough problems without adding a kid in the mix. It should have been me that died, but no, I was the "lucky one." Jack's side of the car took the brunt of the hit.

"I don't listen to idle gossip, and your tough girl exterior is just a wall you've thrown up to protect yourself. Everybody needs to love and be loved in return. That's part of being human. Deep down, you're not the tough girl you pretend to be." Remi reaches for the cigarettes on the console. "May I?"

I shrug, not really caring. Jack smoked, my father smoked and Mama smoked up to five years ago. Besides, I don't want to delay getting to my mom for his smoke breaks. "Go ahead." Curiosity gets the best of me. "Just what type of girl do you think I am?"

He cracks his window and lights a cigarette, taking his time before speaking. The wait for his answer seems interminable, and that uneasy feeling of anxiety fills the pit of my stomach. It hits me full force that despite my self-inflicted isolation, and the stronghold I've built around my heart as a means of survival, it matters to me what *he* thinks. This man of God is getting under my skin.

"Misunderstood. Outwardly you portray this hardened, smart-mouthed girl who doesn't give a damn what others think. But, that isn't the real you. I think you're a passionate young woman with a huge personality, who hasn't figured out how to channel all this gusto for life productively. I'd go so far as to say, you're a visionary who sees things beyond superficial appearances. Yet, for some asinine reason, you're stymied by your fears. You refuse to trust yourself enough to let go and grab life by the balls. You've pigeonholed yourself into this stereotype of the crazy, bad girl. My question for you, is why?

"Sure, it's true, you've veered off course through some bad decisions, but you have it within yourself to know your true path. Someday, if you drop this wall of distrust you've built around your heart, you'll find someone worthy of your love. And when you find him, let the poor guy in that cuckoo head of yours, past all the superficial *I don't give a damns* and *I'm a crazy bitch* layers. If he's the right guy, he'll love you in spite of your flaws and imperfections. He won't mold you to change, he'll help you to embrace your idiosyncrasies and learn how to control them so they don't become so self-destructive. You, *Evangeline*, are your own worst enemy."

I look at my hands clasped in my lap and shake my head, wondering just who the hell he's talking about. This girl with potential, it can't be me. I snort with derision. "Not everyone is good, *Father*. I didn't figure you to be the type to toe the company line, spouting canned platitudes. I thought you were a straight shooter, not like Father Asswipe. He'd tell me I was a '*good girl*,' but I know he didn't truly believe it."

"No. *You're* the one that doesn't believe it. So talk to me." He stares at the road and takes a deep draw off his cigarette, careful to blow the smoke toward his open window.

"What? Like confess my sins? I don't think so." Nervous energy builds inside of me. My leg bounces, and I twist a lock of my hair around my finger.

"No, just talk. Sometimes it helps —"

"Oh good God, would you stop? I've talked until I'm sick of talking about my pathetic life. I've seen countless shrinks, counselors, therapists and even Father Asswipe. *No*, I don't want to talk about it. I'm done talking." I move to flip on the radio, but his hand catches mine. My body trembles in response to the contact as I stare at our fingers, now interlocked. Energy crackles between us, and the heat of my embarrassment flushes my cheeks. I jerk my hand from his as if burned.

"Back away from the radio. Driver rules," he growls, but he's grinning at the same time.

"What?" I blink, incapable of focusing on the words coming out of his mouth after the jolt of desire that just coursed through my body.

He smiles as if unaware of the carnal electricity sizzling in the car. Maybe he hadn't felt it, and it's all in my mind. I press my knees together.

"The driver gets to pick the music."

"If I have to listen to monks chanting for over three thousand miles I'll truly be certifiable by the time we get there," I grumble.

His head snaps toward me. "Seriously? Do I strike you as the type to listen to that? What did we listen to last night?" His affronted look is comical as he concentrates on the road again.

True. Looking at his muscular arms in the T-shirt, his sunglasses and his disheveled hair blowing in the wind, I have to admit, classical would never be his style. But I don't want to let him off that easy. I kind of like this verbal sparring and pushing his buttons. It makes me feel normal. I shrug. "Well, yeah."

His lips curl in a grin. "If that's what you think, you *are* two beers short of a six-pack. I never said Bach is my homeboy." Raising his hips, he digs his phone out of his pocket and plugs it into the car stereo.

I find the simple action mesmerizing. I'd love to see those hips thrusting toward me…"Homeboy? That's a little *dated*, Father."

"I'll make note of that. I have a special playlist named *Evangeline*. I made it last night, just for you."

Gnarls Barkley begins wailing about being crazy and I burst out laughing. It's refreshing to be around someone that doesn't pussyfoot around my mental illness. I admire and appreciate his straightforwardness. Even though I've only known him for such a short time, I realize when I'm with him I'm almost comfortable in my own skin. Maybe I *can* let down my guard and just be myself around him.

"Nice." I hide my grin from him with my mop of hair.

"Don't cover that pretty smile, Crazy Girl. You can't hide from me. I'm here for a reason."

"Yeah, yeah, I know. To save me."

"Is that so bad?"

I shrug. Yesterday, I would have said yes. Today, I'm less sure. I decide to play the indifferent card. "Whatever suits you, it doesn't matter to me."

"That's precisely the problem. You're so self-involved nothing matters to you. It's really quite selfish the way you don't give a damn about anyone else. Let me remind you once again, the world doesn't revolve around *you*. Did you ever consider that your suicide would be detrimental to your mother?"

No, I hadn't. His harsh, accurate words hit a bull's-eye in my heart, and all of my hidden insecurities slowly bleed into the tension in the car. "You think you know me so well, don't you, *Father?* You think all of your religious bullshit training and college education makes you an authority on suffering." Hot tears threaten to spill down my cheeks and I struggle to maintain control, sucking in a ragged breath. Turning my back to him, I stare out the passenger window so he can't see how much he's just hurt my feelings.

"Here are some more platitudes for you. Life ain't fair. Truth sometimes hurts. And love isn't always enough. What are we doing in this car, if you don't care about your mother's wellbeing?"

He's right, after everything Mama has been through, my death would be a nail in her coffin. However, I refuse to let him pull me into a heart-to-heart. "Trust me, you don't know a thing about me."

"I don't claim to know all your truths, just what you've revealed to me and what I've observed." He sighs when I refuse to look at him, and we drive in an uncomfortable silence for a couple of hours listening to his *Evangeline* playlist. Just about every damn song has the word crazy in it, the son of a bitch.

"Evie."

His use of my preferred name instead of my full name catches my attention, and I turn to face him.

"It's a long drive, and I don't want it to be spent in silence. I'm not a Trappist monk."

I let out a huff and reply, "Too bad. I like silence."

"Talk to me, please?"

"I have to pee," I confess, twisting in my seat. When will I learn my stubbornness never serves me well? I should have asked to stop an hour ago.

His warm laughter fills the car and melts a little of the ice wall I put into place. "Well, I guess that's a start."

He drives a few more miles before finding a gas station. Before he cuts off the engine, I throw open my door and damn near trip over my own feet trying to get to the bathroom, only to find it's locked.

I knock and someone grunts, "I'm in here."

Remi walks in and pays for the gas, laughing as I rock on my heels, doing the gotta-pee dance of agony. I pound on the door, again.

"I said it's occupied."

I groan at the muffled response. I'm at the point of serious pain and it's going to get ugly in a minute.

I glare as Remi walks past me straight into the men's room. He's right, life is unfair; you never see a line at the men's room. Two minutes later he walks out with a smug smile. "Ready?"

"No, dammit! She won't get out of there." I beat on the door again only to be told, in no uncertain terms, she'll get out when she's ready and for me to go away.

Remi peeks in the men's room, grabs my arm, and shoves me inside. "All clear, go. I'll stand guard." Without hesitating I dash in the stall, holding my breath due to the stench. Men are such disgusting pigs. I wash my hands, drying them on my jeans since the blower is broken.

"Thank you." I breeze past Remi to the candy aisle, picking up a chocolate bar and a pack of gum. Remi shakes his head at me, his arms crossed over his chest.

I frown, wondering what's crawled up his ass. "What?"

"How much money do you have?" he asks.

I shrug. "I dunno, a couple hundred dollars, more or less. Why?" *Probably a lot less.*

"Hand it over. We're pooling it together."

I hand him most of my money, keeping back a twenty. I trust him, but you never know.

"Look, we can't waste money. We have over three thousand miles to travel. That's a lot of gas, food and hotel bills. You don't need candy."

"You're not my mother. What about your wasteful spending?" I raise one eyebrow and stare pointedly at the brand new pack of cigarettes poking out of his jeans pocket. Next to something else that garners my attention. With reluctance, I force myself to look him in the face.

"It's an addiction," he argues.

Mmm, a habit that I might want to try...I shake my head. *Cigarettes, he's talking about smoking. Quit looking at his package.*

"So? Maybe chocolate is an addiction for me."

"You don't need it. After meeting you, trust me, I *need* the cigarettes."

An older woman emerges from the bathroom. As we argue, her head volleys back and forth like she's a spectator at a tennis match.

I toss my chin up in defiance. "My chocolate and chewing gum aren't going to put me in the grave."

"Pity, since that's your main goal in life. Ever hear of diabetes?"

"Would you stop? It's one lousy candy bar and a pack of sugar-free gum. Combined they don't add up to what you just spent on those damn cancer sticks."

"Evangeline—"

"Keep your mouth shut, young man." The dire warning comes from the bathroom lady and Remi's face pales before turning the color of my cinnamon gum. She hobbles toward us with the help of her cane, and I feel bad for having beaten on the bathroom door. A gnarled hand plucks the candy bar and gum from my hands. She totters to the register and pays for them despite our protests. With a smile, she turns around and hands them back to me. "Here you go, hun. Accept this as my apology. I'm sorry it took me so long. I just had a total knee replacement, and I'm moving as slow as Moses in the desert."

Remi coughs and chokes. The old woman turns and pokes him with her cane, hard enough to make him wince. He backs away, a dark look settling across his handsome features.

Guilt makes my cheeks burn. "I'm sorry tried to hurry you. You don't need to do this." I hit Remi on the arm and hiss, "Pay her." Rubbing his arm he glares at both of us as he digs in his back pocket for his wallet, but she stops him with another prod of her cane.

"Keep your money, cheapskate. And pray you don't die from lung cancer." She turns and faces me. "Honey, you need to learn to stand on your own two feet. You deserve better than this tightwad. Like my sister and I always say, you don't need a man in this world. Consider the bigger picture; don't settle just because of what he has between his legs. They make dildos for that." Remi splutters and my mouth remains open as we watch her shuffle to her car where another older lady waits, staring intently at both of us. Remi leaves the store, red-faced, not giving more than a cursory glance at the amused clerk.

I follow him with a smirk. "What a sweet old lady." I wave at the two women, ignoring Father Frowny-face as he hands off the car keys so I can take a turn at driving. "What's your problem? We didn't spend any of our precious money on my dumb candy. You should have blessed her or something. I thought she was a saint." Grinning, I settle my sunglasses on my nose and buckle my seatbelt as he sits beside me stewing. "You're just mad because she injured your male pride, get over it."

Cool, green eyes cut toward me as he fastens the seatbelt. "She's a nosy old witch; she always has been."

I start the car. "You knew her?"

Remi jumps and stares at me with a wild-eyed look before his brow furrows. "What? Uh, no, I meant, her kind, you know, meddlesome old ladies."

"That's not very charitable, *Father*," I reply with a prim simper as I pull out on the road.

"I'll pray for forgiveness." He shoves his sunglasses up his nose, tapping his bouncing leg with his thumb. He's wound up tighter than a two-dollar watch.

Evie plugs her phone in and starts singing off key about knocking on heaven's door. I close my eyes and pretend to sleep, still fuming about the incident at the gas station. I wonder if the Boss sent those two nosy old broads to check up on me, or did the old busybodies take it upon themselves to see what I'm doing? My chest still hurts where Martha poked me with her cane. I'm surprised Mary left His side to drive. She usually likes to cling to Number One Son like stink on shit. Those two brown-nosers have always irritated me. I hope their tattletale report satisfies Him that I'm doing my job. I mean, Evangeline's still alive and kicking. What did they expect to find? Me burying her in the backyard?

However, I'm stubborn, not dense. If He sent the gruesome twosome, it was meant to be a subtle warning that He's watching. I bet no one else gets treated like this. Well, Luc, but that's a whole different story. And I refuse to go all Frank Capra and tell Evangeline about her wonderful life. I mean come on, her life has pretty much sucked ass so far. And I'm certainly not up for any Dickens-like time travel. Besides, it's the end of stinking hot August, not Christmas, and I like being in a corporeal body.

I especially liked it when my corporeal body was next to her smoking hot body. I'd like it even more…The music changes and suddenly we're listening to AC/DC singing about being on the highway to hell. Evangeline mutters under her breath about not having pushed shuffle.

I sigh. I know who pushed shuffle.

Point taken, Sir.

Chapter Seven

Hungry and tired, we pull into a respectable, low-budget motel after driving for twelve hours straight, with very little conversation. Remi heads into the lobby to secure our rooms, and I rub my pounding head. Despite my epic meltdown this morning, today has been one of my better days as far as my *loco en la cabeza* thoughts go, but it's still been stressful.

Time spent alone in peace and quiet is treasured. Time spent in peace and quiet with someone not speaking to you is downright lonesome and triggers my abandonment issues. I don't understand why the incident with the old lady riled him so much. When I think about it, despite spending the last twenty-four hours together, I don't know much about Remi. Picking up his phone, I scroll through his playlists. I watched him thumb in his pass code, which is far too easy to be much protection. Aside from the list entitled *Evangeline*, it has an eclectic mixture of rock and roll, alternative music, and blues. A quick glance through the glass doors of the motel shows him signing the register.

I look to see if he's on social media, but he isn't. Maybe there's a rule about it for priests. I flip to his contact list. He only has one other number besides mine programmed. It has an unknown area code and I wonder who *The Boss* is. A Monsignor? His Mom? It looks vaguely as if it could be an overseas number. *The Pope?* Curiosity gets the best of me. I hit dial and listen.

"Good evening, Evangeline."

My mouth falls open, and I drop the phone before snatching it off of the floor with trembling fingers. "H-How do you know it's me and my name?" I whisper, shrinking into my seat. It isn't like caller ID would work, I'm on Remi's phone. A trickle of cold sweat breaks out on my forehead, and the hair on my arms stands straight up. The hand holding the phone shakes so hard I have to use my other hand to steady it.

"Aren't you with Remiel?" The warm voice sounds rich and uplifting, like hot chocolate on a cold morning.

"Y-Yes. You know about me? What has he said?" Why would Remi talk about me with his boss?

"Yes, of course, dear. I know all about you. Everything will be fine, I promise. Just concentrate on getting to your mother. She loves you more than you know."

"Who are you?" My distrust kicks into overdrive. "And how do you know about my mother?" *Is my mom in on this?* Maybe she isn't sick. Maybe she's paid Remi to kidnap me. Maybe this guy is a shrink. I bet they've planned this together to take me back to the nuthouse. Without waiting for an answer, I drop the phone and fumble with the door lock. The damn seatbelt pulls me back, hindering my escape. I manage to unlatch it and bolt from the car as Remi strides out of the lobby.

"Evangeline?"

"Stay away from me!" Backing away from him, I throw my hands out as if doing so will hold him at bay.

"Oh, for Pete's sake. Now what?" He approaches me like I'm a rabid dog.

"I may be crazy, but I'm not stupid," I spit out, walking backward, keeping a wary eye on him. My overwhelming need to get away spikes to an alarming level. I don't want the mind-numbing drugs and endless sessions of talking.

The lights in the parking lot provide a diffuse illumination, but even so, I see a dark shadow rise up behind him. I spin around and sprint toward the safety of the tree line at the end of the property. My heart pounds in sync with the rhythm of my frantic feet. Every sound behind me seems magnified, but I'm too scared to look back, afraid he will be right behind me. Praying I can hide somewhere in the safety of the woods, I forge ahead. At one point, I'm running so fast it feels like my feet aren't even touching the ground. Just as I reach the edge of the trees behind the motel, he catches hold of my hand, jerking me toward him.

"Evangeline, what the hell happened?" The bastard who smokes isn't even breaking a sweat or breathing hard.

I, on the other hand, can't catch my breath, and my heart hammers so fast my chest aches. I attempt to pull away, but he yanks me back and I land with a thud against his chest. The arm that snakes across my chest prevents me from falling. Spinning me around, he grabs me by the shoulders and peers down at me. Away from the lights of the parking lot it's dark, except for the moonlight, but fire flashes in his eyes. I close my eyes and sink to my knees in despair.

"Please don't hurt me, please, leave me alone and go away. Oh, God, I don't want this anymore. Go away, please…just go away and let me die. I can't go back there." I clasp my hands in front of me like a repentant sinner.

"Slow down, you're not making any sense." He kneels so he's level with me. His brows knit together over eyes full of concern.

"Of course I'm not. I'm insane, remember?" A hysterical laugh surrounds us and I realize it's mine. I clutch his shirt with my hands. "Please, Remi. If I mean anything to you, don't make me go—" The sob in the back of my throat cuts off my air and voice.

"Go where, sweetness?" he asks, pulling me to his chest. His hand rubs soothing circles on my back.

"Back to the hospital," I choke out. The thought of the needles, spinning rooms, and the oblivion provided by the powerful psychotropic medications, or worse, the shock treatments, has me terrified beyond reason.

"But your mother needs you."

"She hired you, didn't she?" My teeth chatter around my thick tongue, and despite the summer heat, I shiver with icy dread.

"What?"

"My mother. She hired you to kidnap me and make me go back to the hospital to get regulated on my medicine. Did she get that power of attorney?" Frustrated, I beat on his chest with my fist. "I know all crazy people say it, but I'm not that crazy. I'm not! Just let me go, and I promise I won't tell anyone. Please." I'm trying my best to contain my sobs, but my breathing sounds like a choked engine.

"That sounds pretty damn crazy, Evangeline. I don't know your mother—"

"Please Remi, *I'll do anything...*" I rub against him. This isn't my first rodeo using sex to get what I want. If it keeps me out of the nuthouse, it will be worth shoving my pride aside, yet again. Sometimes loneliness would force me to pick up a random stranger, using sex to feel connected. But in those cases the relationship was superficial, and in the end, it made me feel worse, and worthless. At least Remi's good looking and I like him. Or, I did...

What am I doing? A tiny fragment of my conscience screams for me to stop. I pull away, ashamed of my actions, but my eyes are drawn to the pounding pulse in his neck. I lean in closer, feeling the heat from his body. Almost of their own accord, my lips trail the faint blue vein up his neck. He sucks in his breath and freezes. Pulling his T-shirt out from his jeans, I run my hands up his hard, muscular back. It isn't the only thing hard. His erection presses against me, spurring me on. I kiss and nibble along the stubble on his jaw, up his cheek, until I reach those perfect lips. A needy fire simmers deep within me as his warm breath fans across my face.

Deep in his chest a growl rumbles as he gasps, "No, we can't. Evangeline, stop—"

"Yes, Remi, yes..."

For the first time in a long time, I feel like I'm in the right place at the right time. With every ounce of my being, I know I belong here. We are somehow one and the same. It no longer matters who is manipulating whom. Intellectually, I know it's wrong. In my heart, I don't give a damn. This feels more right than anything I've ever experienced, including my love for Jack. Somehow, he manages to sit and I straddle his lap facing him. "Please, Remi..."

"Please what?" he croaks. His hands have worked their way under my shirt onto my back. The contact fuels my desire. My feverish body pulsates with need and I rock against his hard arousal, escalating my yearning to be with him a hundred fold. A soft moan escapes my lips.

"This is wrong," he whispers as he pulls me closer, his lips nipping at mine. One hand moves from under my shirt and cups my face.

"Oh, God."

He deepens the kiss as our tongues tease one another in an ancient fertility dance. My hard nipples press into him as my hands roam underneath his shirt, kneading and stroking upward until my fingers entangle with feathers.

Her soft lips nibble along my jaw, her hands delve under my T-shirt and every damn reason why we shouldn't be doing this flees my Evangeline-intoxicated brain. I pull her closer to me, inhaling her scent and tasting the nectar of her skin. I'm drunk and out of control as an overwhelming need to devour her consumes me. I somehow manage to sit without falling and position her on my lap with her legs straddling my waist. Her arms wrap around my neck, and only our clothes separate us from being totally connected.

"Please, Remi," she whispers as my lips trace down her neck to the pounding pulse at the base.

"Please what, Evie?" My voice sounds husky because I can't seem to swallow. My hand creeps under her shirt loving her curves, as I trail kisses to her delightful mouth. Her soft moan combined with a purr of pleasure from the back of her throat is the sexiest thing I've heard in the past three centuries, maybe ever. She rocks against me and I damn near explode.

Her head falls back and she murmurs, "Oh God."

Calling on the Boss combined with her fingers grasping a handful of my feathers is like being immersed in an ice-cold bucket of water, shocking me back to reality. This has to stop and it has to stop, *now.*

I grab her face and I see my fire of need reflected in her dark, dilated pupils. "This will be a dream, Evangeline." Confusion settles in her beautiful eyes just before they close and her body goes limp.

Holding her to my chest I kiss the top of her head and rock her, inwardly cursing our fate for what can never be.

"Wake up, sleepyhead."

I'm not asleep, Remi's hands are on me, and I can taste his lips...

Something nudges my shoulder and my eyes fly open. I look around, taking in my surroundings. I'm in the car with the seat laid back, and Remi sits beside me on the driver's side. Still groggy, I rub my eyes and realize we're parked in front of a room at a motel.

"I was asleep?" An overwhelming sense of sadness washes through me, and I shiver as the blood quits racing through my limbs.

"Like the dead. Did you know you drool?" The smile doesn't seem to quite reach his eyes as he rubs the back of his fingers across the corner of my mouth. They linger for a second longer than necessary on my jaw. "You okay?" he murmurs.

Snapping my seat upright, I rub the back of my neck. "Yeah, I guess so. I feel hung over or something. I must've slept too hard." A dense fog seems to encase my mind. I look out the window. It's dark, but by the dim light I see a parking lot and a fast food joint lit by the bright golden arches. I long to slip back into the glorious dream of his lips on mine.

"You've been under a lot of stress. Your body's just trying to catch up. Look, let's get you settled in for the night, and I'll run next door and grab us something to eat. You shower and I'll be back in a few."

"Is your room next to mine?" I find my purse on the floorboard and open the car door, but look back at him when he doesn't answer.

He stares straight ahead instead of looking at me. "Uh, no. That's why we need to orchestrate this carefully."

I narrow my gaze and his cheeks flush under the light from outside the motel room. "What do you mean?"

"We have one room, two beds. I told you, we have to save money."

It's my turn for my cheeks to burn as I recall my dream. "Is this wise? What about your reputation?"

"Mine? What about yours?"

I shrug. "We both know mine's for shit." My self-deprecating laugh makes him frown.

"You're a good person, Evie. I wish you'd believe that." He sighs. "Look, no one knows us here. I'm placing my trust in you that you won't tell anyone, and I'm trusting God to help me remember my vows." He taps his thumbs against the steering wheel. "So help a poor guy out, okay? I may be celibate, but I'm still human. No sleeping naked or sexy lingerie, please." Although his voice sounds teasing, the tic above his clenched jaw betrays his nervousness. He's coiled up tighter than a serpent about to strike.

Too tired and confused by my dream, I nod, but add teasingly as we step out of the car, "Party pooper."

"Shit."

The soft expletive pushes me to have mercy on him. "I'm teasing. I sleep in an oversized T-shirt, and I'll add yoga pants just for you."

He grabs our luggage and hauls it into the room. "Thank you. So what do you want to eat?"

"Whatever is cheapest, and I'll drink water." I rub my jeans nervously with my hands. The way he keeps staring at me unnerves me. I must look like a mess.

"Okay. You get first shower, and I'll be back in a few. Leave me some hot water, okay?" He whips around and points at me. "And no suicide attempts while I'm gone. Promise me."

I give him a smart ass salute. "I promise, *Father*." He leaves and I collapse on the bed, rubbing my aching forehead. That dream had been so real and disturbing on so many levels. I slip the room key in my pocket and set off in search of the elusive ice machine, thinking something cold might help my headache. The dry stifling heat is nothing compared to the humidity of south Florida, but still uncomfortable. I round the corner toward the front office and freeze. The front of the motel looks just like it did in my dream. I hug the wall with a mixture of fear and curiosity as I take in my surroundings. There's the tree line where I ran, trying to get away.

Like a burglar, I creep away from the motel and scurry across the parking lot. The path of trampled grass I'd previously taken disappears in the waning light. Clouds cover the moon, making it too difficult without a flashlight to determine which way I'd run. A bead of sweat forms on my forehead and my knees knock together as I look around, trying to figure out what it means.

Was it a dream?

A hallucination?

If so, they're becoming more life-like, less dream-like. And I've never seen or heard non-human apparitions until I met Remi—unless you count my talks with the angels when I was a little girl. Hypersensitive to my surroundings, I jump at every noise, and a firefly damn near makes me pee on myself. I wish I had a flashlight. Too terrified to walk into the inky darkness alone, I retrace my steps. Despite my trembling hands, I manage to shovel a bucket of ice. I return to the room and sit on the bed, waiting, like a cat outside a mouse hole. A knock on the door propels me off the bed to throw open the door. Remi holds a bag of fast food, nibbling on a French fry. He frowns at my appearance.

"Look, Crazy Girl. You need to bathe. I'm not riding with you for days in an enclosed car in August if you're not going to take care of your personal hygiene. That's just gross."

"What are you?"

His eyes shift nervously for a fraction of a second before he sighs. "I feel like your mother right now. Why haven't you bathed?"

I clench my fists and stomp my foot, my temper exploding with exasperation and fear. Using my index finger, I punctuate each word with a stab to his chest, asking through gritted teeth, "What. Are. You?"

"What I am is annoyed as hell, at the moment." He raises one eyebrow and moves into the room, closing the door. Leaning against it, he digs out another French fry crossing himself with it. "Bless this fast food and nourish our bodies despite the grease with which it was fried. Amen." He takes a bite and chews thoughtfully. "I'm tired, hungry and in need of a shower. What bug has crawled up your ass this time?"

"It wasn't a dream. I saw the motel. I saw the trees." I back away from him, taking deep breaths to keep myself calm.

He sighs and shakes his head. "It was a dream. You were tired and sleeping and probably stirred a bit when we pulled into the motel, making you somewhat aware of where we were. However, by the time I pulled around to our room, you were out cold."

"But I saw the grass bent where I ran toward the trees…" My voice trails off. In truth, I don't know what to believe.

He rolls his eyes and rubs the back of his neck. "For heaven's sake, do you not recognize how batty you sound? Stop and listen to yourself. This is a rundown motel on an interstate that allows pets to stay here. Walking back with the food, I saw two people out in the grass walking their dogs. Now quit working yourself into a tizzy and eat."

He shoves the sack of food at me, his brows drawn together over eyes that appear to snap with anger. "You know what? I'm a pretty patient man, but you're pushing it, Evie. I'm going to go smoke and take a minute to calm down and pray for forgiveness, because right at this moment I'm not feeling very charitable toward you. Go take a bath. You have five minutes." He slams the door so hard the cheap prints over the beds tilt, and I hope we don't get kicked out for public disturbance.

Too tired to think and almost beyond caring, I grab my things and take the quickest shower of my life. After I'm dressed, I crack open the bathroom door and peek into the room. I find Remi lying on the bed, one arm thrown over his eyes. He's removed his shirt, and I pause, wishing dreams did come true. He's placed my hamburger and fries on the bedside table, and poured me a glass of water.

There's nothing unusual about him except for the fact he really is a nice guy. *Or is he?* A momentary fear slithers through my mind. But what if he isn't thoughtful at all? What if my food or drink has been tampered with, either with poison or prescription meds? My sarcastic inner bitch reminds me it doesn't really matter. I want to be dead anyway, don't I?

Do I?

No, not any more. At least not until after I make sure my mom is okay.

"I haven't done anything to your food," he grumbles from behind the arm thrown over his eyes. I watch his other hand rise and fall on his hard, contoured chest with each measured breath.

His perception is uncanny. "I never thought that," I lie, biting my lower lip and twisting my hair.

Remi lowers his arm and stares at me. "Don't ever play poker. You'll lose." Remi sits and his shoulders sag as he scrubs a hand over his stubbled jaw. I remember enjoying the sandpaper feel of his beard under my lips and against my tender skin…He stands and quickly turns his back to me as he digs through his suitcase. The back of his neck flushes.

"Asshole," I mutter under my breath.

The sound of his suitcase slamming closed startles me. He swings around to face me with a scowl. "Your mood swings are spectacular. Do you ever shoot off fireworks after one to complete the show? I'm going to shower and call it a night. I, for one, am exhausted just from being around you. I can't imagine how fatiguing it must be to actually be you. Now eat and go to bed." His voice sounds thick with disgust and sarcasm, unlike his usually affable manner. I realize my illness will ultimately push him away. It drives everyone away.

I manage not to cry, but I can't swallow my meal for the lump in my throat. I'm hurt and angered by his comment about how exhausting it is to be around me. It's reminiscent of why my mother left me. Why Jack was leaving me. He storms into the bathroom, slamming the door.

You're too intense, Evie. Kayla is easy to be with, her emotions don't ping all over the damn place like a pinball machine on crack. I don't have to walk on eggshells around her.

I brush my teeth and crawl into bed, my back toward Remi's bed. I wish I believed someone would hear my prayers. If I did, I'd pray for peace. That's all. Just peace.

The bathroom door opens and he brushes his teeth. To my relief, he leaves the light on in the bathroom so that it isn't totally dark. He approaches the beds and I squeeze my eyes shut. Taking a deep breath, I relax my eyelids and breathe in even, slow breaths, feigning sleep. The comforting smell of pine mixed with cinnamon teases my senses.

He places his hand on the back of my head and whispers, "The peace of God which passes all understanding will guard your heart and your mind." Just when I think he's turned away, his warm breath teases my neck as he whispers in my ear. "You're my Crazy Girl, but you're not crazy." Stillness enfolds me like a cozy blanket and I snuggle under the covers as my eyelids grow heavy.

Something wakes me, and it takes me a moment to remember where I am. I turn toward the clicking sound of rosary beads being counted. It reminds me of my mom and makes me strangely homesick for her. Remi kneels with his back to me beside his bed. A soft light bathes him with a white aura.

"Go back to sleep, sweetness," he murmurs. The light fades as my eyes adjust to the dark and only a sliver of light from the cracked bathroom door illuminates the room. *That light had to have been from the bathroom, right?*

"I like it when you call me that." I smile. I like it when he calls me Crazy Girl even better. It's like he's giving credence to who I am without judgment. "Checking in with the Man upstairs?" Without thinking I lean over and rub his back. He straightens as if shocked by my touch, and I quickly pull my hand back.

"Something like that. Sorry if I disturbed you. Go back to sleep, it's still early." He rises from his knees and crouches beside my bed, gently pushing the hair out of my face. His tender touch feels so soothing, my eyes drift closed again. There's something about talking in the dark that makes one feel safe. Maybe that's why Catholics use the confessional. I open my eyes again and look at him.

"When I was a little girl, I spoke to angels, but Mama said it was my imagination. Lately, it feels like that. It's like I'm seeing things I know are real, but no one believes me."

I swallow the lump forming in my throat. "Or, everyone's right..." It takes me two tries to get the words out. "And I'm crazy." Struggling to keep my tears in check, I whisper, "I'm getting sicker, aren't I? My illness is progressing. It terrifies me. I'm afraid it'll get so bad, I'll be locked away forever in the darkness of my mind, always searching for something and never finding it."

"I don't know. You quit taking your medications," he reminds me.

"I don't like feeling like a zombie. I want to feel alive."

"And yet you want to die," he points out. A hint of sadness laces his voice.

"Sounds crazy, doesn't it?" I chuckle at the irony, dashing away the one tear that escaped, unable to explain, since I don't understand it myself.

"Nah. Not to me." I hear a smile in his voice this time. "You know, there are some people who are more in tune with the spiritual realm than others. Think of the great visionaries. Saint Bernadette, for one, or the children of Fátima. Everyone thought they had bats in their belfries, too."

I think his explanation is farfetched, but I appreciate the kindness behind it. "Thank you."

"You're welcome."

I move over in the bed so he can sit and pat it, invitingly.

"Evangeline, I don't think this is a good idea." His harsh breathing echoes in his strained voice.

"I don't want sex, *Father*." Like a child, I cross my fingers and pray I don't go to hell for lying. "I just want to talk. You'll be on top of the covers, I'll be under them."

"I'm sure Eve had just as convincing an argument," he mutters, running a hand through his disheveled hair. "Just one bite, Adam…" He speaks in a falsetto voice as he climbs on the bed, making me laugh. Lying on his back with his arms crossed behind his head, he stares at the ceiling.

I curl up beside him and place my hand over his heart. It beats in time with mine. Perfect synchronicity. "Why are you on sabbatical?"

"It wasn't by choice, more like a forced vacation so I can take time and reflect on whether or not I want my job."

"Is your boss a good man to work for?" My heart rate escalates as I try to surreptitiously finagle answers.

He chuckles. "Yeah, he's pretty decent, if somewhat of a know-it-all."

Trying to act casual, I ask, "Does he know about me?" I remove my hand from his heart and pick at a loose thread in the bedspread.

"Yes. I check in daily with him, and I've mentioned you."

"Good things?"

"*Everything*. He's easy to talk to." He reaches for me and pulls my head to rest on his shoulder. His fingers trail up and down my arm. "You'd like him."

His easygoing, matter-of-factness eases my apprehension. It's like we're a normal couple talking. *Friends*. I mean friends, not a couple.

"So what have you decided about your job?"

He doesn't answer right away, and I count the ancient air conditioner's clicks and groans as it strains to keep the room comfortable in the summer heat. "I'm still working on my decision."

"Did you always want to be a priest?"

His bark of laughter fills the room. "Hardly."

"What made you decide, then?"

"Predestination, I guess. I don't know. Enough with the twenty questions; I have a few of my own for you."

I fake yawn loudly to stall, not wanting to break the spell of friendly intimacy. "I'm tired."

He rolls to his side facing me. "You never fight fair, do you?"

Closing my eyes, I tentatively take his hand in mine to prolong this connection. I refrain from kissing it like I want to. "Nope. All is fair in love and war."

"Are we in love or at war?" he asks softly, almost as if he's asking himself, not me.

I don't answer.

For in truth, I don't know.

I watch Evangeline sleep, holding her hand, and listening to her soft snores. I'm headed for deep trouble, and I know it. I've tried getting in touch with the Boss using my phone, prayers, rosary...*Nothing, nada, zip.* Did I really complain about life in heaven being boring? If so, I take it back.

Boring sounds good right now.

Anything would beat this state of hell, not knowing how to reach out to offer hope and comfort to this sad girl. Evangeline has touched me in a profound manner, unlike any human before. Maybe it's those haunted eyes, the way they look at me with a glimmer of hope. Or her inherent sweetness, that is as addictive as the nicotine in my favorite vice. Whatever it is, I'm in trouble. I can't do this alone. I'm floundering.

I desperately need some guidance. I don't want to "go rogue." *Tell me what the fuck to do!*

There is no wind.

There is no thunder.

Silence is my answer.

I pull Evangeline closer, holding her tight.

I'm alone.

And I'm scared.

Chapter Eight

Something tickles my nose and I drift awake, feeling a weight around my waist. When I open my eyes, I realize I'm wrapped under Remi's arm and my nose is buried in his chest. For the first time in two years I feel at peace. Without thinking, I place a small kiss over his heart, just as a thank you for being him. He doesn't stir and I'm sort of disappointed, I'll never know if this spontaneous kiss would have had an effect on him. *What am I thinking? It's for the best.* I slip out of bed and head to the bathroom. When I return, he's dressed and standing in the open door to the motel, smoking a cigarette.

I smile and offer him half of my cold hamburger and fries for breakfast. He shakes his head and doesn't meet my gaze, instead tossing me a carton of milk and a box of Froot Loops.

"Very funny. Keep your day job; the comedy club won't be calling any time soon. Where did these come from?"

He grunts in response and sips his coffee. "It's this dump's idea of breakfast. It came with the room."

I attribute his cold attitude to guilt. He's right; I don't fight fair. I've been selfish my entire life, and it was grossly unfair to test him like that, drawing him into my bed. It's just that I feel so complete with him. There's like an invisible bond or a magnetic pull between us, and I don't mean in a physical way, although my mind invariably drifts in that direction.

He's compassionate, funny and straightforward. He gets me, the way no one *ever* has. And no doubt about it, he's as handsome as the devil. But this strange, convoluted relationship we have has disturbed him, and it's taxing our friendship. His aloof manner has re-established the godly/ungodly barrier between us and I now wonder if it will survive this trip.

He's still giving me the silent treatment after breakfast, and it's starting to wear on my nerves. Quite frankly, it pisses me off. His barked one syllable grunts in answer to my questions brings out the snarky sarcasm in my replies. I also add a few evil-eyed glares, which he pointedly ignores. We drive in total silence if you don't count my exaggerated sighs of frustration. He even refuses to turn on the radio, grumbling about my off-key singing being a distraction. Just when I'm ready to scream to get his attention, he pulls off the interstate to get gas.

As he strides into the station to pay, I call to check on my mom. She's in good spirits and sounds anxious to see me. Her heart test is scheduled for next week, giving us plenty of time to get to her house. I skirt around my travel arrangements, telling her I'm driving with a friend. Before Mama can ask me too many questions, I plead the old "losing signal" excuse and break the connection.

It's hot as hell and I roll down the window, wishing Remi would get with the twenty-first century and use either a debit or credit card to pay for gas at the pump. Something lunges at my window. Startled, I duck and cover my head. Dear God, now what?

A whimper and the distinct smell of dirty dog drifts through the open window. Turning around, I look down and find a scraggly, muddy mutt staring back at me. He's pitiful with his matted, wiry hair, and glazed, soulful brown eyes. I instantly bond with him.

"Hey, sweet boy," I coo. His tail wags and his pink tongue rolls out of his jaw. He looks like he's grinning at me, and I can't help but smile back. "Where did you come from?" I step out of the car and kneel beside him, petting and scratching him behind his ears. He pants and the effort draws my attention to his skeletal frame. Grabbing my purse from the car, I race into the gas station and find Remi leaning against the counter discussing an alternative route around some road construction with the clerk.

"Excuse me, is this your dog?" I point outside to where the poor thing lies with his head resting on his paws.

The gray-haired clerk, whose name tag reads "Franco," smiles and shakes his head. "No, miss. Someone dumped him here last week. We've been giving him some water and scraps because we feel sorry for him." I love the guy's musical accent and his brown eyes appear kind and full of love.

I look out the door at the unfortunate mutt who lifts his head, cocking it to the side when he sees me looking at him. His tail wags and he gives a happy bark. I turn to Remi.

"No." Frowning, he shakes his head.

"But Remi—"

"Look, we barely have enough money for our own food, gas and sleaze bag motels."

"But he'll *die*. He's hungry, and this is a busy place next to an interstate," I argue with just a hint of a whine.

"No. He's a mangy old dog."

"How can you be so cruel? Aren't we supposed to love all of God's creatures?"

The clerk nods, smiling widely in agreement. I cast Remi a shy glance and twist a lock of my hair for good measure, trying to look all innocent and shit.

He rolls his eyes, not buying it. "Evie—"

"Please?" It's time to pull out the big guns. *Yes, I'm going there.* It's the most lethal weapon a woman can use against a man. I let a single tear slip down my cheek.

"I'll give you a bag of dog food and a case of water if you take him," Franco offers. Remi shoots a lethal look toward the helpful clerk. I sense Remi's hesitation borders on acquiescence, so I throw in a trembling lower lip for good measure.

Hands on his narrow hips, he lets out an aggravated sigh and glares at the ceiling before pointing at me. "Okay. But you're responsible for taking care of him."

The clerk claps and I do a victory dance, grinning like a fool.

"Thank you," I squeal with delight, throwing myself into Remi's arms, hugging his neck. He catches me around my waist.

I don't want to let go as every cell in my body acknowledges awareness of Remi as we connect in a weird, almost primal way in the middle of a gas station. I stare into his hooded eyes and revel in the simmering passion reflected there. Sliding down his hard body to stand on my own unsteady feet, I'm grateful for the strong hands still wrapped around my waist. Otherwise, I might collapse at his feet in a puddle of needy goop. My nipples harden and my face flushes hot with embarrassment. *Or is it desire?*

Remi shoves me away and steps back, the color draining from his face as he glances nervously at the clerk. You'd think he was wearing his clericals instead of jeans and a black *50 Shades of Grace* T-shirt. His reaction seems a bit over the top, considering we just slept in the same bed a few hours ago. I'm confused by his mixed signals.

"Bless you, son. It's good to have someone to love and care for. It makes you a better person, no?" Franco responds with a wide, knowing smile. Remi's faced darkens with a scowl and the telltale tic in his cheek has returned. He settles his sunglasses over eyes that appear to flash with anger, and his lips press together in a straight line. The clerk steps out from behind the counter handing him a forty-pound sack of dog food, a case of water, and the bowls used to feed the poor dog. Using some of my dwindling funds, I buy a pretty blue collar and leash. It doesn't take any encouragement to get the neglected mongrel into the back seat. He hops in and settles as if he's been with us for the entire trip.

Remi grimaces and gags as we drive down the interstate. "That dog stinks like camel ass."

"Yuck, that's disgusting. Don't say things like that, you'll hurt his feelings. And how would you know what camel ass smells like, anyway?" I reach into the back seat and scratch the dog's ears talking to him like he's a baby. "Don't listen to the cranky Father. You're our sweet boy, aren't you?" The dog wags his tail, which spreads his noticeable odor throughout the car. I'll never admit it to Remi, but it's pretty damn gross. "What should we name him?"

"We? He isn't *ours*, Evangeline. He's *yours*. If it was up to me, I'd call him Goner."

"Goner?" I frown and look at the poor mutt. "Why Goner?"

"Because as soon as we get to your Mom's, he's a goner, unless you plan to take care of him. And since you can't even take care of yourself, I'd say it's a done deal he'll end up in a shelter." He cracks the sunroof to get some fresh air into the car.

His brutal honesty is like a slap in the face. "That's so mean. I can take care of myself, and I'll take care of Goner, too. I can tell you're not a Franciscan. Haven't you ever had a pet?" *Hell, I'll now take care of this damn dog just to prove Father Self-Righteous wrong.*

"No. Did you?"

"Mostly cats. Mama has our latest cat, Duchess. She didn't want to leave her with me, because…" I bite off the sentence with a shrug, angry with myself.

"You wouldn't take care of it?"

Reluctantly, I admit, "That was her fear."

"But you want to take care of this dog? What's changed?" He glances over at me waiting for my answer. An answer I can't give him. I refuse to let him in and give him the power to hurt me.

You. You've changed me. Life doesn't seem so bleak since I met you.

I gaze out the window, staring at the scenery. I've never been out of Florida before, and I find the green hills of Tennessee intriguing. Peeking at him out of the corner of my eye, I sigh when Father Persistence raises an eyebrow, waiting for my answer.

"I dunno." I cross my arms and stare at the road ahead.

"Well you can't leave me with this dog. If you kill yourself, the dog will truly be a goner."

I gasp and face him, my mouth open with disbelief at his callousness. "That's blackmail. You're the most unethical priest I've ever met."

He smirks as he pulls a cigarette out of the pack. Rolling down his window, he lights it, inhaling deeply. "If you only knew, Crazy Girl."

"Oh? Is there scandal in your past, *Father?*"

"Nothing compared to yours."

I huff with indignation. "Smart ass."

"If you can't take it, don't dish it out." He plugs in his phone and hits his *Evangeline* playlist, cranking it up full blast. I pretend to fan the smoke out of my face, even though in fact, the open window pulls it out of the car. Ozzy Osbourne wails about a crazy train, and Goner starts howling as if he's singing along. Tension broken, we laugh and Remi drums the steering wheel with his thumbs, while I play air guitar, joining Goner's howling on the chorus. After a few more songs about crazy people, Remi turns the music off and we drive for over an hour in a comfortable silence listening to Goner's rhythmic snores. The dog's heavy breathing, combined with the hypnotic rumble of the car engine, and boring landscape lulls me into an almost meditative state.

"Tell me about Jack."

The question snaps me out of my car-induced stupor, and I stare out the window. I knew he'd ask sooner or later. My respirations cease for a moment as the dull roar in my ears escalates in direct correlation to my increasing anxiety level. Dry as desert sand, my tongue feels stuck to the roof of my mouth. I look down at my clenched hands and white knuckles, forcing myself to breathe in slow, deep breaths.

"What about him?" My voice sounds like a frog. The stabbing pain in my heart makes it seems like only yesterday I lost Jack, instead of two years ago.

"How did you two meet?"

My bitter laughter sounds shrill and on edge. "There was no *meeting* Jack, he was always in my life, until he went away to college. That's when he met Kayla."

"His wife?"

I nod and using my thumbnail, push at the cuticle of my other thumb. I don't want to discuss this.

"How long were they married?"

"They never should have married," I snap, my cheeks flaming with indignation and hurt. "He was *mine*, first." I don't attempt to hide my bitterness as I rub my face with my hands. *Why does everyone want me to talk about this? Why can't they just let it go?*

"Then why did he marry her?"

"I don't know." I rock in my seat, my arms wrapped tight around my middle.

"Yes, you do." He reaches over and peels my fingers apart, taking my hand in his, giving it a comforting squeeze. "Tell me your story, Evangeline. It's time."

I swallow, and try to speak, but nothing comes out. It takes me a full minute to formulate the words. "I loved Jack all my life. He was always there for me—when my Daddy died, when I broke my arm rollerblading, even when I wrecked my first car. I can't remember a day I didn't love him. He was as much a part of my life as my parents were." I sigh and stare at the passing scenery. "My shrink called it an unhealthy obsession." I glance over at Remi. "I've never understood that. How can loving someone be unhealthy?"

"Go on." He lights a cigarette, once again cracking the window.

"We grew up together. He didn't have a father at home so he used to bug my dad to teach him about cars and motors. You know, guy stuff…"

Remi's brows draw together as he exhales a smoke ring. "How much older was he?"

"Five years."

I smile as memories flip through my mind like turning the pages of a photo album. The way Jack would shove his glasses up his nose when he concentrated. And how he would pull at his lower lip when irritated. His walnut brown hair was always in need of a trim and he usually had scruff on his angular face. Not because he thought it made him look sexy, but because he'd forget to shave when wrapped up in some new project.

"It wasn't just sex, you know," I defend hotly, having been through this before with countless therapists.

"I didn't say it was."

"Jack took care of me in lots of ways, even fussing when I wouldn't balance my checkbook. He'd sit and work on it for thirty minutes, figuring it to the penny. Whenever I saw him, he'd check the oil sticker in my car to make sure I changed it on time." But I also loved the way his kisses made my toes curl, and the lingering smell of his cologne on my neck after we snuggled. It was these silly little things I missed most.

"What happened to your car?"

I sigh. "After Jack died, Mama sold hers and took mine. She was afraid I'd…" I don't need to finish. He knows.

"What was he like?" Remi asks, breaking into my thoughts. I drag my attention from the past and stare at him. Jack was the polar opposite of the man sitting next to me.

"Quiet, with a dry sense of humor. He was tall and lanky, but not athletic, a total geek, complete with glasses and ink stains on his hands. But to me, he was beautiful. He had the most amazing hazel eyes that would light up with excitement over dumb stuff, like jigs and bell cranks. He loved tinkering with machinery. Whenever he came home from college he'd cut our grass, do odd jobs for Mama. Like I said, he was always part of my life. I thought he was my happily-ever-after." I can't suppress the sigh or stop the tear that escapes down my cheek. I wipe it away.

I hear that distinct sound of ruffled feathers and turn to face Remi. He's staring at the road with a scowl on his face. "When did you become intimate?" A small part of me wonders if he's jealous, but I erase the thought. Of course Father Blackson isn't; he can't be.

Heat rises in my cheeks as I recall the first time Jack and I had sex. For months he'd come home from college on the weekends and sneak in through my bedroom window. We'd get hot and heavy with the petting, but we always stopped short of doing the actual deed. Until the night Mama had to work a double shift...

I suck in a deep breath and whisper, "My fifteenth birthday."

"Ass wipe." Remi slams his fist on the steering wheel and pitches the cigarette out the window. It's a few seconds before he asks, "So what happened to the great love affair?"

"*Kayla happened.*" I don't attempt to keep the bitterness out of my voice. It's impossible for me to be rational when I think about her.

I hated her from the first time Jack mentioned her name.

I hated her more when he married her.

I hated her no less after he died.

And I hated myself for continuing to hate her after she died...

"So Jack married Kayla."

I ignore his statement of the obvious. I refuse to talk about *her*.

"Why did he marry her?"

I stare at the passing scenery, wishing I were anywhere but in this damn car.

"Why," he persists.

"Stop," I cover my ears and close my eyes. I can't talk about this. It makes me feel like my heart will implode from the pain. Like a shattered mirror, my mind provides a distorted image of myself and it isn't pretty. I was obsessive, difficult to deal with.

Jack didn't want me.

"Tell me why he married her."

"I don't know," I scream. "She entrapped him somehow. I think he was lonely." I shove the truth away. Jack loved *me*. He had to have loved me. Otherwise, my entire existence has been for nothing. Even now, I'm nothing without Jack.

"He was lonely?" He shoves his sunglasses on top of his head and glances at me for a few seconds. Those few seconds is all it takes for his intense gaze to strip me bare. I know what he's doing, restating my statement in a question so I'll open up. I've endured enough counseling sessions to recognize the technique. I'm the fucking Queen of Therapy. Instantly, my guard is up and standing at attention.

"Because I wasn't there," I hiss with frustration. Frowning, I look at him through narrowed eyes. Why is he being so persistent? Has someone instructed him to ask these questions?

Remi shrugs his shoulders as if to say, *so?*

"At college," I stress, frowning with annoyance at his blank expression. "I was at home, he was at college." I throw my hands up and roll my eyes.

"How could the jerk be lonely? He had you as his secret tryst at home and Kayla at school. He used both of you."

I gasp at his impudence and jump to Jack's defense. "Take that back. You didn't know him. How dare you! He didn't get to come home every weekend. We couldn't be together because I was still in high school and then beauty school. I wasn't there—"

"Oh, *ex-cuse* me. Where did he go to college? The University of Timbuktu?"

"Where the hell is that? No, the University of Florida."

"Oh, wow, that's all of what, five hours away? This is the twenty-first century. Didn't he have a car? A computer? Or a phone?" His sarcasm strikes like a venomous viper and the truth I've managed to suppress surges forth. I'm falling fast and I hang on to my denial like a rescue rope over quicksand.

"He was busy. After college he went straight into the Masters program. I wasn't *there…*" The interior of the car spirals as my mind splinters into a million shards. Can't he see I'm falling apart? I rock faster, squeezing my eyes tight, holding my arms across my chest as if I can keep my heart and mind from shattering.

"So? If he loved you, he would have made it work, Evangeline. Jack took advantage of you and used you. Technically, what he did when you were underage was statutory rape."

My eyes snap open. "It was *her* fault. She seduced him. We were together for years until she pranced into his life with her blonde hair and easy ways and *normalcy*. He was mine, first."

He snorts with derision and frowns at me. The car swerves from his inattention. I dig my nails in to my palms, bouncing my right leg in time with my pounding heart. *Stop, stop, stop…*

"Jack *loved* me." I want to hit this man of God. He knows nothing of love. I sit on my hands to keep from acting on impulse. I know how disastrous lashing out in a moving car can be. Been there, done that and lost Jack because of my careless actions.

His voice softens, "I'm sure he did in some way, but the point remains he *married* her. He *used* you and was *unfaithful* to his wife—"

The dashboard Virgin Mary mocks me with her serene smile. Since I can't hit him, I strike at the next best thing, and she falls to the floor as the hula girl sways seductively.

"Shut up!" I cover my ears with my hands. My heart sits firmly lodged in my throat. He reaches out to me, but I shove his hand away. "Leave me alone! Let me out of here. I have to get out of here."

"Shh, just relax, you're getting too worked up, Crazy Girl."

"Don't touch me, and quit calling me that. I don't want to hear for the millionth time how stupid I am. Do you think you're the first to tell me how wrong it was for me to love him? Why is love wrong?"

"Calm down," he barks, glancing my way. He presses his lying lips in a tight line. The tic in his cheek flexes several times as he taps the steering wheel with his thumb.

He might be pissed, but I'm livid and my world is spinning out of control.

A wave of nausea sweeps over me, and I clench my teeth to keep from spewing. "Don't tell me to calm down. Pull over. I want out of this damn car, right now." I try to open the door, but he punches the automatic door lock. I struggle trying to get it unlocked and his hand grabs mine.

"Stop it! What the hell? Do you want us to have a wreck?"

I freeze as my surroundings twist and twirl. A voice from the past whispers tauntingly, *Stop Evie, you're going to cause us to wreck.* I whimper and clutch my stomach. *Not again, not again, not again...*

"S-Stop the car," I croak. Is it déjà vu or just some sick coincidence? Closing my eyes, I refuse to watch us wreck. *Not again.*

"Holy moly, hang on, sweetness." The car stops moving, but my world continues to spiral. Remi leaps from the car and yanks open my door just in time. I fall to my knees onto the rough gravel as my stomach heaves violently. He holds my hair as I vomit and sob. Still in the car behind us, Goner whimpers before dashing out on to the side of the road.

"Goner!" we both scream, but he takes off into the woods. I struggle to my feet, but the ground rolls underneath me and I collapse. Remi catches me and holds me tight as my world falls apart.

"Shh, everything's okay. I'm so sorry, sweetness. I shouldn't have pushed you."

*I'm sorry Evie; I should never have led you on. I love you, but Kayla is my life now. I love her and we're going to have a baby...*Jack's voice haunts me and pushes me over the edge.

Everything is my fault. "I'm sorry, I'm so sorry. Oh God, it's my fault you wrecked..." My shoulders shake with my silent sobs, and I bury my face in Remi's T-shirt. Jack's gone. In a rare, startling moment of truth, I realize he was never mine. He belonged with Kayla. And like a tempestuous three-year-old wanting a toy that didn't belong to her, I'd tried to steal him from his wife. I was responsible for his death, her unhappiness and ultimately the worst tragedy of all. The weight of my guilt makes my knees buckle.

Remi scoops me into his arms and leans against the car. He rests his cheek on top of my head, murmuring soothing words. I cover my face with shame. "I nearly killed us. Just like I killed him."

"No, you didn't. I had full control of the car. You got nauseated and it made the car seem like it was out of control. And you didn't kill Jack; it was an unfortunate accident."

"I wish you were wrong, but I did. I was mad at him and we argued. He told me Kayla was pregnant and he wouldn't leave her. I hit him and he lost control of the car." I squirm out of his arms and stand before him, a broken girl. I hang my head with shame. "I'm a horrible, evil person."

"You are not a horrible, evil person. You're a sweet girl with a good heart and you've shouldered this guilt for far too long. It was an accident," Remi reaffirms as he cups my cheeks in his warm hands and forces me to look at him. "It was an *accident*, Evangeline. A tragic, horrible accident."

I shake my head and stare at the ground. "You don't understand. I'm responsible for Kayla's death, too..."

He tips my chin back up and his brows pull together. Those mesmerizing eyes search mine, compelling me to tell the truth. "Kayla was in the car with you?"

"No." I look away, not wanting to see his condemnation or the hatred in his beautiful face. "She found out I was in the car with

Jack the night of the accident." I can't continue, he'll hate me and then I'll lose him, too.

He rubs my arms. "Tell me. Get rid of this guilt you've carried around once and for all. Ask for forgiveness, mean it, and be done with it."

"There is no forgiveness," I whisper. "I'm responsible for Kayla's death and—" The overwhelming burden of my culpability makes me shudder. "And I killed Jack's unborn baby." I turn away and vomit again, as if my self-hatred can no longer be contained. I want to curl up on the side of this godforsaken interstate and die.

"You had an abortion?"

I laugh hysterically. "No. God knows better than to ever let me be a mother. Kayla's baby."

"What makes you think you did that?" He squats beside me, placing a hand on my back. His voice is calm, non-censorious. I stare at him, wiping the spit off my mouth with the back of my hand. Fire rages for a moment in his pupils but quickly burns out, and it's like staring into a calm green meadow.

"I exist," I sneer, preparing for his condemnation, determined to withstand it.

"Don't give me that over-dramatic-woe-is-me bullshit. Just tell me in plain, simple words, what you did. Did you pull a trigger? Poison her? Push her off a balcony?" He pulls me to my feet and the look on his face isn't one of hatred or disgust. I see concern and patience as he shakes a cigarette from his pack and lights it.

I blink, taken aback by his objectivity. Father Asswipe had been full of pompous disappointment. My mother hasn't been able to look me in the face for almost two years. The shrinks have all spouted psychobabble that's left me feeling more confused than ever. "No, of course not. Kayla overdosed on pills. It killed her." I swallow and look at the ground. "And the b-baby."

"My goodness. Aren't you the All Powerful Queen of Shit?"

Startled, my mouth drops open, and I'm shocked speechless. He nonchalantly takes a puff on the cigarette as he watches the cars driving past us.

"What did you say?" Surely I must have misheard. Why isn't he disgusted? This is where he's supposed to leave me on the side of the road with Goner. I'm prepared for the abandonment. My life is a series of being left behind by those I've loved. What's one more?

I gasp at my own revelation. *Am I falling in love with Remi?*

"Sad and heartbreaking as Kayla's death was, you're not responsible. You made some pretty bad decisions and tragedies occurred, but you have to let all of this guilt go and move on." He smiles sadly and pushes a strand of hair that's blown across my face behind my ear.

"You don't understand. I'm bad. This wasn't the first time I was responsible for someone's death."

Remi pauses and exhales the cigarette smoke. I'm pretty sure he just checked an eye roll. The look he levels at me makes me fidget and rock on my feet. The poor man doesn't have a clue just how sinful I am. My soul isn't black. It's non-existent. Despite his bad language, smoking, and irreverence at times, he's too good to understand true sin and wickedness.

"What are you talking about?" His tone of voice suggests that of a patient parent.

"I killed my daddy."

Chapter Nine

What a morning. It started with another spy from above. Francis enjoyed pawning off that pathetic mongrel, Goner, on us. And in the guise of a foreign gas station attendant, *please*. How cliché. It ticks me off to no end that The Boss won't take a phone call, answer a text or a prayer, but can take the time to send nosy old Francis of Assisi to do His reconnaissance. Not because He doesn't already know what's going on. It's a warning, like a horse head in the bed. He's the ultimate Godfather, after all.

A red Porsche 918 Spyder flies by and the Driver leans on the horn. It's tempting to flip Him off, but I refrain, knowing better. I glower for a moment, wishing He'd given me that car instead of the five-year-old Altima to drive. I guess a priest wouldn't have a car like that. His lack of trust annoys me. I might not be going by the book of Saving Lost Souls, but she's standing here, still alive and hasn't tried to kill herself since I arrived on the bridge.

I draw on the cigarette and sigh. That's not why He's checking up on me, and I know it. On second thought, this kind of warning isn't so bad. And truthfully, He's right. I'm skating close to the edge and about to fall in over my head. This chick is getting under my skin.

Actually, I want to be all over her skin, inside and out. I stare at Evangeline. Her shoulders slump, bearing the weight of her guilt, making her look like a lost little girl. Sure, she made some terrible mistakes and bad choices, but she's not inherently evil. I haven't seen Jack hanging around heaven, and I hope he's serving some time for being such a jerk taking advantage of her, not to mention his adultery.

I watch as the wind blows one of her curls across her cheek. She's just about the sweetest thing I've ever seen. Her warm, chocolate eyes melt my heart when she peeks at me from under those ridiculously long lashes. Not to mention those full, dusky-rose colored lips the same color as her tempting nipples...

An eighteen-wheeler drives by this time, leaning on the horn. I draw my attention away from her smoking hot body and back to how I can make her understand she isn't the reason for all the bad things that have happened in the world.

Nope, just a few bad thoughts from yours truly.

An eighteen-wheeler speeds by and blows the horn, making Remi jump. "Don't be ridiculous, you were just a little kid, you didn't kill your father." He blows a perfect smoke ring before stubbing out the cigarette with the toe of his boot, and folds his arms across his chest. I like his forearms, they're defined without being too muscular and the light dusting of hair on them glints in the sunlight.

"I did." I raise my chin in defiance and place my hands on my hips.

"Proud of that fact, are you?" He snorts and mutters, "What a pretentious little brat."

"What?" I stare at him with a mixture of horror and disbelief at his blasé manner. "You don't believe me?"

"Hell no."

"You sure cuss a lot to be a priest."

"I didn't prior to meeting *you*." He chucks me under my chin, and the wide grin he flashes makes my skin tingle. "Now you can add corruption of a priest to your pathetic, self-indulgent list of sins. Feel better? Wanna go pick some old lady's flowers or throw a candy wrapper on the ground to add to the catalog?"

"You're not taking me seriously," I huff with indignation. Meanwhile, my warped mind plays out images of corrupting him on the hood of the car.

"Oh, don't worry. I take you very seriously. You, on the other hand, take yourself *way* too seriously. You can't take on the sins of the world. Last time I checked, you hadn't been appointed a savior, unless you received a memo I didn't get."

"But, it's my fault…"

"For crying out loud, stop this *mea culpa* shit. You were *six* when your father died. It was an accident with a chainsaw, Evie!" I hear the distinct sound of flapping feathers, but don't see any birds around.

"But I was fooling around instead of working—" My eyes widen as fear plummets to the pit of my stomach. My mouth tastes like a rusty nail. "H-How did you know? I didn't tell you any of that."

"It doesn't matter how I know, who told me, or why I know. The only thing that matters is this—*it wasn't your fault*. Get that through your thick skull. You're not responsible for all the death and tragedy in the world. Quite honestly, while you *are* important, you're not the end all, be all."

"But—"

He whistles and Goner runs toward him from the woods. Picking the happy dog up, he carries him to the trunk of the car and opens it. I watch, confused as he pulls out a lug wrench. Remi walks toward me, the dog in his arms, and the lug wrench in his hand. My heart pounds in my constricted throat. He isn't wearing his sunglasses and I see the cold, deadly intent in his eyes.

"W-What are you doing?" I croak, my eyes widening. *Dear God, no.* I shake my head and reach toward him, palms up in supplication. Has he snapped? Have I driven the priest over the edge? I'm trembling so hard it would only take a slight breeze to knock me over. "No, put the dog down—"

"I'm going to kill this dog. I told you his name was Goner. He's lived a good life, he'll eventually die anyway." His voice sounds cold and lethal, his eyes appear distant and soulless. Goner whimpers and squirms in his arms, his tongue hanging out of his sweet face, tail wagging nervously. I must be in some sort of parallel universe. Why would Remi hurt a poor, innocent dog?

"What? No! You can't do this. Please, I'm begging you." I lunge to grab the dog from his arms, but Remi sidesteps me. "If I take this lug wrench and bash this poor mongrel's brains out it would be wrong, wouldn't it? You might even say it would be a horrendous act of evil?"

Nodding, I fall to my knees, blubbering like a baby. "Please, please, don't hurt my dog. He's innocent." Drowning in my sobs, my breathing stutters. Is there no one to stop him? Frantic, I look up and down the road but there are no other cars. I'm alone with a madman. My heart hurts for the poor little dog. They'd been feeding him at the gas station…If I'd just left him there…Please God… someone, anyone stop this insanity…

Remi kneels with the dog in front of me and puts down the lug wrench and releases Goner. Instead of running for the safety of the trees, the stupid mutt runs straight in front of the lone car on the interstate. I scream and jump up to run after him, but Remi stops me, yanking me against his chest. Everything happens so fast I can't comprehend.

The sound of screeching tires and a blaring horn sickens me. "Noooo," I scream sagging against his chest. I can't look. The car doesn't stop. I clutch his T-shirt, soaking it with my tears.

"Shh, he's fine, Evangeline. Look." A bark sounds across the interstate. I wipe my face and risking a peek, see Goner sniffing the ground, his tail wagging.

Relief leaves me feeling weak and my knees buckle. I'd no doubt fall if it weren't for him holding me. "I don't understand. Why did you do that?"

"If I'd killed that dog, it would have been a sin, a malevolent act done on purpose to harm an innocent. If the dumb dog got run over because he ran into traffic instead of the safety of the woods, it would have been a tragic accident."

Now that the relief has faded, anger rises from the pit of my stomach and I can't contain it. He did this to teach me a lesson? "Are you insane?" I scream at him, my fists clenched at my sides. I smack him hard, causing him to flinch, but he doesn't budge.

He raises one eyebrow and smirks, "Are you, Crazy Girl?"

I stomp around cursing him with every profane word I'd ever heard and throw in a few made up ones for good measure until my anger sputters and dies. I wind down, now emotionally, physically and spiritually spent.

"God forgives you for your mistakes, Evangeline. Would it help if I assign you a gazillion Hail Marys and Our Fathers as penance? Or told you to go work in a homeless shelter, a soup kitchen, or an animal shelter? All of these things are good, but mean nothing if you don't internalize it and forgive yourself. Quit using your craziness as a crutch and take responsibility for your actions, not your perceived sins."

I swallow and remain motionless, trying to comprehend, but finding it difficult to erase years of self-retribution. Is he right? Do I use my mental illness as a means to punish myself? "But I feel so guilty." I hang my head with shame. I'm about to start ugly crying all over again.

"Then channel that guilt and do something for someone else. Quit wallowing in your self-pity. For God's sake, quit being afraid to live."

He trudges back to the trunk and throws the lug wrench into it. He stands for a moment leaning against the car, looking as exhausted as I feel. When he returns to stand in front of me, he's wearing his priest's stole over his *50 Shades of Grace* T-shirt. I fall to my knees and wince as the gravel digs through my jeans. This physical pain is minor compared to the crushing mental anguish I've lived with most of my life.

"Ask for absolution, forgive yourself, and be done with it. You can't carry this around forever. It's killing you, and I've already told you, I won't allow you to die on my watch."

His gentle voice and the hand caressing the back of my head comfort me. He's right. The weight of my shame and regret has emotionally crippled me since I was six-years-old and watched Daddy bleed to death before my eyes. I've been sinking in the quicksand of my guilt, and he's offering me a lifeline.

Ready to be free of the mire of this self-imposed torture, I reach for the safety he offers and bow my head. The words I haven't spoken in far too long come without prompting. "Bless me, Father, for I have sinned." My guilt has festered in my heart and poisoned my mind for years. Remi's compassion has lanced it, allowing it to drain and heal.

"I know, Evangeline, I know."

He cups my cheeks and I look up at him. His unwavering gaze holds mine, and in the depth of his eyes I see forgiveness and love.

"God, the Father of Mercies, through the death and resurrection of his Son has reconciled the world to himself and sent the Holy Spirit among us for the forgiveness of sins; through the ministry of the Church may God give you pardon and peace, and I absolve you from your sins in the

name of the Father, and of the Son, and of the Holy Spirit. Amen." My forehead burns where he places the sign of the cross, and a halo of light surrounds him, blinding me. As the sun bathes my face, the darkness in my soul bursts with light. It's similar to the feeling I had on that dark night, flying down a back road screaming with joy.

I'm free.

I'm alive.

It takes us an hour to round up Goner, who seems to hold no grudges, judging by the jubilant sloppy kisses he bestows upon Remi. My emotions ping all over the place, vacillating between feeling drained and carefree. Physically, I ache all over and I'm in definite need of a bath. I'm not sure if Remi has the sunroof open because of the dirty dog stench, or the soured vomit stink of my clothes. Probably, it's a combination of both.

Due to my mental breakdown, or breakthrough, depending on how you look at it, we don't make it to St. Louis as planned. Remi pulls over to a motel on the interstate in the middle of nowhere. After getting us checked in, we sneak Goner into the room, determined to give him a bath.

Goner has other plans.

"Hold him still," Remi grouses through clenched teeth. He winces and wrinkles his nose as Goner shakes his nasty, wet dog hair. I giggle and the murderous look Remi shoots me makes me laugh harder. I'm glad the lug wrench is secure in the trunk of the car.

"I'm trying. It's like trying to hold a basket of snakes. You hold him, I'll scrub," I complain in return. After several swear words offered by the good Reverend and myself, the stupid dog is finally scrubbed clean, while we look a lot worse for wear. Using the detachable shower nozzle, I rinse off, wiggling my toes and feeling strangely lighthearted.

Remi has Goner on the leash and is brushing at the muddy streaks on his jeans, making it worse instead of better. "Yuck, this is disgusting."

I can't contain my grin. "Why? I would think this would be right up your alley."

Remi frowns and furrows his brow. "I'm filthy thanks to this mutt. How is stinking like a wet dog up my alley?"

"Because right now you're a dirty white boy." I take the shower head and squirt him, singing the words to the old *Foreigner* song. "And don't you dare reference me to any song that says bitch in it."

He laughs so hard he doubles over and tears track down his ruggedly handsome face. When he is finally able to stand upright, he peels off his wet T-shirt and runs a hand through his damp hair, oblivious to his effect on me. I swallow and turn off the water as I stare at the water dripping down his body. One drop hangs for a second on a brown nipple before sliding down and disappearing beneath the waistband of his jeans. A desire to lick him dry from head to toe makes my tongue snake across my lips. Blushing, I spin around before he can see the lust written on my face.

"So, I think I'll grab some clean clothes and get a quick shower. I'll clean up this mess, too." I move to head out of the cramped bathroom, but Remi's blocking my exit. Goner's leash is wrapped around his legs. His piercing green eyes stare at my chest and I realize too late that even with a bra on, it looks like I could enter a wet T-shirt contest. My nipples are as hard as marbles, and I'm sure he knows why. Without saying a word, he tears his eyes back to the panting dog at his feet. He unwinds Goner's leash and stomps out of the room grabbing his cigarettes as he leaves.

Guilt washes over me, leaving me feeling as dirty on the inside as I am on the outside. He's warned me repeatedly he's a man as well as a cleric. I know he's on leave for a reason and I don't need to add to his problems by lusting after him. Not to mention, I certainly don't need to add more stupidity to my life.

After I shower and clean up the bathroom, I find Remi stretched out in the chair with his feet propped up on the bed snoring loud enough to drown out the doggie snores beside him. I gently shake his shoulder. "Shower's all yours."

His eyes open and crinkle with his sleepy grin. "Thanks. I don't know about you, but I'm exhausted." He groans and stretches, affectionately rubbing the sleeping head of the dog beside him. How could I have ever thought he would harm Goner? Sadness sweeps over me. In this moment I'd give anything in the world for us to be two different people. To be a man and a woman who could get to know one another, fall in love, and grow old together.

How many times has he told me I need to move on and start living? I desperately wish it could be *him* to move on with. It seems unfair, but I guess it fits in nicely with the story of my life—wrong place, wrong time, and wrong person. I'm sure there are plenty of studies of women who fall in love with men who should be off limits, like married men and priests. It's probably a hazard of his job. Who hasn't seen *The Thorn Birds*, after all? I cast a wistful smile at him.

Even if he were available, why would he want a girl like me? I have enough problems to pack a landfill. Tucking my wrong, immoral thoughts away, I cross the room to the vanity to dry my hair, and start chattering to get my mind off his chiseled chest and my unfulfilled desires. "I wish we didn't have to eat cheap tonight. I'm starving. My mama's a great cook. Her cranberry biscotti and lasagna are to die for. Uh, well not literally, I mean I don't want to die any more. Of course, I know we all die at some point…" My voice trails off when he doesn't answer.

Without saying a word he walks up behind me and his gaze meets mine in the mirror. We stand staring at one another, not saying a word, yet saying everything. I wonder if he knows how much my newly discovered soul yearns for his. A barely audible sigh leaves those lips I long to kiss, and his green eyes appear as turbulent as a stormy sea. *Yeah, he knows.*

When he looks away, I feel like part of my heart has been ripped from my chest.

"I won't be but a few minutes," he murmurs. When the door to the bathroom closes, I grip the sink and wonder how I'm going to get through the night, much less the rest of my life.

I stand in the cold shower for at least fifteen minutes, attempting to get my warring emotions under control. One minute I want to throttle her, the next I want to kiss her. I'll never forget her look of fear and abject horror when she thought I was going to hurt her silly dog. I'd never admit it out loud, but I love that mangy old mutt. I didn't want to threaten him, but I didn't know how else to break through her guilt. Guilt she shouldn't be carrying. If I ever see Jack, I plan to kick his ass for taking advantage of her. I sigh and tiredly scrub my face. Who am I to judge? Can I really blame him? I'm right there with him, having forbidden thoughts about Evangeline.

It's more than just a sexual attraction, I argue with myself. I love her. I lean my head against the side of the shower and close my eyes.

I love her and I can't have her. What the hell am I going to do? I can still see the outline of her lace bra trying to conceal those perky nipples under her wet T-shirt. The girl I love is one hundred percent hot sex in a five-foot-four package, and Christmas has always been my favorite holiday. I want nothing more than to unwrap that present. But it isn't an option, and the icy shower isn't helping.

I sigh and take matters into my own hand.

After a quick, fairly normal blessing over the food, Remi digs into the basket of chips on the table.

"I'm going to say it one more time. You are the most unethical priest I've ever known."

Remi grins. "Are you sure you weren't raised Jewish with all of this guilt you carry? If it bothers you, then don't eat." The look of unadulterated bliss on his face as he dunks a chip into the cheese dip makes me smile.

I snort and shake my head. "With a name like Salvatore? Nope, I'm Roman Catholic through and through. I'd put my Italian Catholic mama against a Jewish mama any day. Nobody does guilt like Rosa Salvatore. I said *you're* unethical. I may be crazy, but I'm not *stupid*. No way I'm passing up this meal." I shove a chip loaded with salsa into my mouth.

"*Padre,*" the waitress murmurs placing in front of him the biggest damn plate of sizzling fajitas I've ever seen.

"*Y para su hermana.*" She places my taco salad down and clasps her hands together, waiting for us to take a bite. I guess she wants our approval.

"*Gracias,* Maria. Mmmm, *muy deliscioso.*" He flashes the waitress his mega-watt smile. I look down at my plate so he won't see the jealousy plastered across my face. I wish I could be the recipient of his smiles, instead of his frowns and concerned looks. A pretty blush suffuses her brown cheeks. The waitress bobs her head and gives him a small, shy grin in return before leaving.

"How many Hail Marys will you have to say for that lie?" I ask, digging in to the food with gusto.

"What lie?" He loads his tortilla with the sizzling hot steak and grilled onions.

"I'm now your sister?" I dump the rest of my salsa on the salad and peek at him from under my lashes. Why does his clerical collar only add to his attractiveness?

Remi puts the loaded tortilla down and places a hand over his heart, giving me a fake, pained expression. "That hurts, Evangeline. We are all brothers and sisters in Christ." When I roll my eyes at his sanctimonious, craptacular answer, he gives me what my Daddy used to call a "shit-eating grin" and a wink.

"Are you fluent in Spanish?" I ask, trying to wheedle more information out of him, since he seems to know my entire pathetic life story, yet I still know very little about him.

"*Sí.*" His eyes crinkle and he grins widely.

I decide to test him. "Okay, say something that doesn't involve a Taco Bell menu item."

"*Te adoro Chica Loca.*"

I have to laugh. Only he would say he adores a Crazy Girl.

He takes a bite of his food and closes his eyes, savoring the taste. "Mmm. This is really good. I may have to ditch the whole blue jeans and T-shirt idea and go back to wearing the collar full time."

I'm looking at that delectable mouth of his and thinking "mmm," too. "Do you get a lot of meals comped?"

He shrugs and laughs. "It's like being a cop or a marine. Women just can't resist a guy in uniform."

"Do many women make passes at you, *Father?*"

My abrupt question has him choking on his food. Maria hurries over and pounds him on the back, as the owner of the restaurant looks on, wringing his hands. The poor guy's probably praying there isn't a lawsuit in his future, or a black mark on his ticket to heaven.

Remi holds up his hand and manages to gasp, "I'm fine. I'm okay. *Gracias.*"

The interruption prevents him from answering the question. The owner's family visits the table throughout our meal, discussing everything from football to the local bake sale at their church. We finish the meal and the tab is "on the house." Remi thanks them profusely, blessing the owner, his family and his business. As we're leaving, three of the children cling to him, calling him *Padre* in singsong fashion as he hugs each one. At the insistence of a petite little girl, he even offers a blessing over a stuffed bear. They adore him and he's relaxed with the children, tousling their hair, and crouching on their level when he speaks to them.

Truthfully, when he isn't in his clerics — and even sometimes when he is — he acts like a big kid. But he isn't a kid. He's a man. A kind, sexy, funny man that I wish was in any profession but his chosen one. Seeing the ease with which he handles the kids makes me a little sad, knowing he'd be a great father. I wonder if he regrets he'll never have children. It will never happen for me. I rub my stomach where the scars remain. For the first time ever, I feel a momentary pang of *what if,* but quickly shove it aside. If there is a God, I'm sure it's for the best. I still need to learn how to take care of myself.

It's late and the sun has already set when we leave the restaurant and head back toward the motel. We pass one of those itinerant carnivals and Remi slams on the brakes. I'm thankful I have my seatbelt on, or I'd be kissing the windshield. His eyes light up like a five-year-old's on Christmas morning as he stares in awe at the Ferris wheel in the distance.

"We *have* to go, Evie. We can check on Goner, I'll throw on some jeans and we can come back to this."

"But what about our money? You said we have to be careful." I want to go, but I also don't want to end up sleeping in the car, or going hungry. I like my creature comforts.

"We'll just ride a few rides. Come on, you need to relax and grab life by the balls. It's been a tough few days for both of us. Let's just chill and enjoy being alive."

The thought of grabbing his balls and being alone with him in the motel, doing things a girl shouldn't think of doing with a priest, runs through my mind like a DVD on fast forward. Heat floods my cheeks. Maybe being out in a crowd instead of alone in a motel would be a good idea. "Okay."

By the light on the dashboard, I see the excitement spread across his face and he cranks the music up loud. The wind from the open sunroof ruffles his highlighted brown hair, as The Ramones sing about evil thoughts and private hell. It might be my imagination, but the Virgin Mary looks a little wary, as the hula girl's hips sway seductively.

Chapter Ten

"I've never been to a carnival." His wonderment is kind of cute as he turns around looking up at all the different colored lights of the artificial happiness. He grabs my hand, and I have to practically jog to keep up with his long stride toward the entrance. Seeing him wearing his jeans, boots, and a faded *Jesus Christ Superstar* T-shirt, more than one woman turns around to steal a second glance at the good-looking man beside me. A cigarette hangs from his lips and his eyes appear awestruck as his gaze darts back and forth between the rides, the vendors, and the interesting assortment of people illuminated by the colorful lights.

He points up at the Ferris wheel. "Isn't that great? We have to ride it, if nothing else." He's so excited he doesn't see my scowl. Just the thought of it makes my stomach fall to somewhere around my knees.

The smell of funnel cakes, cigarettes, and popcorn hangs thick in the air. Laughter and the excited squeals of happy children mingle with the calls of the barkers trying to dupe people in to playing their rigged games. He inhales deeply and pats his flat stomach. "I swear I'm full, but I could eat again. Sugar and fat combined, so good it's gotta be a sin. Let's sin a little."

"You do realize the amount of grease in this food could clog a sink pipe don't you?"

"Don't be such a Debbie Downer. Come on. I want to ride a couple of the rides, and I'll even win you a stuffed animal."

"No you won't, those games are rigged."

"See? It's providence, we were meant to be here." He points at the *Free Admission, tonight only* sign.

Despite my protests, he buys a string of tickets for the rides. For this, he'd better be wearing his clerical collar for more free meals tomorrow. But one look at the excitement on his face makes my foul temper dissipate. His infectious enthusiasm reels me in and my own face almost hurts from grinning so much. I can't remember the last time I truly enjoyed myself.

He pauses to watch some little kids playing in a pit of colored balls. "This is perfect." He turns to the carnie covered with tats. "We want to go in there."

The woman ignores him, thumbing through her cell phone.

He clears his throat.

With a heavy sigh, she stops staring at her phone, looks up and says, "No."

"Why not?" he asks.

She cocks her head to the side, sizing him up. "It's for little kids."

My eyes widen when he starts arguing with her. I tug on his hand.

"Remi, stop. She said no. We're too old."

"It isn't posted that there's an age limit. Quit acting like you're ninety and live a little, it'll be fun." He hands the tattooed woman a string of tickets and an extra five dollars.

Her attitude instantly changes. She pockets the fiver and nods for us to enter. Like a gentleman, he opens the netting and motions me to enter. Rolling my eyes, I pause at the entryway only to be unceremoniously pushed in. The kids start squealing with laughter, jumping up and down all around us.

He jumps in on top of me and starts tickling. I squeal and squirm, trying to get away, but he's too heavy. The kids around us double over laughing.

"Say it," he commands.

"Uncle!" I scream through my laugher. I lob balls at him but he only grins wider.

"That's not it."

"Rumpelstiltskin," I gasp, squealing.

He stops tickling and grins down at me and whispers, "Did you say rumpled foreskin?"

"No." I can't stop giggling.

"Okay, well wrong again. Say, 'Remi is the best thing to have ever happened to me.'"

"Have you lost your mind?"

He sits up and begins pelting me with the colored balls, making the three kids clap and laugh harder. I finally manage to wriggle my way out from underneath him. Grabbing a handful of balls, I lob them back, encouraging the two boys and little girl to join me.

Remi collapses in the balls, grinning. The kids and I scream and dance in triumph until his hand grabs my ankle and I fall on top of him with a loud *oomph*. He smiles up at me and brushes the hair out of my face. The rest of the world seems to fade away as I stare into his eyes. We're breathing heavily but for a different reason now.

"See?"

"See what?" I croak. I see a beautiful man staring back at me. I see lips I want to kiss, smiling at me. I shift a bit and his pupils dilate, his nostrils flare and his erection hardens beneath me.

The kids start screaming, "Kiss, kiss, kiss."

He gently, but firmly, rolls me over and stands, offering me a hand. I grab it and he leans close and whispers, "Taking life by the balls. It's the only way to live."

I can think of some other balls I want to grab, but this is definitely neither the time, nor the place. "Okay, okay. Lesson learned." We leave the pit, waving to the kids as we go. The carnie shakes her head, but there's now a smile on her face.

Pulling my hand, he hurries us toward the merry-go-round.

I raise one eyebrow. "Seriously? Isn't this for toddlers? We're not in kindergarten," I complain.

"Come on, you know you want to. You want the horse with the pink roses."

I freeze as a dull roar rises in my ears drowning out the happy chatter, squeals of excited kids and tinny carnival music around me. It's like I'm in some sort of a carnival-from-hell-time-warp. I double over and place my head between my knees to keep from blacking out.

"That one, Daddy. She's the prettiest."

"But that horse doesn't go up and down, Evie."

"I don't care; she has pink roses, like Mama's. Pretty please, I want to ride that one, she's my favorite…"

"Evie." The male voice sounds alarmed, and I wonder if I've done something wrong. Two strong hands grip my shoulders. "Come back to me, Crazy Girl."

He pulls me upright and snaps his fingers several times in front of my eyes. Slowly, I make my way through the thick mist of my past back to the present and stare at Remi's concerned frown.

"You okay? You look like you've seen a ghost."

I shake my head, shoving the memory away. Sweat trickles down my back, and as hard as I try to speak, no sound comes out of my parched throat. I blink and look around for my daddy.

"You don't look well. You're not going to puke again, are you? I hate puke." Remi grimaces.

"N-No, I'm fine." *Am I fine?* "I thought I saw my…" I close my eyes, pressing my fingertips into my eyelids. "I just got a little dizzy," I reply, opening my eyes, scanning the crowd for Daddy. Of course, he isn't here. I swallow my tears and force a smile for Remi.

"Good grief, you haven't even gotten on the tilt-a-whirl, yet. Come on, I'll stand next to you and make sure you don't fall off the merry-go-round. Knowing you, you'll pick the bucking bronco horse." He nudges my shoulder, and some, but not all, of the tension eases from my body.

True to his word, he lifts me onto the horse with pink roses. When the ride starts, he frowns up at me. "Hey, this horse doesn't move. What a rip-off. Do you want to move to another one?" He holds on to the pole, waiting for my answer. A little girl next to me squeals, kicking her feet with delight as she rides up and down, and Remi smiles at her.

"No, this one is perfect." And it is. I close my eyes and it's like being five-years-old again and Daddy's laughter fills my ears, bringing a sense of serenity to my unease. When I open my eyes, I see my father standing on the outskirts. Grinning, he gives me a thumb up and disappears as the ride moves around. I search for him in the crowd as the merry-go-round slows, but I've lost him. Instead of feeling sad, I feel thankful and strangely tranquil. A warm hand rubs my back. I smile at Remi and brush a strand of hair off his forehead.

"Ready to try something a little more daring, Calamity Jane?"

I laugh. How can I not when staring into those beautiful eyes? "Sure, let's grab life by the balls. You up for bumper cars?"

His eyebrows shoot up and he laughs long and hard as he helps me off the horse. "I don't know. I'm pretty sure I'd be in for some whiplash; I've experienced your driving, after all."

I smack him and laugh. "My driving? At least I use headlights." He snickers and ruffles my hair.

We end up skipping the dodge cars, opting for cotton candy and a candied apple, much to my chagrin. There goes more of our money, but Remi insists we enjoy the full carnival experience, and that includes a little junk food.

"Want a bite?" I hold out my cotton candy and he pinches off a piece.

"It melts and is hardly worth the effort," he grumbles. In return, he offers me a bite of his candied apple, taunting me with it several times before I manage to snag a bite. "Now this is something you can sink your teeth into." A breeze blows over us and the air is heavy with the smell of popcorn, sweat, greasy food, and rain. Again, a tantalizing lock of hair falls rakishly on his brow, giving him a devil-may-care look.

The hard candy shell sticks to the roof of my mouth as I savor the sweetness mixed with the tart apple. "Candied apples are good, but not compared to cotton candy. When I was a little girl I believed the angels lived in clouds made of cotton candy." I lick my finger and pause when I catch Remi staring at my mouth. A rumble of thunder, or maybe it was one of the rides, draws his attention upward.

He chuckles and shakes his head. "You're such a whimsical girl."

"Well I know it isn't theologically sound. I mean, cut me some slack, I was four or five. And angels probably don't even exist. I'm not even sure God exists."

"Trust me, they all exist." He nods with authority, closing his eyes and smiling with enjoyment over his apple.

"Why should I trust *you?*"

He cracks one eye open and pinches my nose. "Ingrate."

We both snicker and I bat his hand away when he steals another pinch of my spun confection. His lips are shiny and wet from his candy apple and the breeze continues to caress his hair into a delightful, tousled mess. His Adam's apple bobbles as he returns my stare.

It's just a nanosecond, but I swear fire sears across the depths of his meadow-colored eyes. When I blink, it's gone and the moment of acute awareness is over. We dump our trash in a garbage can and wander through the carnival, people-watching.

"Come on. I want to do two more things before we leave. Ride the Ferris wheel and win you a ridiculous, cheap stuffed animal."

"But our money—"

Remi stops short and turns around. My body slams into his and of its own accord molds into it as if made to be there. He cups my face with his hands. "Just for tonight, let's pretend I'm not a priest and you're not crazy. We're just two normal human beings having a good time. Just a man and a woman at a rip-off carnival, living in the moment." Laced with forbidden promises, his voice seduces me. I grip his biceps so hard I'm sure I've left imprints of my nails.

"But—"

"Don't over-think this, Evangeline. *Carpe diem*. It's the only way to live. We're all on a fast track to death, born to die, so to speak…" He taps my nose with his index finger and smiles. "Some faster than others. Don't rush it, just breathe and enjoy each precious moment. The good and the bad." He leans in and whispers, "And this is definitely the good." His warm breath on my neck makes me shiver. I pull away staring at those lips I want to taste.

"Okay." Was that my voice, oh so soft and breathy? My cheeks burn, yet goose bumps skitter across my skin.

His lips turn up into his blindingly beautiful smile. "Good, let's go fly."

The ride operator buckles us into our seat on the Ferris wheel, and the car sways back and forth. I grip the handrail and hold on tight despite my sweaty palms. Closing my eyes, I attempt to focus on my breathing, but the pounding in my chest escalates in direct correlation with our height. Remi lets out a rebel yell that's loud enough to pierce an eardrum as we ascend higher and higher.

"What's the matter?" he whispers in my ear. His breath tickles my neck.

"N-Nothing." I swallow the bile of fear bubbling its way to my throat.

"Are you scared of heights?" The incredulousness in his voice would be funny if I wasn't so damn scared.

I elbow him in the ribs and nod.

"Why didn't you say so? You're really scared of heights?"

Still not opening my eyes, knowing I'll vomit if I do, I nod again.

"What the hell? When I met you, you were standing on a bridge getting ready to jump."

"But it was dark and I couldn't see exactly how high I was. Plus I wanted to d-die," I stutter through numb lips, my heart pounding in my ears.

"You mean to say, you could've just gone to the bridge during the day and looked down? Easy peasy, drop dead of fright?" His whoops of laughter fill the air.

"If I wasn't too scared to let go, I'd hit you right now," I mumble, my teeth chattering.

"Look, we're on the downside now, we're really not that high." He nudges my shoulder.

I open one eye and peek. At least he hasn't lied to me. We're almost at an even level with the uninterested carnie who had buckled us in the seat. The guy stands there watching us, looking bored as he smokes a cigar. "Do you think he'll let me off?"

"No. Just take your mind off it. Embrace the feeling, it's like flying with training wings."

We swoop past the carnie and sure enough, the guy ignores my frantic waving motions to get me off this death trap. The seat sways gently as we once again move toward the top.

"I think I'm going to be sick." I close my eyes again, praying to a God I'm not even sure I believe in, to get me off this damn ride.

"Oh no you don't. I'm tired of cleaning up puke."

"You're a lousy priest."

"I never claimed to be a good priest, or a good man, and I certainly never claimed to be a nurse." He pulls me closer and wraps his arms around me. Of their own free will, my hands loosen from the guardrail and wrap around his neck. My fingers curl and entangle in the waves of his soft hair. His mouth blazes a trail across my jaw, and I catch my breath and freeze, unsure if I'm lucid, hallucinating or dreaming. Opening my eyes I find stormy green eyes ignited with fire deep in their depths staring back at me. I start to sputter my protest, but his lips capture mine. They're warm, inviting, and wickedly delicious. He tastes of candy apple, cigarettes, and sin. It's an intoxicating combination.

A soft moan escapes my lips. "We can't...you're a priest—"

"Shh," he whispers. "Just for tonight, it's just you and me." The wind picks up and rocks the seat and I grip his neck, terrified of falling, whether of the ride or where we're headed, I'm not sure. Maybe both.

"Just you and me," he repeats, nipping my lower lip with his teeth before deepening the kiss. Our tongues dance as we explore each other's mouth, and our breathing is as heavy as the air around us. I lean in to him, craving more. Thunder rumbles in the distance and lightning snaps across the sky, making me jump and close the last inch of distance between us. The heavens seem to open up as torrents of rain slant down upon us.

When I was a little girl, Daddy told me when it rained the angels were crying. If that's true, they're sobbing inconsolably right now. In the distance I hear various carnies shouting to shut the rides down, but I don't care. The only thing that matters right now is being in his arms, tasting his lips. I'm flying free, living in the moment.

Her soft lips taste of cotton candy. Now that I've tasted her sweet mouth and experienced her kisses, I know I'll never get enough. I'm thankful she's scared and has her eyes closed because I'm pretty damn sure a moment ago she saw the fire of my arousal in my eyes. If she'd look down, she'd see it in my jeans, too. I fight to regain control, but her soft sigh and sweet moan are like a lit match on dry tinder, sparking my desire. I'm immersed in my infatuation.

I want her like I've never wanted anything before in my life, and I've been around for a long time. With Evangeline, I've found the part of me that's been missing. I've always felt disconnected, dissatisfied, knowing there is something more out there. Evangeline Salvatore is my something more, my everything. She's that last satisfying bite of dessert after a seven-course meal. I'm in love with her, and damn the consequences. I will literally risk heaven and hell to hold her in my arms like this forever and kiss her like there is no tomorrow. Deep within me burns a need to protect her, to keep her safe and love her the way she deserves to be loved. This is no longer a stupid job. This is now my life's mission. I'm going to do everything in my power to make her realize her life means everything to me. She is now my reason for existing. I love her for who she is, including every crazy idea in her beautiful head. I've never felt more alive and at peace than when she is in my arms. Not meaning disrespect to the Boss, but she defines my heaven.

A loud crack of thunder shakes the Ferris wheel and she clutches my shirt, whimpering. From the intensity of the boom, I know I'm in deep trouble. Normally, He's slow to anger, but when pissed, He's a force to be reckoned with. I don't care. I'll take the punishment. Nothing matters but Evangeline Lourdes Salvatore. I want to be her second chance. *There has to be a way for us to be together.*

I meant it when I told her I just wanted to be a man. Not a priest. Not an angel. Just a man, with the woman he loves and adores. We're on top of the Ferris wheel, alone in our own little world of discovery, and she's oblivious to the maelstrom brewing above and below us. Rain pelts down upon us as our car lowers to the ground. Reluctantly, I disentangle from her arms as the operator barks for us to get the hell off the ride and get a room. It sounds like a plan to me. How I'll execute it, I have no idea. One doesn't go against orders from the Boss. It just isn't done. But I'm determined to try to figure out a way.

As we make a dash for the exit, I see the milk bottle game and remember I promised to win her a stuffed animal. I tug on her arm and she crashes into me, which isn't so bad since I get to feel her warm, wet body next to mine. The game worker curses a blue streak as the wind whips at the drop down curtain he's unsuccessfully trying to secure.

"Hey, I'll help you if you let me have a go at knocking over the milk bottles first."

"Look we're closing up. You see that storm, dickhead?" he barks, glaring at me.

"I'll pay double what you charge. Just one chance. Please? For my girl." I cock my head toward my bedraggled girl, maintaining eye contact with the reluctant carnie. I'm not above cheating and using a little subliminal mesmerizing if needed. Luckily, my charm wins out. Or, more likely, he thinks I'm an easy mark.

"Yeah, sure." He gives me a smug *you're-so-gonna-lose* smile and holds out his hand for the tickets. I hand him the rest of them, which is quadruple what he charges.

"Remi, these games are rigged, it's a waste of money," Evie sputters in protest, tugging on the hem of my soaked T-shirt. "They put lead in the bottom of the bottles and the ball isn't hard enough to knock them down." She looks like a pitiful drowned kitten as she fidgets back and forth.

"Look, we already paid for the tickets. We're gonna lose 'em anyway."

Her color pales and her eyes widen so that the whites can be seen completely around her warm chocolate irises. The pulse in the base of her neck beats so fast it looks like her heart has jumped into it. I glare at the apparition that has startled her.

Once again He's run interference, and this time He's playing dirty.

Chapter Eleven

"You need to move on and be happy," a familiar voice speaks. I spin around, the hair on my arms standing on end. My heart races so fast I can't breathe. Desperately, I scan the soaked people running for cover, searching for Jack. It's his voice, I'm positive…Or not… Maybe it's just the noise from the rain and the crowd making me confused. I shake my head to clear it and turn back to watch Remi throw our money away on a stupid game.

He tosses the ball up in the air a few times, a smirk lurking at the corners of his perfect mouth.

"Hurry up, mister."

"Remi, please. Listen to me, this thing is rigged." I glare at the game agent. This is Remi's first carnival, and in some things, he's so naïve. I guess priests aren't allowed to go to crooked fairs.

"Oh ye, of little faith. I got this, Crazy Girl." He draws back and pitches. The ball flies by so fast you'd think he was a pitcher with the Tampa Bay Rays instead of a man of the cloth.

All of the milk bottles tumble over, and even the startled carnie whistles in appreciation. "How the hell did ya do that? Are you a sharpie?" The comical look on the guy's face with his mouth hanging open and eyes bugged wide provides further proof it was probably rigged.

I jump up and down, clapping and shouting like a cheerleader. It only takes me a second to choose the stuffed angel-bear, which makes Remi roll his eyes. I guess a teddy bear is too girlie for him. Remi insists it be wrapped in plastic to protect it from the rain, and even slips the guy a couple of dollars of our dwindling cash. After helping the guy secure the drop down curtain on the game, he grabs my hand. Dashing toward the car, we kick through mud puddles laughing like little kids. This has been the best day I've had in forever, and my face almost hurts from smiling so much.

Just before we reach the exit, I look to my right and halt. Standing by the tilt-a-whirl, I see Jack again. I tug to get loose from Remi's hand, but he holds tight, pulling me through the exit, urging me to hurry. Looking back at Jack, I reach out with my free hand toward him and watch with a sense of finality as he blows me a kiss and waves. Whether Jack was real, or a damn hallucination, I know in my heart this was the final good-bye. My life is moving forward, and I'll never see him again. Lightning streaks through the sky and Remi tugs harder.

"Evangeline, come on, quit lagging."

I nod and follow him, but sneak one last glance behind me, but as expected, Jack's gone. A bittersweet feeling of sadness envelops me and tears mingle with the rivulets of rain running down my cheek as I follow Remi to the car. He unlocks my door, tossing the stuffed animal in the car, but before I can climb in, he stops me. Rain drips down his face, and I answer the concerned question in his eyes.

"I saw him."

He doesn't ask me who, he just nods, as if he knows. With one hand wrapped in my hair, the other on my waist, he tugs me to his strong body. Truthfully, there's a magnetic pull to him that my body can't fight; his hands aren't even needed. Warm lips brush my forehead. "You're going to be okay, sweetness. Trust me."

I nod. He doesn't think I'm crazy. Or if he does, he accepts it without judgment. Trusting him is the easy part. Trusting myself, not so much.

My teeth chatter and I can't stop shivering when I step into the cold motel room after my hot shower. Goner's snoring at the end of the bed, but Remi isn't here. I figure he's stepped outside to smoke so I peer out the window, searching for him. Like a tiger in the zoo, he paces the walkway, smoking as he talks on his phone. He rolls his shoulders and his brow furrows as he pauses to listen, his mouth set in a grim line. Resuming his restless pacing, every so often he punctuates his words with the lit cigarette and rolls his eyes. Curiosity gets the best of me, and I turn off the a/c unit to see if I can eavesdrop on what appears to be a heated conversation.

My heart hammers as I strain to listen. Paranoia is an insidious thing. It creeps in and takes over all normal thought processes in a matter of seconds. Perhaps my hallucinations at the carnival have driven Remi over the edge and he's reporting my instability. Or worse, he's been conspiring all along with my mom and the doctors to have me committed. I clutch my stomach as the knot of fear tightens at the thought of his betrayal.

When his pacing brings him in front of the window, I can hear his muffled conversation over the raging rainfall. "Please stop running interference." He stops and listens for a few minutes, pinching the bridge of his nose. "Punishment? Really, you're going there?"

Cold sweat breaks out on my brow and the metallic taste of fear nauseates me. Will it be shock treatments? Stronger meds? Or will I be locked away forever?

He throws the cigarette down and stomps it out, grinding it with a bit more force than necessary. "I respectfully disagree, sir. I don't think your way will work this time. Please let me try it my way." He listens for a moment and rolls his eyes. "Perhaps you should try something novel, like trusting me." The booming crack of thunder makes me yelp and the immediate, scary arc of lightning signifies it's close. He needs to get off the phone and come inside where it's safe. He jumps and glowers at the night sky lit like a laser light show. "Yes, *sir.*" Sarcasm drips from his voice as he hangs up, his face contorted in a mask of fury.

Shoving the phone in his pocket, he runs his hands through his wet hair. With his head thrown back and hands on his hips, he glares as the rain slants down fast and furiously. In a moment, he spins on his heels and marches away. I press against the window, squinting to see. Dark, ominous looking wings engulf him. The trees across the parking lot whip and bend with the force of the wind. He moves out of sight, and I back away from the window shaking like the leaves on those storm swept trees.

Nervous energy surges through me as I try to process the events of tonight. Mimicking Remi, I pace back and forth, clenching and unclenching my fists. The vision of his dark wings doesn't terrify me like it did the first time I saw them. If indeed, they are real.

The door handle turns and I throw open the door to find him standing there, scowling, his eyes blazing with fury. Literally, I see flames leap in his eyes. *No!* I rub my eyes, trying to make sense of everything. When I look again, his features are schooled into a pleasant, if somewhat strained smile, and there are no flames in those amazing eyes.

Trying to maintain a sense of normalcy, I blurt out the first inane thing that comes to mind. "I'm done in the shower." Twirling a lock of my wet hair, I warily watch him as he sucks in a deep breath and nods. Continuing with my stupid comments, I add, "It's really raining hard."

He looks up for a second and one eyebrow rises with amusement as if to say *duh*. "Yeah, I checked the weather. It's the wettest summer on record around these parts."

His blasé response calms me, and throwing my shoulders back, I dig up the courage to confront him. "So, who was on the phone?" I glare at him and block his entrance to the room, crossing my arms in front of my chest.

"My boss."

"Are you in trouble?" *Or am I?*

He laughs and his eyes crinkle at the corners. I wonder again how old he is. "Trouble is my middle name, Crazy Girl."

"You know, you could give me a complex calling me crazy all the time. I wish you'd just tell me the truth. If you're in cahoots with my mom or the shrinks, just tell me. I'd rather know than not know and be caught off guard." My voice raises an octave higher than normal and sounds pressured, even to my own ears.

"Your paranoia has no boundaries does it? When will you learn to trust me?"

"Promise me that wasn't my mom, a hospital, or a couch doc on the phone." I grip the front of his wet T-shirt, searching his eyes for the truth.

His gaze never wavers as he smiles down at me. "I promise. It was my boss giving me hell, which is totally par for the course."

I let out the breath of fear I've unknowingly been holding. I may not trust myself, but I can trust him. At this point in time, I don't care if I'm seeing things or not. He accepts me as I am.

"Need a hug?" he asks with a teasing smile.

I move into his arms and mumble, "You probably deserve the tongue lashing from your boss. You're the most unpriestly priest I've ever met." Standing in his arms, a rare feeling of contentment makes me sigh with happiness. I squeeze him tighter, feeling safe and loved, never wanting this moment to end. "And I'm glad."

He cups my cheeks in his hands forcing me to look up at him. His beautiful lips smirk and fire leaps from the depths of his eyes before simmering down to a smolder. "So you've told me, numerous times. Now, let me in so I can get out of these wet clothes." I blink as an image of him stripping off naked and me licking him dry from head to toe makes my cheeks burn and my breathing hitch. I trip over my own feet as I step out of his way, causing him to chuckle. Goner raises his head and stretches before settling back into a deep sleep.

"Stupid dog," Remi mutters shaking his head, slinging moisture much like the very dog he's grumbling about. He grabs his sleep pants and heads toward the bathroom.

I pet my dog with affection. "St. Francis of Assisi would be ashamed of the way you treat poor Goner."

"Who, Frank? Nah, I'm positive he knows Goner's a fleabag." With a wink and a wicked grin, he closes the door behind him, ignoring my indignant and prolific praises of Goner's merits.

I brush my teeth and climb into bed and pat the bed for Goner to sleep with me, but the little ingrate responds with a loud doggy snore from Remi's bed. Fine, maybe he'll join me when Remi kicks him off his bed. Turning out the light, I snuggle under the covers, unable to turn off my thoughts after the ups and downs of this long day. The bathroom door opens, and I sneak a peek at Remi in his low-riding, black pajama pants. He has wickedly delicious hipbones underneath the muscle definitions of his abs. He brushes his teeth and glances my way in the mirror, but I close my eyes, hoping he didn't catch me spying on him.

The light over the vanity snaps off, and I open my eyes. He's left the bathroom light on and cracked the door, leaving a bare sliver of light for me. Stretching and rolling his back he collapses on the side of his bed looking like he's carrying the weight of the world on his shoulders. Through lowered lashes I watch him nudge the snoring dog, but Goner doesn't budge.

For twenty minutes he silently prays the rosary. The gentle clacking of the beads intermingles with the soft snores from Goner. A soft glow of light from the bathroom surrounds him, but his face is concealed by the shadows. It occurs to me this man is the light in my darkness. The peace in my tortured soul. The room is warm with the air conditioner off, but I don't want to kick off my covers and draw attention to myself.

With a loud yawn, he stands and kisses his rosary. I close my eyes, reliving our kiss on the Ferris wheel. His lips had tasted of candied apple and been so soft, yet firm. Even now, my body feels like a furnace, burning with a desire to feel that mouth exploring my body. I berate myself for the wrong, sinful thoughts that I can't seem to shut off. The man has just prayed and yet I want him to sin against his God. For once I wish I had the mind numbing medications that made me unable to think or feel. Is there a special place in hell for people like me? Or will I reside in purgatory? Or is it all a bunch of bullshit?

Nights have always been hardest for me. Like pain, my delusions seem exaggerated at the fall of darkness, as if they are too shadowy to deal with by light of day. I saw both Jack and Daddy, and I know in my heart today was significant. It was like a closure of some sort, and sorrow hangs over me like the smell of incense on Easter Sunday. It lingers in the air, and I grieve my losses all over again, but without the usual sense of despair. A frustrated sigh escapes my lips, and I roll over so my back faces Remi. I squeeze my eyes shut and a lone tear makes its way down my heated cheek. Although I'm sharing a room with another human being and a dog, I've never felt so alone. Does he regret the kiss? Probably.

Remi turns the air conditioner back on and I feel the bed dip with his weight. Feigning sleep, I attempt to even my breathing despite an overwhelming urge to reach up and take hold of his strong, comforting hand. I need to feel connected to someone. Wrong and forbidden as it is, I long to feel his arms around me, his lips on mine. If God exists, He has one sick sense of humor. Why else would I be attracted to this man? As he has done every night, Remi offers a quiet blessing over me. His warm hand strokes the back of my hair. His touch is my demise.

"Please, don't."

"Don't what, sweetness?" His husky voice holds all the promises I want, and know he can't, and shouldn't deliver.

"Just go away and leave me alone. I'm already damned to hell."

The scent of Christmas moves closer as he whispers in my ear, "But I thought you weren't a believer." His soft chuckle pushes the button on my frayed temper. I sit up and wrap my arms around his neck, pressing my body into his bare chest, wanting there to be no space between us. My lips crash into his, exploring his beautiful mouth. He's right, if I don't believe how can this be wrong? Or if I'm insane, how can I be held accountable?

He doesn't move for a few seconds and it's just enough time for me to regret my impulsive move. Shame pulls me away, and I hide my face in my hands.

Remi stretches out beside me and gently pushes me back, rolling me to my side, facing him. He brushes the hair from my eyes and his thumb sweeps across my lips.

"I'm sorry, *Father*," I whisper.

"*Remi.* I'm not," he whispers in return. My eyes widen as his lips capture mine. One hand strokes its way down my body, creeping under my T-shirt and up my back, pulling me closer. His touch leaves a trail of fire on my skin as our souls connect on some cosmic level. Two becoming one. I've always thought it meant the physical act. I now know it is so much more. It's the twisting of our very being into one like the coils of DNA or barbed wire.

I loved Jack, and I'm sure he loved me. But he hadn't loved me *enough*. He hadn't loved me enough to wait for me, or perhaps he'd loved me too much. Who knows? All of that is irrelevant now. He's gone. He's my past.

This love I'm sharing with Remi can't be measured, or compared. And it isn't just lust, although I have a healthy desire for this man beside me. No, I want more. I need more. Lying here with him, I realize love is so much more than silly words or actions. It is all encompassing and unfathomable until experienced. It is darkness intertwined with light, good with evil.

The kiss deepens and his tongue explores my mouth and a moan sounds, but whether it's his, or mine I can't say. We are no longer two separate entities. One last shard of guilt spears my conscience in a weak attempt at stopping the inevitable.

"Remi, I don't think—"

His fingers rest on my mouth and I see fire blazing in his eyes. "Then don't. If we do this, we do this without recriminations or regrets. We do it for love. Yes, I said it, and you need to hear it, and more importantly, believe it. I love you, Evangeline. Tonight there are no labels; we're just two people who need each other for a few stolen moments." His lips smile against my forehead. "And you have to promise to never kill yourself, because your life is precious to me." As the storm outside escalates, an inner sense of calm settles on the inside. I kiss his fingertips and he rolls over on top of me.

"Promise me and mean it." His lips skim my jaw. "No matter what the future holds, you have to carry on. You have to live. You're strong enough to live, Evie."

At this precise moment, I'd do anything he asked, even if it means we only have one night of heaven in exchange for a lifetime of hell. "I promise," I whisper in his ear. "I love you, and I need you."

He pauses and looks down at me, the back of his fingers stroking my cheek. "I feel the same way, but I don't want to take advantage of you."

"That's weird. Because all I can think about right now is how much I want to take advantage of you." I grin and lick his jaw.

"You have to understand; I don't know what the future holds for us. I can't promise you anything."

"I understand, now quit stalling."

He chuckles. "Crazy, impatient girl, come fly with me, and I'll show you a glimpse of real heaven." He peels my T-shirt off over my head and it floats to the floor. The dusting of coarse hairs on his chest tickles my nipples, making them pebble to the point of aching. An overwhelming need for this beautiful man courses through every cell in my body.

This need to connect, to be loved, to be one with him in mind, body and soul has developed over the past few days and now explodes with his touch and his kisses. He kisses my neck and I arch to give him greater access. His hands explore my body like a blind man reading Braille, sending a current of raw desire straight to my core. My fingers tangle in his tousled, damp hair and the sound of my soft moans mingle with his heavy breathing, filling the air with the seductive sound of lust.

"You're so beautiful, and you've changed me in more ways than you can comprehend. I'll never, ever forget you. When I look into your eyes, I see your truth, and your truth is good and pure. You never cease to amaze me or amuse me." He kisses my chest over my heart. Feeling shy and nervous, I roll my eyes, but inside I'm soaring with happiness over his words. I'm not bad. He wouldn't love me if I were bad.

"You won't believe me, but you have the biggest, kindest heart of anyone I know. You think you're wicked but you're the polar opposite. You're not crazy. You're not bad." He grins and nips my hard nipple, making me gasp. "Although you're definitely naughty. I like that about you. A lot. You're the love of my heart, my soul, and my life. If you remember nothing else, I will make sure you remember this, *you are worthy of love.*"

The raw emotion and tender words leave me speechless.

"You have my love, and you own my heart." His lips find mine, demanding yet tender as they tease and taunt my mouth in a give and take primal dance. "Do you have any idea the fantasies I've had over these full lips? They drive me insane with desire. One sweet smile from you can light up my world and at the same time lead me down a forbidden, dark path of carnal desire."

When I start to protest, he places a finger over my lips and whispers, "Hush. I'm not afraid of the dark, and forbidden fruit is my favorite dessert."

His lips move to my closed eyelids and he places a gentle kiss on each one. "I love the way your eyes soften when you look at that stupid mutt. And the way you roll them when you think I'm not looking." I open my eyes and he smiles at me. "And the way your pupils overtake your irises when you kiss me. I love you, Evangeline. I love you so damn much it hurts. I know we've only known each other a few days, but you're part of me. You're mine and I'll fight through heaven and hell to make sure you know how much you mean to me." Fire simmers in his eyes, but I'm not scared.

I murmur, "I love you, too. I didn't think I was capable of loving again. I didn't think anyone would ever love me…" I can't speak for a moment—his words have seduced me more than his skillful hands and lips. "But you do. You love me, all of me, even the parts of me that aren't lovable. You've shown me life is worth living and one moment with you *is* a lifetime and so very precious."

His hands skim down my sides as his tongue pays attention to my needy breasts. My yoga pants soon follow my T-shirt. I should feel shame, but I don't. He isn't Father Blackson. He's Remi, my lover and my savior. I will worship him with my body and live in the moment, embracing life. I will be his sacrificial lamb if need be. The God of my childhood, the one Remi serves, might damn us in the end, but it will be worth it.

His tongue dips into my belly button and I laugh nervously. My giggles are soon replaced by a sigh when he smiles against my skin as he explores every inch with his perfect lips. I hold my breath with fear when his hands trace the scars on my stomach.

"They're ugly," I choke out, attempting to cover them with my hands.

He moves my hands and his lips trace the scars lower and lower. "No, they're not. I think of them as a road map to something better," he teases. Light, soft strokes from his fingers skitter across my ribcage making me squeal so loud, Goner wakes up and barks a warning. Leaping off the other bed, the dog shoves his cold wet nose in my side, and I scream with laughter.

Remi shoves the mutt away with a laugh and covers my mouth with his hand. "Shh, you'll get us thrown out. I'm pretty sure this is a lot more comfortable than the backseat of a car, because regardless of where we do it, I refuse to stop."

I frown and turn serious. "I can't have babies. And I don't have any protection, but I'm clean. I get tested—"

"We're fine. No worries," he whispers as he skims my panties off and drops them to the floor.

I scramble to sit up, bringing him with me. My legs wrap around his waist, his hard erection presses and teases me with only his thin pajama pants separating us. His hands grasp my waist and our foreheads touch as we gaze at each other by the hint of light in the room.

"Don't tickle." I bite his full lower lip for emphasis. He chuckles and I rock against him and damn near explode on contact.

"Hush, or I'll do precisely that, with you tied to the bed and unable to move."

I gasp with a combination of surprise, longing, and dread. "Please, no tickling."

His laughter rumbles deep in his chest. "Are you saying no tickling, but the other is okay?"

I bury my face in his neck and pray my burning cheeks don't scorch his skin.

"Want a side order of flagellation with your bondage?" he teases.

"W-What?" I freeze in a combination of fear and curiosity until I peek at him and see the smirk on his beloved face.

"Silly girl, I'm not a Brother of the Cross. No worries."

I smack him on the back. "You have on entirely too many clothes."

"Oh that can be remedied, very easily." Fire simmers in his eyes and this time I know I'm not imagining it. I blink and it remains, flaring as he gazes at my naked body with a look of undeniable lust and longing. It's like gazing at a wildfire burning out of control as it engulfs a green field.

"Remi—" All further thoughts escape me as he flips me on my back and stands, shucking his pajamas to the floor. I've seen beautiful men before—those airbrushed, Photoshopped models and actors in magazines and on the Internet—but I've never seen anything like him. He's almost too much to take in and a blinding light surrounds him, making it difficult to keep my eyes open and focused on him. He moves to turn out the light in the bathroom and my breathing stops as my eyes sweep up and down every perfect inch of his carved body.

But it's the dark wings expanding from his back that render me speechless. The bed dips with his weight and I scoot toward the headboard pulling the sheet up around me as if it can shield me from whatever is about to occur. My voice breaks in a hoarse whisper as my heart pounds like a jackhammer in my chest. "What are you? Who are you?"

His hand brushes down the side of my head and moves to behind my neck. The fire in his eyes dies down and burns red, like smoldering hot coals. His warm breath fans across my cheek fueling my desire. "I'm yours," he whispers. "Close your eyes, there's nothing to be afraid of. I love you." His reassurances seem to hypnotize me as he pulls the sheet away. There's no way I could refuse him if I wanted to.

"Are you real?"

"Learn to trust yourself, Evangeline." Remi stretches out beside me on his back and pulls me on top of him. He pushes my hair behind my ear and cups my cheeks in his hands. "You have a choice. You always do. We can stop this right now."

"No! I don't want to stop. I just don't understand...you have wings, and sometimes I see fire in your eyes."

"I love you, Evangeline."

I run my fingers across his rough jaw line, my thumb dipping into the hollow of his cheek. There's no light in the room and yet he seems to be bathed in an incandescent glow. "You never answer my questions. Answer me just one. Are you real?" *Please be real.* More than anything, I want him to be real and to be mine, if only for this one night.

"Yes, I'm real, just different."

Throwing caution to the wind, I kiss him soundly. His skin is warm, his lips soft and inviting. If this isn't real, I don't care. I need him as much as I need air to breathe, and water to survive. I want to live in the moment, even if it means spending the rest of my life in the darkness of my mind. "I know loving you is wrong, but I don't care…"

Laughter fills the room as he rolls over on top of me. "I'm not going to lie to you. This is wrong on so many levels, it's epic in proportion. The earth may very well move off its axis and swallow us whole."

He brushes my hair from my face and the fire once again burns brightly in his eyes. In their depths I see my fear explode and dissipate. My fingers rake down his back, finding only hard muscles and skin as his lips devour mine. He consumes me like an expensive meal, taking his time to taste and appreciate. His hands skim down my body and his warm mouth follows. And when his lips and talented tongue delve into my essence, I do indeed soar to heaven before crashing back to reality onto a bed as soft as feathers.

Remi travels leisurely up the length of my body, his hands and lips leaving no inch untouched, marking me as his. I run my fingers through his disheveled brown hair and whisper, "I need more."

"Tsk, tsk, greed is a sin, Evangeline." He teases and taunts my hardened nipple with his wicked tongue.

"So is lust. I guess we're both damned."

"No, we're blessed because we have each other. Tonight, we are one." His hands grasp mine and holding them over my head, his lips cover mine as he buries himself deep inside me, completing me. Making me whole. My body echoes every move he makes. Effortlessly, we move as one. Our breathing becomes synchronized, our bodies in tune with one another. We soar and yet are immersed in one another, reaching a height of connection I've never felt with another human being. It's exhilarating and scary, like that damn Ferris wheel.

I'm falling, but I'm not afraid.

And when I climax, I die just a little.

And begin to live.

He rolls to his back bringing me with him. With my head on his chest, I listen as his heart rate slows. He strokes lazy circles on my back as we slowly descend from heaven back to earth.

I kiss the cross that lies against his heart and whisper fiercely, "He's mine."

"He knows," he agrees with a note of sadness.

When we're able to move, we shower, once again exploring each other's bodies. He gasps when I cup him and feeling powerful, I smile and stare into those fathomless green eyes.

"Just taking life by the balls," I tease, sinking to my knees under the spray of water, trailing kisses down his chiseled wet body.

"It's the only way to live," he agrees, laughing until my mouth makes it where he can no longer speak in intelligible words.

Afterward, we cuddle and as I drift to sleep, he whispers, "I love you, Evangeline."

Lying with my girl in my arms, I feel replete and at peace for the first time, ever. She sighs softly and snuggles in, purring in her slumber. I stroke her soft hair, watching a curl wrap around my finger. I don't want this to end. I love watching her sleep. It's the only time she's truly relaxed. As my mind works over the consequences of my actions, I sigh as cold, stark fear encompasses me. The high from making love to Evangeline has dissipated like adrenaline after a marathon race. Reality crashes down around me. What I have done is so wrong I can't even begin to fathom the depth of my depravity. I love her, but I can't have her. Truth be told, I'm no better than Jack.

Earlier, the Boss bent my ear with a thirty-minute tirade. To say He's unhappy with my behavior would be the understatement of the millennium. When He expresses His disappointment by throwing your name in with Judas, you're in deep shit. He's given me forty-eight hours to right my so-called wrongs or face the wrath of Him face-to-face. I argued with Him to no avail and selfishly forged ahead with my own desires and plans, not thinking about the consequences. Free will, the very thing I longed for, has now damned me.

My phone buzzes with an incoming text and my heart sinks.

We need to talk. Rectify this situation ASAP.

I delete the message and cold, stark fear now oozes into my conscience. I didn't think about how my actions will impact the woman I love. Breaking four out of seven deadly sins in a matter of hours and placing her in danger is unforgivable. This isn't buyer's remorse. This is serious shit and there's only one thing I can do to try to rectify the situation, and it's killing me. I have to protect her and face the consequences of my actions on my own.

I hold her close and kiss her forehead, her eyelids. My mouth closes over her soft lips. She smiles sleepily at me and returns the kiss, without waking from her deep sleep and dreams. Leaning in I whisper in her ear, "I love you, Evangeline. When you wake, you will think this was a dream."

She sighs and rolls over in her sleep and I leave her bed, feeling empty and bereft.

Chapter Twelve

I awake to the sound of the steady hum of the air conditioner and sit up with a start, feeling disoriented and hungover. The angel bear I'm clutching reminds me we're somewhere in the Midwest, and we wasted money at a carnival last night. My head pounds, but I don't remember having anything to drink last night.

Goner and Remi aren't in the room, and I experience a momentary sense of a panic at being alone. I ease up in bed, careful not to jar my aching head. A quick glance around the room reveals Remi's bed already made, as if it had never been slept in, but that's the norm. He's a fanatic about bed making, never leaving it for the maid, like I do. His suitcase is packed and stands by the door with Goner's bowls. I allow myself to take a deep breath and clutch the stuffed animal to my chest. At least I haven't been abandoned. *Yet.*

With a loud yawn, I shove my hair behind my ear and climb out of bed, taking the bear with me to pack in my suitcase. Strange, I hadn't noticed she had one black feather in her wings. It looks out of place so I pull it out and throw it in the trash. Something niggles at my memory, but without the benefit of coffee, it's too much to process. I toss the bear in the suitcase without another thought and grab some clean clothes, heading to the bathroom for a quick shower. Feeling relaxed and strangely happy despite the headache, I smile and hum as I bathe.

When I exit the bathroom, I find Goner seated at Remi's feet, wagging his tail and begging for food. Remi sits at the rickety table by the window dressed in his clericals, sipping a cup of coffee. He feeds the dog his last bite of biscuit. His wary gaze follows me and makes me pause for a moment. *Is he mad at me for sleeping in?* Tucking my foot under me, I sit on the edge of my bed, accepting the cup of coffee and ham biscuit he hands me.

"Thanks and good morning." For some strange reason, heat rises in my cheeks. "What, no Froot Loops?"

His eyes don't meet mine and he grunts in response. There's a strange vibe in the air between us and my paranoia creeps in, putting me on guard. *What's he up to? What have I done?* I take a breath and calm myself down. Plastering a smile on my face, I decide to "fake it till I make it" with casual conversation.

"I must have slept like the dead. I didn't even hear you leave. Did you get a free breakfast?" I motion toward his priestly garb.

He stares at me for a few seconds. "It came with the room." The dark circles under his eyes make them appear a deeper green than usual, and the disturbing, haunted look makes a shiver of unease creep up my spine.

"You look tired. Didn't you sleep well? Did I snore, or something?" The food and coffee have helped ease my headache, yet my stomach rolls, feeling queasy. Maybe something we ate yesterday has given us both a bug.

His hand fumbles and he sloshes coffee on his shirt. With an exasperated sigh, he drags himself to the sink to rub it with a damp washcloth. "I, uh, no. I didn't sleep at all."

"I'll drive and you can catch a nap."

He looks at me in the mirror and his brow furrows. "Are you sure you're okay?" His eyes search my face with an intensity that makes me squirm a bit.

"Aside from a slight headache, I'm fine. Better than fine. I feel great, actually." I take a sip of my coffee and grin at him. "I even promise not to kill myself today." I wiggle my eyebrows, but my smile fades when he doesn't immediately laugh or give a smart ass reply. Something's wrong but I can't put my finger on it. "Are *you* okay?"

"Yeah, yeah, sure." Remi smiles at me in the mirror, but it doesn't quite reach his tormented looking eyes. He's distant this morning, as if he has a lot on his mind. "I'm fine. I can relax a little knowing you're not planning any suicide missions today. That's progress."

I cross the room and stand behind him, rubbing his neck and back as I peer around him and stare at him in the mirror. "I haven't done anything to make you mad, have I?"

His color blanches. "No, not at all. Why would you say that?"

"Because you're acting all weird and shit." It hits me why he's mad. The kiss on the Ferris wheel. My toes curl just thinking about it. "Hey, we just got caught up in the moment. It's okay," I lie.

It's not okay. I'm falling in love with him.

"Caught up in the moment?" Sweat beads on his brow and he drops his gaze.

I wonder if he's coming down with something. He looks downright sick. The muscles in his neck and back tighten even more. I work with my thumbs to loosen them and he closes his eyes, humming in the back of his throat. An image of his lips on my body mingled with the sound of his moans causes something akin to an acid flashback.

"It was just a kiss…" The pounding in my head escalates, as if a marching band has taken up residence there. I struggle to pull something from my memory that seems to be just out of reach.

Or was it a dream? I drop my hands and turn away, confused and a little frightened. Am I now suffering blackouts? My brain feels more muddled than usual, and I can't seem to remember anything after leaving the carnival. I try to hide my escalating terror. *Fake it till you make it.*

"Sit down, Crazy Girl. You look like you've seen a ghost." He has the decency to blush at his insensitive blunder. After all, seeing ghosts is the crux of my problems. His discomfort is nothing compared to the sudden physical reaction I've just experienced with my hallucination. My cheeks feel like I have a second-degree burn, and my body tingles with a sexual awareness of Remi that is even more unsettling than usual.

"Just a kiss. You're right. It was reckless and I apologize. I'm, I just…" he stumbles on the words looking defeated. "I'm sorry. Truly, truly sorry. Forgive me?"

My heart sinks. I turn my back to him and begin throwing the rest of my clothes in my suitcase. I have plenty of room since our dirty clothes are in his. "Sure, of course. Whatever. It was just a stupid kiss. It isn't like I expect you to declare your love for me, or anything." I slam my suitcase closed, refusing to look at him. "I'm going to step outside and check in with Mama." I grab my phone and run outside, and despite the blast of early morning August heat, it's easier to breathe out here than in the room with him.

"Hi, Mama."

"Evie, how are you this morning?" The unspoken questions are enough to set my teeth on edge. *Are you taking your meds? Have you gone off the deep end lately?*

"I'm fine, you?" *I'm fine except for my X-rated visions, dreams, hallucinations, or whatever the hell you want to call them, involving a priest.* If I were to speak my thoughts aloud, I'm sure it would cause my good Catholic mother to drop dead of a heart attack.

The relieved sigh Mama gives in response speaks volumes. "I'm taking it easy like the doctors told me to."

"That's good. We should be there in a couple of days." Why did I call her? It's not like I can tell her what's bothering me.

"I look forward to seeing you." Mama pauses before adding, "I miss you, Evie."

I hear her sniffling and swallow the lump in my throat. A need to feel my mother's arms around me and hear her tell me everything will be okay makes me unable to speak for a few seconds.

"I miss you, too, Mama. I love you."

"I love you, too, baby."

We chat for a few more minutes about inane nothings before hanging up. For a brief moment, I wonder if having me there and dealing with my *issues* might be too much of a burden for her weak heart. I hope not. I make a promise to myself to be more patient with her and to try harder to repair our relationship. Maybe I'll even go back to seeing a therapist. This latest blackout is a little too scary.

The door opens and Remi hands me Goner's leash as he makes his way to the car with the suitcases. He looks exhausted and makes no protest — which is unusual — when I insist on driving. After getting buckled in, I look over at him in his dark pants, black clerical shirt with the stiff white collar and grin. "Planning to have all your meals comped today?"

He winces and runs a finger around the inside of the clerical collar as if to loosen it. "No, not really. All my civvies are dirty. Although, I guess free meals could be a perk."

"We'll look for a laundromat this evening. Even though we're headed north, those clothes have to be hot as hell in this heat."

His smirk spreads and lingers. For the first time this morning, he appears to relax a little. "You have no idea." He kicks his seat back and grunts when Goner decides to join him in a nap by hopping on his chest. "Stupid dog." The hand affectionately scratching the mutt behind his ears says something else.

"At least the storms have passed."

His eyes looked unsettled as he gazes out at the bright sunshine for a moment. "Yes, it should be clear from now until we reach Seattle." He sighs and closes his eyes, petting the "stupid dog." It doesn't take long for the sound of their combined snoring to compete with the classic rock radio station.

I'm enjoying the drive. The landscape is different from south Florida and I love the wide-open spaces. I'd stop and take pictures, but I don't want to risk waking Remi. Sleeping priests are like sleeping dogs, best left alone. Bright sunshine makes sunglasses a necessity, and the heat gives the pavement a wavy appearance. There's very little traffic on this stretch of road, so I'm surprised when a hitchhiker comes into view up ahead.

As I pass him, dark enigmatic eyes meet my gaze, drawing me in even more than his good looks. His plaid shirt is unbuttoned, exposing well-defined abs and a nice happy trail leading into the waistband of his worn jeans. A duffle bag sits beside his feet and a cowboy hat covers his hair. Looking in the rearview mirror, I see he's standing with the help of crutches. I pull over, slamming on the brakes.

"What the—" Remi sits up with a start, rubbing his eyes, looking like a sleepy little boy. "What's wrong?"

"Nothing, go back to sleep. I'm just stopping to give this guy a ride."

He turns and looks out the back window as the hitchhiker slowly makes his way toward us on his crutches. "Are you insane?"

"I think we both know the answer to that," I reply with a grin.

"Evangeline, you can't pick up a hitchhiker; it isn't safe, or smart," he snaps with a frown, glaring at the stranger hobbling toward us.

"Where's your compassion, *Father?* The guy is out here in a hundred-plus degree heat on crutches. We can't leave him here to die."

"Sure we can." The closer the guy gets to the car, the more agitated Remi becomes, drumming the dashboard with his fingers, making the Virgin Mary and hula girl dance like they're at a rave. His scowl darkens. "He won't die. Look, I'll give him a bottle of water and some money. We are *not* letting him in this car," he says authoritatively.

I roll down my window as the guy draws nearer.

"Thanks for stoppin', sunshine." The cowboy tips his hat and flashes even teeth, made whiter by the attractive dark stubble on his strong jawline. He leans his forearms on the window and stoops down to peer inside the car. His grin grows wider when he sees Remi. "Hiya, Pops."

Remi coughs and gasps, "Pops?" His eyes widen with either horror or indignation, possibly a combination of both.

"Padre, Father, whatever." The cowboy shrugs nonchalantly, turning his attention back to me. After the cold shoulder Remi's given me all morning, my feminine pride enjoys the interest.

"Where are you headed, and why are you hitchhiking?" I ask, trying not to stare at the expanse of bare, well-defined pecs in front of my face. I may have an unhealthy attraction for the priest sitting next to me, but I'm not blind. This guy is gorgeous.

"Well, to make a long story short, my girl dumped me out here in the middle of nowhere. I was headed to Billings to see my grandmother."

Remi snorts next to me and I glare at him, wondering what his problem is. Turning back to the cowboy, I smile. "Why did she dump you? What's your name?"

He holds out his hand and takes mine in his firm grasp. "Rafe. Rafe Goodman, ma'am. I haven't been able to work since I got out of the service. I'm still recuperating from the sniper shot I received trying to rescue some orphans in Afghanistan. Me and my girl got into it about money and me not being able to take her dancing."

Rafe sighs and looks down for a few seconds. "Unfortunately, we were in her car on the longest, loneliest stretch of highway around. She put me out like yesterday's garbage." When he pulls his gaze back to mine, tears fill his dark eyes. Even though I'm a little suspect about the whole story, I feel sorry for the guy. Besides, it takes crazy to appreciate crazy.

"That's terrible. How could anyone do that to someone who's sacrificed so much for his country?"

"Maybe he beat her, or he's a raging alcoholic," Remi offers. "We don't need to get his entire life story. It's hot and we need to get going."

Remi shoves a bottle of water and a twenty toward Rafe. "Here you go, buddy. Call someone who cares."

My mouth drops open and I glare at Remi. "Good God, why are you being such an ass? What's wrong with you? Why don't you go back to sleep, Father Grumpy Bear." I turn back to the cowboy. "Please, excuse him, Rafe. Somebody woke up on the wrong side of the bed this morning."

Rafe's eyebrows shoot into his cowboy hat and his mouth drops open. Remi sounds like he's dying as he hacks and chokes beside me. I pound him on the back and give him the bottle of water he just offered Rafe. Glaring at the cowboy, he manages to take a drink and stop coughing.

"Why don't you take a picture, it lasts longer," he snarls at Rafe. Remi's lack of compassion confuses me. It's totally out of character for him. Well not totally, he didn't take any of *my* bullshit, but I've never seen him be downright rude to anyone, myself included. I elbow him in the side and return my attention to the poor crippled man.

"Is there anyone you can call? I can let you use my phone," I offer.

"No, my grandmother's sick, plus my phone was in my girl's car. I can't remember any phone numbers due to my TBI after the sniper attack."

"TBI?" I ask blankly.

"Traumatic Brain Injury."

"It means he's bonkers. You two should get along beautifully," Remi remarks with an eye roll. "Snipers, an orphanage, and a sick grandmother? Really? You can't come up with a better story? Buddy, I think you've watched too many Lifetime movies. Look, Crazy Girl, we don't know anything about this guy. He could be a serial killer for all we know."

"I didn't know you, but I trusted you."

"But I'm a priest!" he defends hotly, running a finger under the white collar.

"Then act like one. Get in, Rafe."

Rafe throws his head back and laughs. Stepping back from the car, he balances on his crutches. The sun highlights every perfect dip of his six-pack abs. I count again, yep, six. *Damn.*

"You're staring," Remi mutters, drawing my attention back to the conversation.

"I'm not armed. Anyone wanna frisk me?" The cowboy holds his arms out wide.

Me, me me... Any woman with a pulse would volunteer. He's *that* gorgeous. Plus, I'm mad at Remi for giving me the silent treatment most of the morning. Yep, call me a bitch. I want to make him jealous.

"Of course not," Remi snaps.

"I could, but it would upset the good Father's sensibilities." I smirk when I hear the hiss of annoyance next to me.

Out of nowhere, an image of Remi kissing my neck flashes in my mind. Like steel to a magnet, I turn to face him as a searing heat creeps from my chest to my cheeks. Remi refuses to meet my gaze, staring out the window as he taps the side of the car. Is it my imagination, or is he blushing, too? I can't seem to get the image of him naked on top of me out my head, and my heart stutters in reaction. These dreams feel even more real than the ones involving my father and Jack... Remi scowls and presses his lips together in a straight line. *I want those lips pressed to mine.* The tic in his cheek works overtime as he clenches and unclenches his jaw.

"I-I'm just kidding, Father. Get your rosary out of a wad." My lame attempt at humor falls flat, and he continues to ignore me, staring straight ahead.

The stranger clears his throat, and I drag my attention back to him.

"Do you mind if we see what's in your duffel? You know, to make sure there aren't any weapons or severed limbs? It might make Father Blackson feel better." I smile sweetly, and nudge Remi hard in the ribs when he starts to protest. I'm ready to go. It's hot as hell and my pounding headache from this morning has returned with a vengeance.

"Sure, anything to set your mind at ease, sweetheart." Rafe hands me the duffel, but Remi grabs it out of my hand and rifles through it. I want to laugh and hide my face at the same time when he pulls out a box of condoms. A dark scowl crosses his face and his whispered obscenity makes me raise my eyebrows. He quickly shoves them underneath the jeans, underwear, and cowboy shirts. He zips the duffel and shoves it back in my lap.

Rafe chuckles. "Sorry about that, Pops. I believe in covering up."

I'm certain my cheeks are as red as a hooker's lipstick as I throw the duffel in the backseat next to Goner. My attention-whore dog wags his tail in anticipation of some company.

Saving Evangeline

I look at Rafe and nod toward the back. "Get in."

"Evangeline, this is *my* car," Remi sputters in protest, running a hand through his hair making it a tousled mess. I clench my hand to keep from reaching out and finger-styling it into place. I'd like to think it's because I'm a hair stylist, but I'd be lying to myself.

"We can't leave him out here, Remi."

"Why not? Someone else will come along and give him a ride."

I look at the long stretch of empty road in front of us and behind us and raise an eyebrow. There's not a single car on the road. "Seriously? If we were in an old western, there'd be buzzards circling in anticipation of their next meal. I don't want his death on my conscience."

"I thought you didn't believe in the hereafter," he mutters in return. He sighs and I know I've won this battle. He unlatches his seatbelt. "Fine. But I'm driving. How come when we're in the city you drive like an Indy driver, but when you hit an open stretch of highway you meander like an old lady leaving church?" He throws open his door and storms to the driver's side.

With my pounding headache, I'm relieved by his offer, but I can't help grumbling a little. "There's nothing wrong with my driving. You know, I didn't wake up suicidal this morning, but I swear, dealing with your snarky attitude today could change that by nightfall. What is your problem?" I slam the car door and immediately regret it as the sound rumbles in my aching head.

"You promised me…"

"I'm kidding." I glance embarrassedly at Rafe who stands there with a shit-eating-grin on his face, watching us like we're stars on some crappy reality television show.

"I'm sorry. I'm just tired." Remi pauses and frowns at me. "Aren't you the least bit tired?"

I hadn't been until we started arguing. "Physically, no. Tired of your attitude, yes." Before the image of him kissing me became lodged in my mind, I almost felt *normal.*

Remi lights a cigarette and smirks when Rafe waves the smoke away with a grimace. "Hurry up, Evangeline, we don't have all day. We have to get to Billings."

I stomp to the passenger side muttering obscenities under my breath. With the mood he's in, I'm pretty sure we'll arrive two hours ahead of schedule.

Rafe crawls in the backseat, and of course, Goner starts whimpering to get out of the car to do his business. Taking his leash, I walk him into the grass, and look back at the car. Remi slams Rafe's door and the car shakes from the impact. He stands for a moment with one hand on his hip, smoking and glaring off into the distance. Stubbing out the cigarette, he climbs in the driver's seat and turns toward Rafe. From the look of it, he's giving the poor guy a piece of his mind. The wind picks up and a dust devil swirls, blocking my vision of the car for a moment. When it clears, Rafe tips his cowboy hat back and stretches his arms out across the backseat appearing unaffected by whatever Remi's saying.

"Why are you here? And that had to be the most ridiculous story I've ever heard. You're a wounded soldier who rescue orphans and has a sick grandmother? *Puh-lease.* Couldn't you find any more clichés to pull out of your ass?" I slam the car door and glare at Raphael, keeping a wary eye on Evie and Goner. I can't risk her overhearing what is bound to be an explosive argument.

"I rescued a kitten from a tree, too. Using my crutches to help the poor thing down," the asshole quips with a laugh.

I'm not the least bit amused.

Raphael sighs and his dark brows furrow. "The Boss didn't give me all the details. He just said for me to keep tabs on you, because you're treading in dangerous water. Which is ironic since you can't swim. What's going on?"

"None of your damn business."

Raphael shakes his head and clicks his tongue against his teeth. "You know He doesn't like that kind of language."

"Fine, why don't you run home and tattle like a whiney little girl." I close my eyes and take a deep breath. Arguing with the Boss's right hand stooge is probably not the best way to get the jerk to leave. "Look, I had a little misstep, but everything's cool. I handled it. She hasn't tried to off herself since I got here and even woke up *happy* this morning." Out of the corner of my eye, I watch her stretch, her shirt rising to expose a stomach I long to kiss and nibble. I shift uncomfortably in my seat since one source of her happiness wants to stand up and be counted.

Raphael pinches the bridge of his nose and groans. "Tell me you didn't go there."

When I don't respond, his anger explodes. "Remiel! You can't toy with the humans. It's His number one rule. You know how much He puts into free will and all that it encompasses."

"I didn't plan it and I didn't toy with her. It just happened," I say through gritted teeth, ready to tear him apart in an all-out celestial war. My wings bristle. The wind whips outside, and a small dust storm ensues. Even the trees rustle from the impact. Evie looks up and tucks her windblown hair behind her ears as she tugs on Goner's leash urging him to go. I have to calm down before she grows suspicious.

I rub my face, feeling exhausted. "Shit. I'm in deep, brother. I love her..."

"Oh, no." Raphael doesn't say anything else for a moment. It's the first time I've ever seen him at a loss for words. It only lasts a few seconds. "No, Rem. You *can't* fall for a human. How could you make such a stupid mistake? You know it isn't allowed. What are you going to do?"

"I don't know," I reply with a despondent sigh.

"You need to go home and talk to Him. I'll babysit Evangeline."

"I'm not leaving her. Besides, I didn't agree with how He wanted this handled to begin with."

Raphael shakes his head and his mouth forms a perfect O. "Please don't say you tried to tell Him how to run His business. That never goes over well."

"It isn't fair. She thinks she's crazy and has been carrying around all this guilt—"

"You know what He says. Life is beautiful, but not necessarily fair."

"I won't have her shouldering that burden any longer. I'm going to finish what I've started. I'm teaching her to grab life by the balls and to enjoy it. She's been lost for too long and now she's making progress. Like I said, she was happy this morning." I smile, watching the woman I adore cussing like a sailor as she tugs on the leash, urging her silly dog to hurry. "*I love her*, dammit."

Raphael blows out a deep breath. I don't like the look of pity in his dark eyes. "I'm here to make sure you don't mess up and overstep the boundaries. I have to report back to Him in two days. You know I can't lie to Him, so make this right and tend to business only."

I sigh, knowing I don't really have any other option. "Just let me get her home to her mother." I shut up when Evangeline approaches the car, her dark brown eyes narrowed with suspicion.

"Forty-eight hours. That's it. And you're stuck with me as a chaperone," Raphael whispers.

"Hurry up, dammit." I tug at Goner's leash. He finally pees and bounces toward the car, greeting Rafe with a lick to the face and happy bark. I barely get my seatbelt buckled before Remi hits the gas, jerking the car forward. I'm positive he hit seventy miles per hour in three seconds. His sunglasses obscure his eyes, but I bet they're blazing with anger. I can practically count his pulse by the tic above his clenched jaw.

"So where y'all goin'?" Rafe drawls.

Remi smiles the first real smile I've seen all day, glances at me, and replies, "Crazy."

I smack his arm, but can't help but snicker. *Smart ass.*

"O-*kay*." Rafe's brows knit together a little. "Well that sounds like my kind of place." Rafe strokes Goner's rough fur. The happy mutt collapses on his lap with a contented sigh.

Rafe yawns loudly and we all laugh when Goner joins in before going back to sleep, his head still in Rafe's lap. "I think I'll just catch a nap if y'all don't mind." He settles back and tips his cowboy hat over his face and in a matter of seconds appears to be asleep.

Remi turns on his *Evangeline* playlist, but a strange vibe remains between us. I gaze out the window, reflecting on how different this trip is from my last trip. It was on the way home from a stolen weekend to Key West that Jack told me Kayla was pregnant. He took me away to tell me good-bye and ended up dying on the side of the road. I now see Remi's point. Jack was pretty shitty to both Kayla and me. God, it seems like such a lifetime ago. In the space of a few days, with the help of the man beside me, Jack's gone from being a painful memory to a bittersweet one. I have a choice. Dwell in the past or move forward. The past no longer holds any appeal, but my future is scarily uncertain.

As if sensing my discomfort, Remi reaches over to hold my hand. I realize in this moment, I never want him to let go. We'll soon be at my mom's, but I don't want him to leave. Ever.

I'm in love with a priest.

I swallow several times to keep my tears in check and curl into my seat.

"Hey, you okay?"

No, I want to scream. *I want you to stay.*

"I just hate good-byes," I whisper, so as not to wake Rafe.

"Me too." His thumb gently strokes my palm. "Let's not think about it right now."

"What's going to happen to me?"

"You're going to take life by the balls, remember?" He squeezes my hand reassuringly.

"And what about you?"

Remi doesn't answer for a moment, glancing in the rear view mirror at Rafe and Goner.

"I have some difficult decisions to make. This so-called break was supposed to help me as I wrestle with what to do with the rest of my life."

I swallow and gaze down at the warm, strong hand holding mine. I'm afraid if I let go of him, I'll lose a part of me. "W-Would you consider leaving the priesthood?" I hope Rafe is truly asleep. If not, that the air conditioner and Goner's snoring drowns our whispered conversation.

He doesn't answer for a full minute and sighs. "Last night I did." He gazes at me through his dark sunglasses for a second before returning his eyes to the road.

I frown, trying to remember anything after the carnival, but all I remember is our one stolen kiss in the rain. Our one brief glimpse of what life could be like if we weren't who society labeled us. A kiss that changed me in some way, I know it did. I struggle to pull up more memories, but all I have is the dream of him telling me he loved me. I contemplate asking him what happened, but I'm both terrified to let him know I blacked out, and scared of the answer.

I assume he stayed up late pondering his life and his calling to serve his God. That must be why he's so on edge today. My cheeks burn, knowing I've contributed to his guilt. What's wrong with me that I continue to choose men I can't have? The shrinks will have a field day with this latest development.

"There can't be an us, can there? You've decided to remain a priest." I try to contain my disappointment, but fail miserably. My voice sounds like that of a sullen child.

He looks straight ahead and his shoulders sag when he exhales. Squeezing my hand, he whispers, "I'm sorry, Evie." Letting go of my hand, he fumbles for a cigarette.

Chapter Thirteen

"*I love you, Crazy Girl.*" *His lips brush against my ear and his husky, whispered confession makes my body tingle all over. I feel safe and loved. He's mine and I'm his. Nothing can separate us. I arch into his body and wrap my arms around his neck.*

"*I love you, too...*"

"Wake up, Evangeline."

I sit straight up and rub my eyes, disoriented. Why can't my dreams ever be real? I see Rafe standing with his crutches outside of a motel scowling at us through the windshield. Goner whimpers in the back seat, wanting out of the car. I drag my gaze to meet Remi's and find my profound sadness reflected in his eyes.

"Where are we?" I rake a hand through my tangled mess of hair.

"We didn't make it to Billings. Rafe's leg hurts, my head aches, and you slept most of the way. I think we might have a touch of food poisoning or something from the carnival." Remi's eyes look everywhere but at me.

My limbs feel like lead. Every mile we drive we're getting closer to my mother and ultimately to Remi leaving. I want to turn the car around and go back, but my mom needs me. I have no choice but to move forward with my life. As we step out of the car, the air between the two men crackles with an unspoken tension that only adds to my nervousness. I need to get away, to put some distance between Remi and me and get my shit together. I refuse to fall apart. I pull Goner from the car.

"Where are you sleeping tonight, Rafe?" Remi leans against the car and takes out another cigarette and lights it. Judging by the almost empty pack, his tobacco consumption has more than doubled today.

Rafe stands beside him balancing on his crutches and tips his hat back. "I dunno, where are *you* sleeping, *Pops?*"

Exhausted, my mouth engages before my brain. "We've been sharing a room to save on expenses."

Rafe raises one eyebrow and his lips thin. Remi's eyes narrow in an unspoken challenge. I feel like a spectator at the O.K. corral. Goner whimpers and hides behind my legs, probably in response to the overabundance of testosterone bouncing around in the air.

The strange sound of beating wings has me looking around, but nothing seems out of the ordinary. I don't see any birds and clench my teeth. *Not now.* Not when I'm trying to deal with two stubborn men intent on having a pissing contest.

"In separate beds, of course," I offer in a belated attempt to smooth things over. What's wrong with these two?

Rafe's lips curl in a smile. "Of course. What wonderful restraint you must have, *Christian Grace.*" I roll my eyes wishing Rafe would stop with the digs toward Remi. He's under enough stress dealing with his own situation.

The tic in Remi's cheek beats several times before he answers in a measured voice. "This isn't any of your concern and certainly none of your business. I can assure you, Evangeline is safe with me. I'm acting as an escort to make sure she arrives home safely because her mother is ill. Now as for *you*, I'm sure we can call around and find someone to give you a ride to Billings. We're only a few hours away. As a matter of fact, you can use my phone. If that doesn't work, I'll drive you myself. Evie can stay here until I get back."

"No!" Both men turn to look at me after my outburst. "I mean, we're all too tired to drive any further." *No, what I really mean is I don't want Remi to leave me. Ever. Not. For. One. Second.* God, I'm such a co-dependent mess.

Rafe stares straight at Remi and his expression looks as stubborn as my mulish priest. "It was just a simple question, no one is going anywhere. I don't know anyone in Billings except my grandmother and she can't drive. My leg is killing me from being cramped up in the backseat, and I'm not up to another two-hour drive. I beg your *pardon*. I didn't mean to imply anything happened that would compromise your calling, *Father*. I have no problem sleeping on the floor. I've slept in worse places."

I'm not buying Rafe's exaggerated look of pain and his excuses, but my head hurts too much to listen to their arguing.

"While you two battle out the sleeping arrangements and who's sleeping with whom, I'm going to get some fresh air and walk Goner. Try not to kill each other while I'm gone. I get squeamish at the sight of blood." Yanking Goner by the leash I stomp toward the grassy area.

As handsome as Rafe is, I wish I'd listened to Remi and not given the cowboy a ride. He acts like he knows something I don't, and I'm starting to have doubts about him.

My days with Remi are numbered, and spiritual counseling is the last thing on my mind. Nope. I want him, and not in a platonic way, either. I want my dream to come true: to experience his bare skin on top of mine, feel his hands buried in my hair, and hear his moans of desire in my ear.

Goner and I have wandered too far to hear what looks like a heated argument judging by the way Remi paces, puffing on the cigarette in his mouth. Every so often he punctuates a point with the lit cigarette. If I had a joint I'd give it to him, maybe it would chill him the fuck out. Not that Father Blackson would ever do anything illegal—illicit, maybe, unethical, positively. Again, the vision of his naked body on top of mine sneaks in, making me feel hot and bothered. I'm in desperate need of a bath. That thought leads to a vision of us wet and naked in a shower.

Depravity. My new middle name.

Rafe stands leaning against the car with his arms crossed in front of his chest, the crutches at his side. He points at Remi and then at *me*. The wind picks up and it sounds like a summer storm blowing through palm trees, yet there isn't a cloud in the sky.

The pounding in my head has increased to the point I feel nauseated. Remi opens the trunk, takes out my suitcase and puts it on the sidewalk. Goner's stuff follows and then he throws Rafe's duffel at him. A cold sweat of fear trickles down my back when Remi throws himself in the car and starts the engine. Gravel spins with the tires as he peels out of the parking lot.

"No," I scream, scrambling back toward the car, dragging Goner with me. *He can't leave me, he can't leave me, he can't leave me...*My heart hammers in time with the constant refrain as I watch him drive away without looking back. Utterly devastated, I fall to my knees and sob into Goner's neck as an overwhelming sense of loss moves in like an old neighbor. He's left me, like so many others. Once again, I'm an empty shell. With him, I felt whole for the first time in my entire pathetic life.

A hand pats me on the back. Through my tears I stare at a worn cowboy boot. "Why?" I manage to choke out.

"Why what, sweetheart?" The concern in his voice makes me angry. This is his fault.

His use of a nickname only serves to remind me Remi will never again call me Crazy Girl, or sweetness. Rafe hauls me to my feet and tips my chin up to look at him. I childishly squeeze my eyes tight and spit out bitterly, "I hate you."

"You hate *me?*" He sounds genuinely surprised. "Why? Besides, hate is a pretty strong word."

I open my eyes and shove him. Despite being crippled and on crutches he doesn't budge. "It's your fault he's *gone.*"

"You're this upset over Father Fractious going to do laundry?"

"Laundry?" I squeak. Thanks to the unrelenting pounding in my head, I'm having a hard time keeping up. "He just left to go do laundry?" Rafe nods. "Why didn't he let me do it?" Relief floods through me.

"He said he needed some time alone." He frowns and rubs my arm, pity registering in his dark eyes. "Wow. You've got it bad for Justin Believer."

Embarrassed, I squat next to my dog, making a great pretense of straightening his collar and leash. "It's just..." *Come up with a reasonable lie, stupid.* "I have to get home to my mom's. If he leaves me, I don't know how I'd get there."

Rafe grunts and sits down next to me. "Honey, you realize this can't go anywhere, right? He's a priest. No hokey-pokey, horizontal slides, bumping the uglies, or mattress jigs allowed."

After my initial shock, I giggle and wipe away the tears on my cheeks. "That has to be the longest list of sexual euphemisms I've ever heard." And they sounded funny and awkward coming from him. They were much more suited to Remi. As a matter of fact, Remi seems more like the cowboy type and Rafe the priest.

"Yeah, well, just trying to get my point across." He pulls at some grass as we sit for a moment in an awkward silence. "So tell me, how did you and Judas Priest meet?"

I shrug and glance at him from under my lowered lashes, standing to end the conversation. "He's a priest, I'm a lapsed Catholic. That makes us a match made in heaven."

He struggles to his feet, and I look away from the sympathy in his dark eyes.

"I'm going to lie down. I don't feel well," I mumble, but he catches my hand before I can leave.

"Look, I'm going to tell you something and you can take it for what it's worth." He squints up at the clear sky and sighs before dropping his gaze back to mine. "He cares about you. He cares more than he should, if you know what I mean. And he's struggling at the moment. You know in your heart it can't develop, not the way you two want it to. It just can't."

I swallow the bitter pill he's giving me, even though I want to spit it out and live in my delusional world. "I know." I sigh and look at the ground. "I'm not going to stand in the way of his calling. I just…" My voice falters. My mouth had once again been about to activate without my brain in full gear, but I've managed to stop it in time.

"Just what, Evie?"

I shake my head.

"Tell me."

"I just wanted to pretend for a few days I was normal and he wasn't a priest." I blurt. "I know it's wrong. I know it will supposedly damn my soul for all eternity, but I don't believe in that shit."

Rafe releases a long, deep breath before speaking. "Look at me."

I glare at him in response.

"Evie, the problem is *he does believe that shit.*"

My dreams crumble like a cookie in a child's hand. He's right and I know it. I swallow my disappointment, knowing what I have to do. I have to let him go. Together we walk back toward the room we've rented for the night.

The sun sits low in the sky, but being this far west, it isn't close to sunset. However, a different type of darkness seeps into my brain, the shadowy feeling of hopelessness. My depression, which has been blowing like a fresh laundered sheet on a clothesline, settles like an old comfortable terrycloth robe around me. I'm once again in the skin I know and wear well. Perversely, it's like the feeling of coming home after a tiring trip. That brief moment of happiness and contentment wasn't me. My grandmother once said I suffered from *melancholia*, a nicer sounding word than the clinical term depression. Like rain slipping down a window, I return to my melancholic comfort zone.

Rafe sits on the curb outside the room with Goner while I shower, giving me time to think. After I'm done, I call my mother to check on her but hang up before she can start with the twenty questions. I just don't have the energy to talk. Drawing the curtains, I turn out the lights and crawl into bed, pulling the covers up over my head like a shroud, emotionally dead. Closing my eyes, I try my damnedest to block out the memory of Remi's kiss on the Ferris wheel and the dream of him making love to me.

I now understand what hell is. It isn't a physical place with flames and a red devil. It doesn't matter if you're good or bad, if you believe or don't believe. It's the total and utter isolation you feel when you have to let go of the other part of your soul, the one you love.

The bed dips under his weight and the smell of Christmas makes me smile. I've just had a lovely dream of playing in the snow with Remi.

"C'mon, Evie, wake up. We're hungry, let's go find something to eat."

"I wish I could see snow," I whisper, keeping my eyes closed.

I hear the sound of ice clinking in a glass. "It's the middle of summer, Crazy Girl. This as close as we can get." He rudely yanks the cover off, sprinkling me with ice water. So much for dreams.

"Stop, please stop, I have to pee," I whine between giggles. He looks devastatingly handsome in his jeans, and *50 Shades of Grace* T-shirt. His damp hair waves and falls on his forehead, adding to his mischievous, boyish look. The room is dim, lit only by the light over the vanity.

Remi grins as he crunches an ice cube. "Pee on the bed and you'll be sleeping on wet sheets."

I peer up at him and can't resist the joke. "Why do girls prefer dildos to men?"

"Not possible. No way a girl would prefer motorized rubber over a real man. It's a sin to lie, Evangeline." His stern admonishment is lost in his wide grin.

"Dildos don't make girls sleep on the wet side of the bed."

He laughs that full, gusty laugh that I'm going to miss. "Masturbation constitutes a grave moral sin. I will pray for your soul." A bark outside the door has him bolting to sit on the other bed, and I pull the covers up to my chin just before Rafe walks in with Goner.

"She still isn't up? Let's go, I'm starving."

I yawn and stretch. "What time is it?"

Remi answers, "After seven and he's right, we're hungry. You slept so hard we were getting worried. *Are* you okay?" He sits with his elbows on his knees, his hands clasped before him, staring intently at me. He's back to being serious, and I long for the carefree man that teases me. For a brief second fire flares in his eyes, but he blinks and it's gone.

Casting a nervous glance toward Rafe, I nod. "I'm just exhausted. You two can go get something to eat, I'm not really hungry. If Remi puts his clerics back on, you can get comped a meal."

Rafe raises one eyebrow and shakes his head. "Using the collar for gains? Good grief."

"People are just nice. I don't ask for a free meal," Remi protests.

I roll on my stomach and dive under the covers, closing my eyes. "Bring Goner some scraps." Being forced to be pleasant over a meal doesn't fit in with my current plans for a pity party. Besides, I don't think food would get past the lump lodged in my throat.

Remi stands. "Get your ass out of bed and get dressed, Evangeline. You're not going to wallow in your self-pity. Grab life by the balls, remember? We'll be outside waiting for you." He glances at his watch. "You have fifteen minutes to get ready. Be sure to brush your teeth and comb your hair like a good little girl. Don't make us take you out looking like a hot mess and in your pajamas." His condescending manner kind of pisses me off. I'm not a three-year-old who needs to be told what to do.

"We can just leave her here with Goner if she doesn't want to spend time with us." Rafe gives Remi a pointed look that makes me suspicious. What is it between these two? It seems to be more than just testosterone one-upmanship. It's almost like they know each other, like they're brothers. Maybe it's just a guy thing.

"Please come with us," Remi asks softly, ignoring Rafe's annoyed sigh.

I can't refuse him. Besides, I guess it would be better to spend a little time with Remi—even in the company of Rafe—than no time at all.

"Fine. Get out." I crawl out of bed, running smack into Remi as he stands to leave. The air snaps and sizzles between us, and my skin burns where he touches me in an effort to steady me. I stare at his Adam's apple moving as he swallows. A multitude of emotions wash over me. I want to melt into his arms, collapse at his feet, and throw him back on the bed all at the same time, none of them a viable option.

Rafe clears his throat, and Remi steps around me, shoving the cowboy out of the room. It doesn't seem to bother him that the guy walks with crutches and could get hurt. It isn't until the door closes that I'm able to breathe normally. I have fifteen minutes to get my shit together. I know in my gut I'm at a pivotal point in my life. I either wallow in self-pity the rest of my life, cycling in and out of the mental health system, or I listen to the man that has shown me that life can be fun. The choice is mine. I take a deep breath and square my shoulders, making the decision to grab life by the balls, even if that means doing it alone.

"She's slipping away. I'm losing her. When I first met her, she was suicidal. My job was to save her, but now…" My chest hurts like someone has ripped open my chest and pulverized my heart with a hammer. If I were human, I'd think I was having a heart attack.

Raphael watches me pace. "At the risk of sounding redundant, she was never yours. What did you expect, Remiel? You're skimming this side of shady even in human terms. I mean whatever the heck you two have done may have been consensual when it happened, but you warped her memory into dreams. Now, I realize you did what you had to do to rectify the situation. But man, you've got to pull yourself together. If you don't, you run the risk of either pushing her over the edge, or she'll figure out what you are. And you know The Boss won't be down with either one of those options. So what are you going to do?"

"I'm not asking you. And if I knew, do you really think I'd tell *you?*" I light a cigarette, puffing on it like a steam engine on a one-way track to hell.

"Remiel, I'm not the enemy. I'm here to help. You know the end result. You have to let her go."

"Help? Or spy?"

The concern and compassion in Raphael's eyes makes me uncomfortable. "Call Him. He'll know how to get you out of this mess. You're in too deep."

Refusing to admit I'm wrong and he's right, I lash out. "Do you honestly think I haven't tried to reach Him? He doesn't answer. I guess He's letting me flounder to teach me a lesson. Well, guess what? I don't need anyone's help. I can do this on my own without any interference from you or Him."

Rafe shakes his head. "When will you ever learn? How can you not see what lies ahead? Nothing good can come from your blatant disobedience. Just admit you're in over your head. You have to learn it's okay to rely on others before it's too late."

I ignore his cryptic doomsday prophecies. I'm lost, but like all respectable males, I refuse to stop and ask for directions. Sometimes the scenic route is more enjoyable. Besides, as long as I save her, does it matter if I veer off the chosen path?

Chapter Fourteen

I pull on the only dress I packed, a wraparound red number that used to hug my curves. I'm one of those Italian girls blessed with big boobs, a little waist, and round hips. Yanking my hair into a topknot with a few loose tendrils, I add a touch of makeup. I'm ready in fourteen minutes, a record time for me.

"Wow. You look great, sunshine. Doesn't she look pretty, *Padre?*"

If Remi wasn't a priest, I'm pretty sure he'd flip Rafe off judging by the dark look he shoots him. "Let's go," he barks, opening the car door for me. Silence prevails on the short drive until Rafe starts singing along with the radio, an old George Michael's song about having faith.

"Very funny," Remi mutters.

"What?" Rafe asks, leaning forward from the backseat, sounding surprised, but as always, looking like he knows a secret. He seems to have an uncanny ability to push every button Remi has. It's the one thing the cowboy and I have in common.

In a matter of minutes, we arrive at dilapidated cement block building. Neon beer signs and the sound of loud music from an old-fashioned jukebox make it feel like we've stepped back in time. There isn't a man in the place that isn't wearing a cowboy hat or ball cap, except Remi. Good thing he didn't wear his clericals — he'd stick out like a sore thumb. The place is nothing more than a dive bar with a kitchen. The only saving grace I can see is it isn't fast food. I don't think I could stomach another cheap burger.

"Are you sure we're in the right place?" A glance around the place makes me glad I have two men with me. Several drunken cowboys look me over like a prize cow at the stock show. Two weeks ago, this was just my kind of place. Now, not so much.

"The people at the laundromat said it was the best place in town to eat," Remi replies defensively.

"And I'm sure folks at a laundromat know where all the fine places to dine are," Rafe responds with a wink at me.

"Fucker," Remi mutters under his breath.

"*Father*," Rafe replies with a wicked grin.

I bite my lip to keep from grinning.

We find a booth and I slide in, followed by Remi who practically trips Rafe to keep him from sitting next to me. Rafe sits across from me, which is almost worse, because he keeps staring at me. I decide two can play this game, and I narrow my eyes giving him my best eat-shit-and-die glare, but Rafe just smirks, never blinking. Frustrated, I drop my gaze to the names carved into the wooden table and run my finger over them repeatedly. My left knee bounces with nervousness until a warm hand stills it. A kinetic jolt of sexual energy works its way straight up my leg. I hold my breath, wishing Remi's fingers would follow and delve underneath my panties.

The waitress touches up her lipstick before bringing us our menus and water. Her gaze flickers at Rafe, but lingers on Remi. An unreasonable urge to slap her and tell her to back the fuck off overcomes me. Dammit, now I wish he'd worn his clerical shirt and collar. At least women aren't as blatant in their attention when he appears to be off limits. My conscience reminds me he's off limits for me, too.

Remi removes his hand, leaving me feeling empty. I look up to find Rafe staring at me with his lips pursed. One questioning eyebrow rises, and he shakes his head, like a parent trying to correct a child with just a look. I pretend to study the menu, doing my damnedest to keep my shit together.

Remi leans back in the booth and stretches his arms across the back. His thumb lazily strokes my back in a reassuring manner. *He knows me so well.* I draw strength from the comfort he offers and try to relax. This is our last night together; I don't want to spend it falling apart. I'll do that when he leaves.

Not having much of an appetite, I order a small side salad, but I doubt I'll be able to swallow a bite past the lump lodged in my throat. Rafe orders a burger, and since he's offered to pick up the tab, Remi seems to take great delight in ordering a huge steak, the most expensive thing on the menu. With a devastating smile, Remi thanks the waitress as she bounces off to turn in the order.

Remi nudges my shoulder and leans in, whispering in my ear, "Hey, you okay? You need to eat, especially since we're not paying for it. I'll share part of my steak and potato with you, if you want." His warm breath caresses my neck. Closing my eyes, I take a deep breath, suppressing the urge to beg him to hold me and never let go. I yearn to feel his lips on my skin. Instead, I shrug, staring blankly at the stupid carved names in the table.

"I'm fine." *I'm anything but fine.* I manage a small smile, faking it until I make it.

A jukebox plays in a dark corner and a few couples are slow dancing, wrapped up in each other. The sound of clacking pool balls filters in from another room. Laugher and conversations drift from other tables muffled by the music. It's all very normal, in direct contrast to what's playing out at this table.

The tension between the two men hangs heavier than the cigarette smoke from the back room layered by my dark depression. I'm almost relieved when a bleached blonde approaches the table with a sultry sway of her hips, and a smile of conquest on her bubblegum pink lips. If her boobs are real, I'm sane. She leans across the table showing off her *assets* to her best advantage, her attention focused on Rafe.

"Hiya, cowboy," she purrs, drumming her pink, fake nails on the table. She places her fruity mixed drink with the cheesy umbrella down as if she intends to stay.

"Ma'am." Rafe tips his hat toward her, and only the slight flare of his nostrils betrays his apprehension as the woman slides into the booth next to him. She scrunches in so close they look like they could be attached at the hip like Siamese twins.

Remi's grin grows wider. The tension he's been holding in all night almost magically disappears and his shoulders relax. In direct correlation, Rafe drums the table with his thumbs, sitting ramrod straight as he casts nervous glances toward the woman next to him.

I feel like I've started watching a movie in the middle. The characters are familiar, but I'm clueless to the plot.

Remi whispers in my ear, "Hey, let's go dance and give them a chance to get acquainted."

Rafe's wide eyes and strained smile look desperate as he gapes at the blonde bombshell cornering him in the booth. I cast Rafe an evil smirk and eagerly follow Remi, wanting to feel his arms around me.

Drawing me to the darkest corner of the building, I sink into his arms and it's like coming home. This is where I belong. I feel safe and calm, like he's my anchor in my sea of turmoil. He rests one hand on my hip and the other wraps around my shoulders almost in a protective manner. Wanting to be even closer, I rest my head on his chest and listen to the comforting, steady sound of his heartbeat. I will forever associate the smell of Christmas with sin and love. It's an intoxicating combination, and I long to drink him in and get drunk.

Ironically, the jukebox plays a sad, slow song about lost love, and the words seemed to echo my feelings. I've promised him to grab life by the balls. Surely that means asking for what I want most…

I stand on my tiptoes as we sway to the music and whisper in his ear, "Don't—" The words never leave my lips. I close my eyes, biting my tongue. It would be wrong to ask him not to leave me. I can't place more of a burden on him than he already carries. It's better to live with a broken heart than none at all. For once in my life, I'm going to take the high road.

He pulls away and looks into my eyes.

"Don't what? Step on your feet? Let me lead, then," he teases, but his strained smile tells no lies. He's struggling, too.

"No. Please…just don't forget me," I whisper. His face blurs with my unshed tears.

He rests his forehead against mine, pulling me closer as he peers into my eyes. Fire burns there and I know I'm not imagining it. "Never," he rasps. "I love you, Evangeline."

The dam on my emotions breaks loose, and I weep into his shirt as he holds me, stroking my back, comforting me. We both know this is good-bye, and the pain paralyzes me. I can't move. I can't breathe.

"Shh, hush. Everything will be okay. You're going to be fine. I know this is hard, but you'll get through it."

"What if I don't want to?"

He grabs me by the shoulders. Through my watery eyes I see fire blazing in his. "You have to. Promise me, Evangeline."

I nod and whisper, "I do. I do. I promise. I'm going to take life by the balls." I take a breath and give him a tremulous smile. "I love you, too."

He gives me a sad smile, wiping the tears from my face with his thumbs. Reverently, he kisses my forehead. "I know." Wrapping an arm around my shoulder, he walks me back to the table. The blonde bombshell knits her penciled eyebrows together and purses her lips.

Rafe gives a slow, teasing whistle, incongruent with the worry around his eyes. "Is Papa Roach that bad of a dancer? Did he step on your feet, sunshine?" The blonde elbows him hard enough to make him grunt.

"You okay, honey?" She catches my hand in hers and gives it a squeeze.

I nod, still unable to speak. She hops up and pats Rafe on the shoulder. "I'll be right back, handsome. Come on, love, let's go to the ladies room and get you straightened out. We'll be back in a jiffy, boys." Grabbing a glass of ice water and my hand she drags me toward the bathroom.

Thankfully it's empty, and she locks the door, placing the glass on the vanity. As she rummages through her purse, I look in the mirror and gasp, horrified by my appearance. I am, as Remi would say, one hot mess. Black mascara runs down both cheeks. To top off the picture, my red nose is dripping like a faucet. I've never been a pretty crier. The kind stranger fishes an ice cube from the glass placing it in a paper towel as I splash cold water on my face.

"Here doll, put this on your eyes and forehead for a moment. It will help with the swelling and crying jag headache."

"Thank you," I whisper, pressing the cold compress over my eyes. I choke out the only lie I can think of at the moment. "My mama's sick, I'm on my way to see her, and I guess it's just finally catching up with me." I take the ice off my face and stare at her in the mirror.

The blonde nods and kindly pretends to buy my feeble lie. "I'm Madge. Everything will be okay, honey." She applies another coat of lipstick to her full lips. She's pretty in an overdone kind of way. I wish I could do her hair, add some low lights into the bleach and tone it down a notch. "Your boyfriend's cute. Not as hot as that cowboy, but you two look like you belong together."

I sigh and tuck a loose strand of hair behind my ear. "I'm Evie and he's not my boyfriend." The wistful longing seeps out in my sigh.

"He cares about you. Even a blind person could see it, and you care about him. What's the problem?" Her wide rhinestone bracelets clatter as she drums her fingernails on the countertop.

"His, uh, job prevents us from being together."

Madge frowns and purses her lips as if deep in thought. "That's too bad. I can tell how much he means to you." She rubs my back in a reassuring manner and then draws me in for an outright hug. Aside from Remi, I can't remember the last person that hugged me without an ulterior motive. Although I can't tell Madge the entire sad story, it helps to share just a little of my pain. She cups my cheeks in her hands and smiles at me. "How about I take care of that good-lookin' cowboy for you and give you and your man some alone time. Would that help?"

It isn't much, but I'll take any time I can steal to be alone with Remi. I smile and hug her back this time.

"Why is she here?" I hiss, glaring at Raphael after Mary "Madge" Magdalene hauls Evie to the bathroom.

"Don't ask me, I didn't send for her. Although, I find her new look kind of intriguing, if a little daunting." He takes a sip of his water.

Of course, Mr. Brown Noser didn't order a beer. I, on the other hand, gulp mine down and signal for another. Maybe if I get shit-faced drunk it will help ease the pain.

"You can't drink and drive," Raphael cautions.

"Fine, I'll fly home."

"You know that's not allowed, either. Look, I'm not the enemy here. I'm just here to check on you and Evangeline. You need to let this go. Just sever it nice and clean. It'll be easier than prolonging this. I'll talk to the Boss and He can erase her memory of you together. Let Madge and me take her to see her mom. We'll take over making sure she's okay and learns to live life to the fullest. You can tell her you've been called away on an emergency, *Father*."

I swallow the lump in my throat and stare at the condensation dripping down the bottle of beer. What he suggests makes sense and is the right thing to do, but the thought of her not remembering me at all hurts worse than a sucker kick to the nuts. There's no way in hell I'll ever forget her. *Ever.* And ending up in hell is a distinct possibility. I sigh and rub my eyes. My feelings don't matter. Rafe's right, I have to do this for her sake.

"Okay." I keep my face covered, hiding my emotions. I've never felt this way about anybody. I've always been out for number one. *Me.* I've done my jobs and even guided a few lost souls back to the right path, but only because it benefited *me* in the long run.

God, I'm such a selfish bastard, so full of envy. I always thought it would be better down here on earth. I couldn't have been more wrong. This isn't fun. True life is hard work and full of pain. I never realized how damn easy I've had it. I don't have time to dwell on my ass wipe behavior. I have to do what's best for Evie. She's all that matters. Even if I have to move south, and shovel coal in the proverbial fires of hell for all of eternity, so be it. As long as she's safe and learns to enjoy life and even love again, I can survive.

Raphael taps his water glass to my beer. "It's for the best, Remiel. I'll talk to Him. He'll know what to do. He always does. I know your free will has messed things up, but nothing is irreparable."

"Who are you going to talk to?" Madge asks as she and Evie scoot into the booth. Although Evie's face no longer resembles Ozzy Osbourne after eating a bat, her eyes appear glassy with unshed tears, and her nose remains red and shiny. Lord help me, she's the most beautiful creature I've ever seen in heaven or on earth.

"Remi just received a phone call from his *Boss*—"

"Oh, that's nice," Madge interrupts. "But we're not talking business tonight, cowboy," she purrs. Raphael's eyes grow wide with a look of shocked horror when she leans in, rubbing her generous cleavage against his arm. Her hand disappears under the table—and I'm assuming—lands somewhere quite personal judging by the red tint of embarrassment on his face. If I weren't so damned depressed, I'd laugh. Leave it to Madge to throw Mr. Perfect off kilter. She's always been one of my favorites with her bawdy sense of humor.

The waitress brings our food, and Madge flashes a bright smile at the harried server. "Just bag the cowboy's to go. We're gonna go eat in private, if you know what I mean." She winks at the waitress, who grins knowingly while Raphael sputters his protestation. Evie keeps her head down, finger tracing the carved names over and over.

I'm a bit confused myself and look to Madge for an explanation. She stands and tugs on Raphael's arm, holding his crutches with her other hand. "Come on, handsome. We'll go grab your stuff, and I'll give you a ride to your granny's. I live ten minutes from her, and you never know what could happen. She might need you *tonight*."

"But—"

He never gets the words out of his mouth. She leans in and plants a kiss on him that's almost pornographic to watch. Several patrons whistle and suggest they take it down the road to the motel. I don't think twice and hand Madge the extra card key to the room so he can get his duffel bag. Not that he really needs it, but we have to keep up the charade. I just pray Madge really isn't intending on taking him back to our room for a quick toss in the sack. I now have plans of my own.

"Evie, it was nice meeting you. You too, Remi. Come on, cowboy. Get your crippled carcass in gear. I'm gonna make you forget all your troubles by the time we reach your granny." She plucks the cherry out of her drink, puts it in her mouth, and pulls out a knotted stem. Rafe's eyes bug and his mouth drops open. He doesn't have long to gape because she yanks him to his feet, shoving his crutches at him. Evie raises her head and stares, her eyes wide and questioning.

He gives us both a pointed look before reluctantly holding out his hand. I shake it and meet his troubled gaze with my own.

"Good luck, Father Christmas. Make things right." His smile is one of genuine affection when he looks at Evie. "I hope everything turns out okay with your mom, sunshine."

Evie gives him a tremulous smile in return. She turns to me biting that lower lip I long to nibble on one last time. I wink at her and her smile widens.

"Bye, Rafe. Madge. It was nice meeting both of you. I hope your grandmother's okay." She takes a pen out of her purse and writes her phone number on a napkin and hands it to Rafe. "Keep in touch, okay?"

"Sure thing, sunshine. I have a feeling we'll meet again." He leans over and gives her a kiss on the cheek and whispers something in her ear.

She looks up at him, and her brows pull together in a puzzled frown. A firm pat on my shoulder and he's gone, following Madge to the parking lot. Evie blushes pink, and her long lashes fan out on her soft cheek as she gazes at her untouched salad.

"What did he say to you?" I wrap a loose tendril of her hair around my finger. I want to yank her hair down, preferring it waving in a riot of loose curls.

"He told me I wasn't crazy and gave me a Bible verse."

I smile at her. "You'll always be my Crazy Girl. What Bible verse?"

"Second Corinthians chapter four, verses sixteen to twenty. Do you know it?"

Of course I know the verse and quote it for her. *"So we do not lose heart. Though our outer self is wasting away, our inner self is being renewed day by day. For this light momentary affliction is preparing for us an eternal weight of glory beyond all comparison, as we look not to the things that are seen but to the things that are unseen. For the things that are seen are transient, but the things that are unseen are eternal."*

"I'm not sure what it means." She shrugs, and picks up her fork, pushing her salad around on the plate.

I'm not sure what he meant by it either. And at this precise moment, I don't care. I've been given a reprieve from my death sentence. Although technically I can never die, living without Evie will be like death. It will be my personal, living hell. I only have a few more stolen hours with my girl, and I'm not about to waste one minute of it.

"Eat, Evie. He was just some itinerant cowboy trying to wax philosophic. We have the rest of the evening to relax before we get to your mother's tomorrow."

"I'm not really hungry."

"Me either." I drum the table, feeling like a teenager about to ask a girl on a date. Her liquid gaze meets mine. "I meant it, you know."

She blinks and her eyes light up with hope.

"I love you. I, uh, don't know about the future," I admit.

"I love you, too," she whispers.

"So, now what?" I leave the question hanging.

For the first time this evening, she genuinely smiles. "Let's take life by the balls and live a little dangerously."

That's my girl.

Chapter Fifteen

"Evangeline, we need to talk," Remi pants, lighting his cigarette and collapsing on his back with a satisfied groan.

I curl into his body with my head on his shoulder. We're both slick with sweat. "No," I gasp in response. The man's been trying to "talk" since we arrived back at the room. I let him know right quick I had other ideas for passing the time. "I told you, tonight is about the present, not the future. Besides, you should be ecstatic. I'm doing exactly what you've been telling me to do." I grin and reach down cupping him as I lick his nipple to a tight peak.

"Okay, okay…stop and let me catch my breath." He laughs and kisses the top of my head. "Tell me something. If you could have any three wishes come true—that don't involve our future—what would they be?" Remi stubs out his cigarette and pops a breath mint in his mouth.

"My wish just came true." I peek at him and grin, waggling my eyebrows. "Several times. What's yours?"

"To dance with you in the moonlight." His eyes crinkle softly, and his lips relax in a lazy, replete smile. His hand runs up and down my back in soft, lazy strokes.

"Mmm." I purr and smile in response.

"And for you to be happy and never think about hurting yourself again."

"We said we weren't talking about the future," I murmur, pushing the sadness away, concentrating on the steady, comforting beat of his heart that keeps time with my own.

"Okay. To lick ice cream off your tits."

I raise my head and stare at him with my mouth hanging open.

He laughs, and his abs ripple beneath my hand. "You asked. Chocolate, to be precise."

"I'm shocked, *Father*. Isn't that a sin?"

"After what we've just done, several times over? I'm sure it's venial in comparison, but sinfully good, for sure."

I giggle. True. I've already been his appetizer, main course and dessert. I roll onto my back next to him and lace my fingers behind my head and stare at the ceiling. "My wish is to see snow. I've never seen it."

"Snow? It's way overrated and that qualifies as a future wish. It's August," he scoffs. "If you want cold and wet, let's go for the chocolate ice cream on the girls." He gives me a wicked grin and pinches my already hard nipple.

"Not fair. That's *your* wish. Your third wish, actually. For my second wish, I want you to recite poetry to me."

He groans. "Poetry? You're kidding, right?"

"Poetry," I affirm.

"Even though I'm not a fan of poetry, I'll recite a poem while we dance. Let's go do it." The husky timbre of his voice makes my toes curl in anticipation.

"Now? For real? I thought we were just playing a game."

"Yes, for real, but in a minute." He turns on his side, propping his head on his hand. When he smiles down at me, flames flicker in his eyes. I'm too tired to fight the crazy delusion and just ignore it. I'll have plenty of time to contemplate the state of my mind after he leaves. My cheeks grow hot under his frank perusal and I'm pretty sure I'm red all the way down to my toes.

"Don't stare at me." Self-conscious, I move to turn away, but he captures my wrists and holds them above my head.

"Be still. I want to memorize every last perfect detail of you. With my eyes…" Fire simmers in his hooded eyes. "With my hands…" His free hand cups my cheek, his thumb brushing my lips. I lick his thumb and suck on it. In response, he closes his eyes and moans. My breath catches and even though he's just had me every which way to Sunday, I ache for him again. He opens his eyes, and they are once again dark with desire. "With my lips…" Warm lips capture mine. He tastes of peppermint, cigarette, and me. It's like an aphrodisiac and I buck up against him, needing more.

"Remi," I gasp as he leaves a blazing trail of need down my neck. "Remi—"

"Yes, dear? You never said, what's your third wish?" He raises his head and grins at me.

I laugh and choke on a sob at the same time. Goner rises and pads over to the bed with a whimper and gazes at me with his sad eyes, offering what comfort he can.

"Hey, stay with me in the moment." Remi pulls me into his arms and strokes my hair. A snap of his fingers has Goner curling up on the floor once again.

He reaches over and lights another cigarette, a sure sign he's as anxious as I am.

"I'm sorry. My emotions are more scattered than usual. I'm happy, sad, turned on, and scared…" I frown. "Those things are going to kill you."

"Want one?" he teases softly in an attempt at a lame joke. I'm not in the mood, and before I can stop it, a lone tear hits his chest. "Don't cry, sweetness."

"Why not? This is so unfair!" I dash the tear away with the back of my hand.

"Because quite frankly, Crazy Girl, you're not a pretty crier. Quite the opposite, actually." He's skirting my real question with jokes and we both know it.

"Very funny. I'll remember to curb my tears when I accept my award for Craziest Bitch on the Planet. I'll put it on the mantle next to my World's Most Pathetic Little Girl badge." We laugh, but there's a strained edge underneath it and a quiet air of desperation between us.

I swallow my bitter disappointment. I'm not important enough for him to leave the church. Sadly, I realize I've never come first. Chores were more important to my father. Kayla was more important to Jack. A good name is more important to my mother. And the church is more important to Remi. It's my lot in life to be second best. What's the saying? *Always the bridesmaid, never the bride.*

"I'll miss you."

He starts to sputter a protest, but I cover his lips with my hand.

"It's okay. I understand. Really, I do." I refuse to cry again. It isn't like I haven't known this was yet another impossible relationship.

He sits up and hangs his head. "No. No, you don't understand. You can't possibly." When he looks up at me the torment and pain I'm feeling is there in his eyes the color of a stormy sea. I get the sense of what it must be like to view a battlefield after a skirmish. Grief, death and despair reside there. It threatens to devour both of us, and I can't stand to see him in pain. We're so connected it sucks the breath out of me. I'll do anything to alleviate it, even if it means letting him go back to his God.

Peace settles over me as I'm finally able to take in some much needed oxygen, and I smile through my unshed tears. "I'll be okay. I promise."

He stamps out his cigarette and pulls me into his arms. "I know you will."

"Promise me one thing?" I trace the outline of the cross on his chest.

Remi freezes for a moment. "Anything."

"Never forget me. That's my third wish."

"No way in hell. You're like that song, unforgettable." He picks me up and holds me in his lap, as if he's scared I'll disappear if he lets go. After cuddling for a few minutes, he carries me to the bathroom. "What are you doing?" I nuzzle his neck, enjoying the roughness of his five o'clock shadow and the smell of his skin.

"One of our wishes can be fulfilled tonight and luckily it's mine."

"We don't have any ice cream."

He throws his head back and laughs, pinching my bottom for good measure. "I was referring to dancing in the moonlight, silly. But now that you mention it, we can stop and pick up some ice cream on the way home. Let's get cleaned up and go throw down some moves." He kisses my nose and pulls me into the cold shower with him. I scream and squirm in his arms, trying to get away from the icy onslaught.

"Shh." His mouth covers mine in an attempt to hush me. It's late, and he's right, we don't want to be thrown out of our room. He has me pinned against the wall of the shower, taking the brunt of the cold water on his back. My breasts ache for his touch, and the feel of his need for me at my entrance heightens my arousal. I'm no longer cold. I'm on fire to be one with this man.

"I can't get enough of you, Evangeline. You make me insatiable," he murmurs in my ear as he drives into me. This isn't the tender love making we've just experienced over the past couple of hours. This is wild, desperate and primal. He's fierce in his onslaught and my fingernails rake his back. He moans as he savagely hammers into me against the shower wall. He reaches between us and murmurs in my ear, "Let go and fly, my love."

His touch sends me over the edge and shatters me into a million pieces. My love for him is infinite, indescribable. He's mine, and yet he isn't. His heart belongs to an entity with which I can't compete. Ironically, I call *His* name when I orgasm.

He follows me with a shout and nip to my shoulder, his body shuddering before stilling. Our ragged breathing fills the air as the water from the shower washes away the sweat on our bodies. I shiver, and he blindly reaches behind him, switching it to warm. The sight of his haunted face filled with unmitigated fear distresses me. I watch with a mixture of horror and disbelief as he falls to his knees and buries his head in my waist, wrapping his arms around me, holding me so tight it's almost painful.

"I'm so sorry. I'm so sorry. Please, forgive me…"

I am the worst kind of bastard. Selfish. Undisciplined. Unscrupulous. The list can go on forever and still not come close to describing what a douchebag I am. I've used my free will and pretended that everything will be okay in the end, but it won't. Raphael was right. I've wronged Evangeline and used her like countless others in her short life. This sin is unforgivable. Through my lies and actions, I've blasphemed the woman I love. Eternal separation from her will be my personal hell. I bury my face in her sweet skin and weep repentant tears, not daring to hope for her forgiveness. I tried to talk to her earlier, to confess. But she wouldn't listen and quite honestly, I didn't press the issue, because I can't bear the thought of her hating me.

Please, God. Take care of her. This is my fault, all of it. Punish me, but spare her and send her someone who will love her the way she deserves to be loved.

She's my everything.

My heaven.

My hell.

My torment.

My heart.

My love.

Of course, I don't get an answer. I didn't really expect one.

"Remi." Her hand runs through my hair. The water continues to beat down on my back. It helps to contain my wings. I need all the help I can get at the moment because I'm seriously losing my shit, and He isn't offering any help. I guess I pushed Him too far this time.

"Remi, stop. No tears, remember? You said you'd take me dancing. I want to dance in the moonlight with you."

I remain on my knees, my arms wrapped around her wet, soft waist. I kiss her visible scars, knowing I'll be leaving far worse invisible ones. "Please forgive me, Evangeline. God, I'm so sorry. I'm the biggest shit to have ever walked the face of the earth. I'm no better than Jack. I'm so fuckin' sorry." How I wish things could be different. She deserves a better life. A good life, one full of love and laughter and a man that won't lie to her.

"Please, Remi—" One of her hands plays with my wet hair and the other grips my shoulder. "Stop."

"I don't deserve it, I know I don't, but please, please don't hate me. I'll tell you everything…" I can't bear to look up and see either the pain or revulsion in her beautiful chocolate eyes. I hold on to her like I'm afraid she'll slip down the drain if I let go. She's my lifeline and my grasp is tenuous, at best.

"Look at me." Her hands cup my face and she kisses my forehead.

I swallow and reluctantly look up. Tears stand on the precipice of her warm, loving eyes, and her smile is tinged with sadness. She nudges me a little and scoots down the back of the shower wall and kneels, facing me. Her arms wrap around my neck. "I can never forgive you."

With this pronouncement my heart explodes leaving a gaping hole in my chest. The emptiness surrounding me is like being in a cold, dark cave.

I close my eyes and swallow the lump of regrets in my throat. "I understand."

"No, you don't. I can never forgive you, because there is nothing to forgive you for."

My eyes fly open and search hers. I see only love reflected there, but my mind still can't quite encompass what she's saying. "What? No, you have no idea what I've done, what's going to happen when I leave…"

"I don't care. If you've taught me nothing else, you've taught me to live in the moment. Our lives are just a series of moments strung together like lights on a Christmas tree. You're the light at the top of the tree, the one in the star, shining bright and strong. You brought me out of my darkness. Other lights on my strand had burned out, and I was ready to pull the proverbial plug and throw it away. But not now, because I've learned that even if one bulb goes out, it's okay. There are other options. You can stand back and rearrange, or replace the bulb…or just simply let it be." She brushes the wet hair out of my eyes and I turn my cheek to her palm, placing a tender kiss on it. I'm moved by her sweet, innocent spirit, and undeserving of her love, yet grateful nonetheless.

"You were never mine. Jack was never mine. People can't be owned. They're on loan to us for however long it's meant to be. Your God needs you. You have a job to do. I don't like it, but I understand. I don't know that I believe in Him, but for the first time in a long time, I believe there *is* something more than this thing we call life. And maybe, if I'm lucky, someday our paths will cross again.

"Please, Remi, I don't want to spend our last few moments with regrets about the past or worries about the future. I want to dance in the moonlight with you, and live in the moment."

Her heart-spoken words, although they have an air of finality to them, also give me hope. She's more than my love. She's my salvation, my inspiration. She completes me. One second with her is worth any consequences. I'm going to take her dancing. And then I'm going to tell her everything. She's wrong on one thing, though.

Evangeline Lourdes Salvatore owns me. Every last piece of me belongs to her. I pull my sweet girl to me and kiss her as the water in the shower turns cold once again.

Chapter Sixteen

He's brought a blanket and his phone. Goner sleeps in the backseat as Remi finds a secluded spot off a main road and pulls over. I'm wearing my red dress and heels, which won't be very practical in this terrain, but it's what he wanted. This is his wish, after all. We're once again living in the moment, although the quiet sense of desperation still remains.

He cuts the engine and smiles as he takes my hand in his. "Dance with me, sweetness?"

"I'd love to." I give his hand a squeeze and open the car door, illuminating us with the overhead light.

"Damn."

"Huh?" I look back at him, confused.

"You give in too easily. I wanted to lure you with the promise of chocolate ice cream later." He winks, and I burst out laughing.

I shake my head as we get out of the car. "Next you'll want me to be a naughty schoolgirl with the requisite plaid skirt uniform."

"Rats. I should've made that a wish. Have you been a bad girl, Evangeline?" The teasing hope in his voice lightens the mood. He opens the sunroof and lowers the windows so we can hear the music.

I snicker. "I think you already know the answer to that, *Father*."

When he plugs in his phone, soft romantic music plays instead of his usual rock and roll. "No collar tonight, Crazy Girl. Come on."

The full moon is dropping in the velvet sky and millions of stars surround us because we're so far away from any city lights. It looks and feels magical out here. Pulling me into his arms, he takes the back of his fingers and grazes them along my jawline before placing a gentle kiss on my forehead. He draws me close and I tuck my head under his chin as he moves us in a sensuous, slow dance as Nat King Cole sings "Unforgettable."

He's a wonderful dancer, which makes up for my lack of grace, especially in heels on rocky ground. He dips and spins and then chuckles when I squeal with surprise. I wrap my arms around his neck and his forehead presses to mine as I mold my body to his. We fit together like puzzle pieces. Together, we complete one another.

"It's true, you know," he whispers. "You're unforgettable, Crazy Girl. And I mean that in a good way."

I cup his cheek and gaze into the face of the man I love, the man ingrained into my soul. "I love you and I'll never forget you."

He sighs and pulls me even closer, burying his face in my hair. "I wish that were true." The sadness in his voice tugs at my fragile heart.

His phone starts playing the theme from *Charlie's Angels*. He reaches in the car and turns it off with a sigh.

"Remi, I know we can't be together, but I mean, maybe, we could…" I shrug and lower my eyes. "Keep in touch. Just as friends, of course."

I peer up at him and his eyes appear troubled, his face haggard under the moonlight. I see it again, that fire deep in his eyes. The air around us stirs with the sound of rustling feathers and something dark flutters and folds behind him. My heart hammers in my chest and I can't breathe. Hallucination, delusion, imagination, I don't care what this is. I want to be his whether he's real or not. And I want the truth, no matter the cost.

My mouth is as dry as the desert sand beneath my feet. "I want you to be honest with me. Am I losing my mind? Are you real? If not, what are you?"

A shadow of a smile plays across his lips and the flames in his eyes dance. "Yes, I'm real." He grabs my hand and pulls me to him, his breath fanning across my cheek. "Come here. I'm going to kiss you until you acknowledge I'm real."

His lips make contact with that ticklish spot behind my ear and I moan, but I'm determined to not let him sidetrack me. If I've totally lost it, fine. I'll spend the rest of my days in an asylum weaving baskets and drooling in a zombie-like state. But right here, right now, I'm going to learn the truth.

I shove him away. "Answer me! What. Are. You? A delusion? A hallucination?"

"Let me show you something, and then I'll tell you everything," he begs. The excitement on his face looks like a kid's on Christmas morning. Huge, black wings slowly fan behind him. The fading moonlight makes the highlights of his hair glint like a nimbus.

My eyes widen and I step back. An ethereal light from within brightens his face and my knees wobble in a vain attempt to hold me upright. Tears stream down my face and I turn away, sobbing into my hands. He's behind me, holding me, and it's his strong, arms, not wings that enfold me, holding me close.

"Shh, it's okay. You're okay, Evangeline."

My knees buckle and he catches me. "You're not real...You can't be real..." I've truly jumped the tracks into a full-blown psychotic state. I'm terrified and pissed at the same time.

"No. You're wrong. I'm very real. That's my point and what I'm trying to prove to you. *You're not crazy.* These things you see, they're all real, just of another realm."

I yank myself free of his arms and stomp away with my fists clenched at my side. I spin around and face him, gnashing my teeth. In truth, I'm a little relieved my whole body spun around and not just my head. And thankfully, I'm not vomiting pea soup, either; an exorcism won't be necessary.

"I *am* crazy. I hear things. I see things that aren't real, like...like you starting fire without matches. *I see dead people...Jack...and my Daddy...*And you have wings and flickering flames in your eyes, for crying out loud. *That's not fucking normal, asshole!*"

"Well, if you put it like that..." He rubs the back of his neck, biting his lip, obviously trying to keep from laughing, but it doesn't work. His laughter spills out and echoes against the huge boulders.

I launch myself at him, beating his chest with my fists. "Quit laughing at me, you unreal bastard! I might be crazy, but the fact remains, you lied to me," I scream.

He captures one of my wrists while I continue to struggle against him raining blows upon him. "S-Stop, Crazy Girl, stop!" I kick his shin for good measure and then hop on one rickety heel with pain. Kicking a cowboy boot with an open toe high heel wasn't one of my brighter moves.

"Shit!" After steadying me on two feet, Remi lets go and holds up his hands. "I've got one more surprise for you that might make it up to you."

"Oh great, like I'm not already batshit crazy enough? Now what? You gonna zap me with a death ray? Fly me to the moon? Fuck me with your super-duper penis?"

"You think I have a super-duper penis?" He looks inordinately pleased.

Yes, he *does*, but that's beside the point. I huff with annoyance and cross my arms in front of my chest and glare at this mirage or whatever he is.

"I dunno about flying to the moon, but..." He snaps his fingers.

I blink and swipe angrily at my cheek as something cold and wet hits my face. Another splat on my forehead draws my attention from Remi and I look up. I rub my eyes and open them again, not believing what I'm seeing. Above us, the full moon still shines, and the stars twinkle beside it, but to my complete and utter astonishment, snow is falling.

I've done it now. My fate is sealed. Turning off the phone when the Boss tried to ring me? Not a good idea. I'm exercising my free will at my own peril, but that's just the way the cookie crumbles. And now I've made it snow in August. Mind you, it's just right here, no one but Evangeline knows it's snowing — well, *He* does, of course — but this is my last hurrah and I figure, in for a penny, in for a pound. There must be something about knowing I'm in shit so deep I'll never dig my way out that makes me think in clichés. Or is it proverbs?

Regardless, I'm fucked.

The surprised look on her face is worth it. Being honest with her, begging her forgiveness and giving her happiness these last few hours is my new priority. She won't remember any of this, but I don't care. I'm going to confess everything, and damn the torpedoes, full speed ahead. Shit, I've got to stop with the maudlin corny sayings. I'm starting to sound like that old windbag, Peter.

Excitement brightens her wide eyes, and I smile when she sticks her tongue out to catch a snowflake. *I love her talented tongue…*She shivers and I rein in my dirty thoughts. Grabbing the blanket out of the car, I wrap it around her and press a kiss to her cold little nose.

"Who are you?" Her voice sounds breathless, and her eyes dilate, but I see no fear in them, more like a haunted resignation.

"I'm your guardian angel."

A slight tinge of hysteria laces her laughter. "No, really. I know I'm crazy, just tell me who you are, or rather, what you are. I promise I'm going back on my meds because these tactile hallucinations are fuckin' scary." She runs a hand through my feathers, ruffling them. It feels great, like when someone scratches your back.

"It's true. I'm an angel. God sent me to take care of you because, um, you kind of ignored the other messengers."

"Other messengers?" Her eyes narrow and she chews on that delectable bottom lip, twirling one curl of her beautiful hair around her finger.

"Your father. And even that asshole, Jack."

"What? They were real?" She gasps and her brow furrows. "No. No one believed me…"

"I know. *'No prophet is accepted in his hometown…'*"I quote, hoping *Someone* is listening and appreciates my last ditch effort at sucking up.

Evie pinches the bridge of her nose and rubs her eyes before glaring at me. "I'm so confused. You're not a priest?"

I shake my head and give her a rueful smile. "That was His idea. I, er, was sent here as a kind of, um, a learning lesson. I, uh, got in a bit of trouble back home…"

"Daddy? And Jack? They're okay? What about Kayla and her baby?"

"They're all fine. I mean…it's a big place. I don't know *everyone* personally, but I checked Kayla in. Jack's in purgatory, sort of a halfway house, I guess is how you'd explain it."

"But Kayla committed suicide…" Her voice breaks. "What about her baby?"

"Both fine. She miscarried, she wasn't thinking straight. Her suicide wasn't intentional, it was accidental." I tuck a strand of her hair behind her ear and stroke her arm in an attempt to reassure her.

"And she and her baby are in heaven. It wasn't my fault," she whispers. "So who goes to hell?"

"Contrary to popular belief, it isn't all fire and brimstone. Hell is the absence of love. You've already been there, done that and got the T-shirt, Crazy Girl. Now it's time for you to live and love. Your reaction to the tragedy in your life put you in hell. You just needed a little guidance, a push in the right direction. That's why He sent me. To show you God is love and that life is good. His forgiveness and mercy have no bounds. *'Mercy triumphs over judgment.'*" I glance up, hoping for a sign this time that He's heard me, but there are only the proverbial crickets chirping. No, wait…the crickets are real, but nothing from Him.

"But why was she successful and you stopped me?"

"Sweetness, I wouldn't call any suicide a *success*. It was her time, not yours. Look, I don't have all the fuckin' answers. I'm not whatever the hell you call it when you know everything." *I never can keep all those omni-words straight.*

"Omniscient." She frowns and my heart starts hammering.

This isn't going well. *At all.*

"You're sure cussing a lot more now that you're not a priest. Is that allowed?"

I chuckle. Of all things for her to be concerned about, it's my language? "Actually He doesn't like it. He says those who cuss lack imagination, but it's at the bottom of my list of transgressions at this point," I admit a bit sheepishly. I'm not about to tell her it doesn't matter anymore. I'm going to be toast, so to speak.

"Does my mother know?" Her eyes widen into black pools of fear.

"No, of course not. It doesn't work that way. This is a covert operation."

She shivers. "Can you make it stop snowing? I'm not really dressed for the weather."

"Of course. You okay?" The snow stops and the temperature rises a good fifteen degrees, although it's still cool with the night air.

"*Am I okay?*" She rolls her eyes and marches off—well, attempts to. I imagine it's hard in heels and she's a bit tottery—the blanket billows behind her like a cape. She'll look great with wings. Whirling around, she screams, "*Am I okay?*" The next thing I know the blanket floats to the ground as a hundred and twenty-five pounds of angry woman barrels toward me like a cheetah that's just spotted a tasty gazelle. I double over as her fist makes contact with my stomach. For such a tiny girl, she sure packs a mean punch.

"Shit, that hurt." I gasp for air. "I'm trying to be honest with you, and tell you everything. I thought you'd be happy knowing you're not totally bonkers." This is the second time tonight she's taken to physical violence. It's kind of hot and for a brief second I imagine her in black leather, thigh-high boots…

"I'm not *totally* bonkers?" She crosses her arms in front of her chest, and one eyebrow lifts just enough to let me know I've said something wrong. The calmness in her voice reminds me of that eerie stillness that occurs in the eye of a hurricane.

I swallow nervously and qualify my last statement. "Well, you have to admit wanting to do a priest is a *little* crazy. Not to mention trying to kill yourself. And not owning a car. What's up with that? I mean it's the twenty-first century. There's nothing better than driving fast with the radio blaring." My flippant response covers my fear. Fear that I've pushed her too far. Fear she will never forgive me. Fear she will hate me forever.

"Go to hell. You're a horrible guardian angel." She tosses her hair and raises that stubborn, adorable little chin.

"Yes, that's true. I suck at being a guardian angel." *Soon enough, I'll be in hell, sweetness. No need to hurry, I've already got my one-way ticket punched and ready to go.*

My gaze narrows on the brightness of her eyes. She sucks in a ragged breath and I realize with a sinking feeling in the pit of my stomach she's barely holding on. Maybe this has been too much for her to handle all at once. Rafe and the Boss are right. I *am* a selfish bastard.

"Evangeline—"

"I hate you!" she spits out, dashing a hand at the moisture in her eyes.

The words pierce my heart, hurting more than I would have ever dreamed possible. I know I deserve it, but it doesn't lessen the pain. Keeping eye contact, I move toward her. It's like approaching a feral cat that's been cornered. Sure enough, she snarls and clenches her fists. She stares at my chest and then the ground, everywhere but my face. That hurts, too. I want her look at me and see how sorry I am for every lousy thing that has ever happened to her. And how much I regret misleading her. I want her to know we are one. *Her pain is my pain.*

I kiss her forehead. "I love you. I've been searching for you since the beginning of time." With my thumb, I wipe away the one tear that has slipped down her flushed cheek. Cupping her face in my hands, I kiss each of her eyelids and then settle a soft kiss on her tremulous lips. "I love you, Evangeline. I always will."

"But?" Her eyes open, then narrow.

The pain and distrust I see in her eyes nearly brings me to my knees. I don't want to hurt her, but it seems inevitable in the long run. "No buts. I. Love. You." I smile at her. *"Forever."* And it's true. I've never felt this way before, and it's both exhilarating and scary at the same time.

"But you can't stay here, can you?" Her voice breaks off with a choked sob.

I shake my head. Now I'm the one unable to speak because of the lump in my throat.

"What's going to happen to me?"

"You're going to grab life by the balls and live, making each moment count. You have a wonderful life ahead of you—"

She snorts in an unladylike manner and rolls her eyes. "Do I look like George Bailey? No, I can't do it without you. *I don't want to.*"

Dammit, no! She has to live. Not because it's my job. Not because of some deep religious or philosophical reason. She has to live because I love her and want her to have the life she deserves. "That's not true. Do you wish you'd succeeded on the bridge? Be honest. Do you wish you'd never met me? Never found out you're not fuckin' crazy? Never found out how much I love you? Or that you're special? That you aren't responsible for all the death that has, unfortunately, been so much a part of your short life?"

She hangs her head and mumbles, "I don't know *how* to live. I have *no one* to live for. I love *you.* It's not fair."

"My love, unfortunately life isn't fair. But you've never truly lived, either. I'm not the only one that loves you. Your mother loves you.

Even that stupid mutt loves you. And my darling girl, there will be others if you just let them in. It's a beautiful world if you open your eyes and look around."

"I can't. I can't bear it when people leave me…" Her voice breaks off with her tortured breathing.

"Life is just borrowed time, Evangeline. That's what you told me. You can either waste it, disregard it, or live it." She buries her head in my chest and I hold her, stroking her hair and her back. God, how I wish there was some way I could stay to protect her and love her.

"Will I ever see you again?" she whispers brokenly.

"I don't know." I have no idea what my *learning lesson* will be when I get home, if I'm even allowed in the gates. It may be a straight ride down. "But He's merciful, so I have hope. Remember that, Evie. There is *always* hope. You take life by the balls and enjoy the hell out of it. Do you hear me? Hopefully, when I see you again, you can tell me all about your adventurous life. I don't want to hear a story of regrets and fear. I want you to be happy and loved. Go bungee jumping, climb mountains, scuba dive, and jump off cliffs. Get married, adopt a dozen kids and take in fifty mangy mutts. Live and love like there's no tomorrow."

My memories of her will sustain me for eternity. And her happiness means more to me than my own. As much as my heart hurts at the thought, I want her to be content and in love, even if it's with some other guy. I would lay my life down for this woman. I realize this is the first time I've truly understood the term *agape,* that all encompassing love that is selfless and unconditional.

She hangs her head for a moment, her shoulders sagging. "What happens next? You just poof and disappear, leaving me all happy and shit?"

That's my girl. "I take you to your mother's house." I shove my hands in my pockets and toe a rock, stalling for time. *Honesty sucks.* I want to tell her everything will be fine, but the lies stop here. Taking a deep breath, I look her straight in the eye and give her the cold, hard truth. "And then, unlike before, I will wipe your memory of me. You won't have the dreams you've been having. You won't remember me at all, but you will retain the lessons He wanted me to impart. That life is worth living, and you are worth loving. It will be up to you whether to move forward and enjoy life or stagnate in your guilt and self-loathing."

Her head snaps up. "My dreams were real?" The stricken look on her face twists the knife of my betrayal, ripping my heart in shreds. "Oh my God," she gasps, crossing her arms. "No. You wouldn't do that to me."

She walks away and spins back to face me. "We made love after the carnival, didn't we?" I move toward her, wanting to hold her, to explain further, but she slaps my face. "Didn't we?" she screeches before covering her mouth and closing her eyes.

"Evie…"

Her eyes fly open and the flash of hurt disappears, replaced by righteous indignation. "Don't touch me." She holds her head high. "How dare you judge Jack? You're just like him…You're a *liar!*"

She's right and my gut twists with my guilt. "Yes." Sorry seems pathetically inadequate, but I utter it anyway. "I'm sorry, so very, very sorry. I love you, Evangeline."

"I want to be by myself. Leave. Fly to wherever the hell you came from and leave me alone. Give me the keys." She holds her hand out and stomps her foot. "Give. Me. The. Keys."

"No, you're too upset to drive. Regardless of how you feel about me at this moment, I will make sure you arrive at your mother's safely."

She attempts to spin and leave, but falters in her heels. Angrily she yanks them off and lobs them at me. If I were a rigged milk bottle game, I'd be scattered. I deflect one shoe with my arm and rub my chest where the other heel strikes with amazing accuracy. Hobbling to the car, she yanks the door open and turns to face me. "I need a few moments by myself. If you come near this car before I tell you to, I won't be responsible for my actions. *Capisce?*"

I nod and she climbs in the car, slamming the door. She's so fucking hot when she's angry. I'm taking this as a good sign. If she's mad, she's not shutting down. If she's not shutting down, she's hanging on to life. Taking out a cigarette, I light it—without the pretense of a lighter—and collapse on the blanket. Staring at the multitude of stars, I pray like I've never prayed before.

Chapter Seventeen

I curl into the seat and cover my eyes, rocking. My dreams weren't dreams. My visions weren't hallucinations. My entire life has been some sick kind of joke. And out of all the people that have lied to me, Remi's betrayal hurts the worst. Oh, wait. He's an angel; he doesn't even fit in the people category, *the asshole*. Goner stirs and crawls into my lap, licking my face. At least my dog loves me. I wrap my arms around him, burying my face in his furry neck.

I'm not crazy.

I should feel vindicated. I tried to tell people I wasn't, but a tiny part of me always feared it was true. After Daddy bled to death in front of me following the chainsaw accident, I withdrew and stewed in my guilt. Mama tried to be supportive, but she had her own grief to deal with. Plus, she had to go from being a stay-at-home mom to working two jobs. I now realize I never appreciated the sacrifices she made for me.

At times Daddy would visit me, and I took comfort in his presence. But when I made the mistake of telling people I saw him, I was subjected to ridicule and bullying from the kids at school, which only increased my isolation. A counselor tried to step in, and thus began my foray into the mental health system. It started with grief counseling and then regular visits with a shrink. When counseling sessions didn't "help," the medications started.

As a child, Jack was my only true friend. But in my teens, my friendship developed into what the *professionals* called an *unhealthy obsession*. It supposedly stemmed from my unresolved grief and Daddy issues. I don't care what people say, at one time we loved each other. Sure, it ended badly, but it wasn't solely his fault, or mine. We both made mistakes and at a terrible cost.

And now I'm in love with an angel. Not a priest.

I'm not crazy. But this situation is insane.

I scratch my dog's ears and whisper, "What am I going to do?"

Goner wiggles and paws at the door. I open it and he runs straight to Remi, covering his face with sloppy dog kisses. Warm laughter rings out in the still night. I dash away the tear sliding down my face, ashamed to be jealous of a stupid mutt.

"I hate you!" I'm not sure if I'm yelling at my dog or Remi. Maybe both.

"I love you!" Remi calls back.

"I love you, too," I whisper.

And that's the problem. It's so unfair. The past few days with Remi I've been happy and *living*, not merely existing. He gets me like no one ever has. I can be me around him. I don't want to go back to the way I was, afraid of life. I realize part of my disappointment is my own foolishness. A part of me held on to the hope Remi would leave the priesthood for me. That we would have our happily ever after. Sadly, it was never an option. Nothing lasts forever.

I pause, realizing I have indeed learned from my past. I have a choice. I can choose to be paralyzed by the past, or I can change and embrace the future. My happiness can't depend on other people. It has to come from within. I look out at Remi playing with my silly dog. He says I won't remember him, but I find that hard to believe. How can I forget the best thing that's ever happened to me? Maybe if I'm happy, I'll remember…Happiness, peace, it's right there, I just have to make the choice. Right now, I choose to live in the moment with Remi. I don't know what my future holds, but I refuse to let life pass me by. The darkness in my soul lifts, illuminated by my decision.

It's time for me to step out on the ledge and fly. Throwing open the car door, I wince as gravel digs into my bruised bare feet. "Ouch, where are my damn shoes?"

"Hold on, Cinderella. Let me find them."

He stops playing with Goner and retrieves my heels. He saunters toward me with Goner following.

"You okay?" He tucks a strand of my hair behind my ear, and flames flicker behind the concern in his eyes.

"I'm still mad at you."

"Fair enough." Kneeling before me, he kisses my feet before slipping my shoes on them.

"I'll never forget you," I blurt, brushing the hair from his forehead. "I don't care what your God says or does. Love like this is the real deal. You can't forget shit like this. Right?"

His sad smile gives me my answer. "You won't remember me, but on some level, you will know you are loved. What you do with the knowledge is your decision." He stands and cups my face in his hand. "I pray you choose wisely. Don't waste one minute with regrets. Live, Evie. Live."

Neither of us says a word for a few moments. Even Goner remains silent. Holding hands, we look up at the blanket of infinite stars. "Seeing all the stars makes me feel like we're so small and insignificant," I murmur.

"We are, but we're not."

"You are my world, Remi."

"But I'm not of this world."

I sigh. "I know. Thank you for telling me the truth. I'm going to be okay."

"I know you will. I'll never forget you. And I promise, I'll do everything in my power for us to be together in the end." He kisses my forehead and my eyes, like some sort of blessing.

"Now what happens?"

"I dance with you one more time and recite my lame poem. Then we'll go catch a nap before driving to your Mom's house." He draws me close. I wrap my arms around his neck and he holds my waist, our foreheads touching. In his eyes I see my love reflected and joy infuses my battered soul. I am loved. *Forever.* I stumble in my heels and he swings me in the air and it isn't my imagination when our feet leave the ground. His wings expand gracefully as we soar above the earth. To my surprise, I feel no fear, knowing I'm safe. I scream with exhilaration and laugh as Goner barks racing on the ground below us.

"See? I told you, flying is the best thing, ever," Remi shouts with a wide grin, dipping and gliding until at last we land back on the ground. "Okay, ready for my poem?"

Still a little breathless, I nod. "Ready."

"Roses are red, violets are blue, smile Crazy Girl, 'cause I love you."

I roll my eyes. "You call that a poem? I did better than that in first grade. You suck at being a poet almost as bad as being a priest and a guardian angel."

"Wait! Let me try again. Roses are red, violets are blue, love is psychotic and so are you."

I laugh outright at that one. "I'm sure that's true, and somewhere I have the papers to prove it. I have one more request."

He eyes me with suspicion. "Okay…"

"Let's stop and pick up some chocolate ice cream."

I check the time on my cell phone. It's three in the morning. My life has changed dramatically since we left the room. I'm still trying to wrap my mind around everything. I'm love with an angel, and he has wings, and we flew. My visions were real. It snowed in August. And I am not crazy.

"Come on, Goner, you're taking forever." I tug at the dumb dog's leash, urging him to hurry his nightly business.

When he finishes, we walk toward Remi, who stands waiting on us with his hands stuffed in his pockets. Dark wings flick once and then disappear as a car drives by. The wings no longer scare me. Actually, they're kind of sexy. By the light outside the room I see his smile, but it doesn't reach his haunted eyes.

"Are you okay?" he whispers.

I nod and swallow the huge lump in my throat. Even though I've promised myself to move forward, saying good-bye is going to be damn hard. "Good as can be expected. You?" I search his eyes, but he looks away, pulling out a cigarette and lighting it. No lighter, of course.

"I need to keep you around in case my pilot light goes out again," I joke.

He chuckles and drags his gaze to mine. Cupping my cheek with his free hand, he grazes my lower lip with his thumb. "I have one more surprise." He finishes his cigarette, takes my hand in his, and we walk Goner back to the room like any other normal boyfriend and girlfriend. When I open the door, I gasp and look around. Two mismatched candles light the room and black feathers are scattered across the bed.

"I had to improvise, no rose petals."

"It's perfect."

And it is. He must've bought the candles when we stopped for ice cream. Goner sniffs and moves toward the bed, but Remi snaps his fingers, and the mutt curls up on the floor with a doggie *humph*. Undoing his leash, I toss it on the chair.

Without saying a word, Remi captures me and sweeps the dress over my head, dropping it to the floor. Hot sex and cold chocolate ice cream seems like a good place to start on my journey to living life to the fullest. Wanting to savor every last moment with him, I pull off his shirt, memorizing the way he feels beneath my hands and under my lips.

We quickly shed the rest of our clothes and collapse in bed, laughing, kissing, teasing and whispering silly, romantic nonsense. Grabbing the cup of now mostly melted ice cream, he hums with pleasure when he takes a bite. He spoons some in my mouth and follows it with a cold, chocolate kiss. It's delicious, like him. Licking his lips, he smiles at me, making me want to pounce on him, yet I want to relish every second and make it last. Fire dances in his eyes as he puts the ice cream down.

"I didn't think your kisses could get any sweeter, but that was pure bliss." He brushes the hair from my face and the backs of his fingers caress my jaw line. "I love you, Crazy Girl."

"I love you, too," I reply wistfully.

"As much as I want to make love to you, do you know what I really want to do?"

"Lick ice cream off my boobs."

He chuckles. "Well, after I do that *and* make love to you…"

I raise my eyebrows and wait. He kisses my nose with cold lips making me snuggle in closer. "I want to fall asleep with you in my arms."

"That's it?"

"That's it. It's my personal definition of heaven." His hand strokes my hair.

"I don't want this to end," I whisper, holding his arm with an iron grip, as if I have the power to keep him by my side. "I love you."

The only indication he gives that he's heard me is a tightening around his eyes before he closes them. I'm soon lost in the myriad of feelings as his cool lips sweep across my jaw and down my neck. Despite the ice cream, I'm convinced he's searing me because my body burns like it's on fire. He takes a spoonful of the ice cream and drizzles it on my nipple, which pebbles into a hard peak. I want to keep my eyes open, to remember every minute we have together, but they close of their own accord when his lips and tongue tease and nibble my breast. I moan with an intense need for this beautiful man, angel, apparition, whatever he is. With him, I'm alive.

Warm lips trail lower, his hands following in their path. Every nerve ending in my body is attuned to him, crying out for him. He makes love to me with more than his actions. His words, his sighs and the way he looks at me, all tell me I'm his, and he is mine. Two lost souls, found, if only for a brief moment in time. And when at last our bodies are joined as one, I hold his precious face in my hands and memorize the look of his beautiful eyes simmering with passion.

"I love you." Her whispered confession makes my heart soar and plunge at the same time but I can't let her see my fear. I smile and kiss the tip of her nose.

"I love you, too. *Forever and ever. A—*"

Her fingers touch my lips and she returns my smile. Her eyes are filled with contentment tinged with a quiet, sad desperation. "Don't say Amen. It sounds too final."

"But this feels like a prayer. An answer to prayer." I shush her further protests with my mouth by teasing her pouty lower lip. The vision of her face flushed with passion, illuminated by the candles, the sound of her soft sighs and the smell of her skin is something I'll retain throughout eternity. Her hands grip my biceps as I move inside of her. I close my eyes. This can't be wrong. I'm home. I'm in heaven.

Her hips move and meet my thrusts and her eyes dilate as she trembles on the precipice of her release. She flies over the edge and I soon follow. Our bodies are slick with sweat, our breathing labored as she holds me close, purring like a contented kitten. I kiss the pounding pulse in her neck, unable to summon the energy to move. I know once this connection is broken it's irretrievable. Her fingers run through my hair, and pulling her closer, I roll to my back with her on top of me, still one.

Evangeline kisses my chest where my heart beats for her and whispers, "You saved me and made me fly." Her sleepy eyes close and she snuggles closer, falling asleep in my arms.

I'm in both heaven and hell.

Chapter Eighteen

We haven't spoken fifty words since we made love one last time this morning. A heavy feeling of despondency hangs in the air. Any question I've asked her has been answered with one word. This silence is driving me nuts, and I'm not getting the silent treatment just from Evie. All morning, when I could sneak and use my phone, I've tried to reach the Boss. I've left texts and voice mails pleading my case, but there's been no answer. This is my Gethsemane.

Without asking, I pull into a fast food joint. She follows me, silently watching as I tie Goner to an outside table. Happy with the promise of a biscuit, he wags his tail and sits. We walk in, me in my clerics and Evie in jeans and a T-shirt, no makeup and red, swollen eyes. The girl behind the counter pushes her glasses up her nose, her questioning gaze darting between us.

"What would you like?" I ask Evie.

She shrugs and looks at the floor.

"Two large coffees and three ham biscuits," I order. We step back to wait and I glance over at the play area. It's empty this early in the morning. I nudge Evie's shoulder and motion with my head toward the colored ball pit. Dull, lifeless eyes meet mine. That's it. I'm determined to make her laugh at least one more time. I grab her and throw her over my shoulder.

"Remi," she squeals, kicking and struggling to get down.

I march to the play area and throw her in the pit, diving in after her. One after another, I lob balls at her until she fights back, giggling. We're jumping around tossing the balls at one another and Evie slips, ending up on her cute little ass. Of course I take advantage, and relentlessly pelt her with the colored missiles. "Have you learned yet? Huh, have you? Let me hear it, Evangeline!"

"Grab life by the balls," she screams, laughing so hard she's crying and hiccupping at the same time. It takes her two tries to stand. When she does, she covers her mouth with one hand, and with the other points behind me. I turn and do my best to quit laughing, but I can't seem to stop.

The clerk with the glasses stands slack jawed holding our food. Beside her is the manager, an older man who looks anything but amused. More like scandalized.

Straightening my collar and cross, I work my way through the balls and assist Evie out of the pit. I smile and take our food, handing Evie one of the coffees. With my right hand I bless them. As we leave, I holler, "*He will yet fill your mouth with laughter, and your lips with shouting.* Job chapter eight, verse twenty-one."

Snickering like two naughty children we grab Goner and head toward the car.

We're a few minutes from her mother's and Evie silently stares out the window. The only noise in the car comes from the heavy breathing of the clueless dog in the backseat. I try once again to break through her stony stillness. I might as well be using a spoon to chip through the Rock of Gibraltar.

"Wanna talk about anything?" I ask breaking the tomblike silence in the car.

"No." She turns her face so I can't see it. I reach out and take her hand, giving it a squeeze.

"I wish things could be different—"

She shakes her head and chokes, "Please don't say anything."

Her words spear my heart. I've made a horrific mess of all of this. It was never my intent to cause her pain. The only thing that prevents me from screaming with frustrated anger is the knowledge she won't remember what a douchebag I've been, and she's promised to live life to the fullest.

But I'll remember. It will be my cross to bear.

I pull into the driveway of a small house where a car is parked with a Florida license plate. We're here. We sit, staring at the house, not making a motion to get out of the car.

Evangeline looks down at her hands clasped together in her lap. "T-Thank you—"

"Don't thank me. I've fucked this up so bad, and I'm so sorry..."

She looks at me, eyes bright with unshed tears.

"No, don't be sorry," she whispers.

Life here is so much harder than I ever realized, and this hurts like hell.

But then she smiles at me and I understand why humans allow themselves to fall in love. It's worth the pain. I'd do it all over again, *for her.*

"You love me and I'm not crazy," she huffs out in a voice laced with repressed sobs. "I can thank you for that."

I shake my head, but she unbuckles her seatbelt and leans in to me. "You saved me, Remi. I'm no longer afraid of living. As much as I'm going to miss you..." She smiles and swallows. "I'll be okay. I'm going to start over and move forward. But oh, how I wish you could stay here with me. These have been the most beautiful days of my life."

"Good things are in store for you. Trust me, okay?" My voice sounds husky because I'm choking back my own tears. I only hope I can talk Him into letting me see her in the future. "And no more thoughts of hurting yourself. Promise me."

She nods. I raise an eyebrow. "Say it."

"I promise not to hurt myself."

"And?"

She attempts a smile, although truthfully it looks more like a grimace. "And I'll grab life by the balls."

"That's my girl." I open the door, yank her bag out of the trunk, and walk her and Goner to the front door.

She gazes at me and her eyes search my face. Her fingers follow, and I turn my face into her hands and kiss her palm. I know she's memorizing every detail of my face, because I'm doing the same damn thing. I cup her cheeks in my hands and her hands rest on my forearms. "I love you Evangeline Lourdes Salvatore. *Forever.*"

"And ever," she finishes for me. "Please…I don't want to say good-bye." She's gripping my arms so hard I know I'll have her fingernail imprints embedded in my skin for a while. It's fine. I want her to mark me as hers.

"This isn't good-bye. Trust me, sweetness."

"Don't you want to come in and meet my mom? She'll be all giddy over you in your priest get-up." Her eyes look desperate, her grip tightens to the point I wince from the pain, much like I did this morning when those nails raked my back and tugged at my feathers.

"I love you." My lips linger on her petal soft lips, savoring them one last time.

"But I told Mama a friend was driving me, she'll be expecting to meet you." She's not letting go and my heart splinters into a million pieces. "At least try some of her cooking, you must be hungry. Her lasagna is to die for," she squeaks.

"I have to go. I love you, Crazy Girl." My voice chokes and I can't look at her any longer, her pain is unbearable.

"I love you, too," she whispers, wrapping her arms around my neck. I hold her close, resting my cheek on top of her head as she sobs into my chest.

Goner rises on his back legs and I affectionately pat the dog on the head. He settles with a contented whimper at her feet. She's nuzzling my neck and much as I hate it, I know it's time to leave.

"Trust me," I whisper. She nods and closes her eyes. As I kiss her forehead, what feels like a powerful jolt of electricity passes between us as He works through me like a conduit to wipe her memory of me. I'm drained like a dead battery when I manage to get back in the car. My cell phone beeps with an incoming text. I read:

Luke 15:11-32. Come home, son.

The story of the prodigal son.

I dread going home, but at least I know I'm forgiven. I start the engine and pull away. In the rearview mirror I see Evie open her eyes, looking lost, but at peace.

I stare at the leash in my hand and the mutt at my feet, confused. My mother's car is in the driveway. She's sick, and somehow I'm here… Dammit, I'm having another of those scary black out spells.

Fake it till you make it.

I ring the doorbell and wait, shaking my leg in nervous anticipation. The silly dog looks up at me with love in his eyes, and I wonder why he's with me and where he came from. I stoop to straighten his collar and he licks my face. Surely if this mutt loves me, I'm not so bad. Dogs know. My heavy heart lightens a bit, and I stand as the door opens.

"Evie," my mom cries out with a smile. I find myself enveloped in her arms and my neck feels damp from her tears. I kiss her cheek and look at her. Worry lines crease her face and I realize with shame that most of them are probably my fault. My mother looks down at the dog and pats his head and then looks behind me. "Is your friend here?"

"My friend?" I look around. Can't she see it's just me? Usually I'm the one seeing people that don't exist.

"The friend who brought you here." Mama's eyes cloud with worry as she searches my face.

What friend? *Fake it till you make it…*

I force a sunny smile. "Nope, they had to leave and just dropped me off." I used the generic *they* because I have no idea how I got here. I'm struggling not to panic over this latest loss of time and awareness. I know Mama is sick and has to have a heart test, but for the life of me, I can't remember anything else. I shove the rising panic down; I have to be strong for my mom. She needs me.

"How are you feeling, Mama?"

"Fine, fine…" She pauses with tears in her eyes. "Better than fine now that you're here." Wiping at her eyes, she turns and extends an arm into her cozy living room. "Well, come in, dear. I've made your favorite meal for supper. Lasagna. What's your little dog's name?"

I look down at the dog, clueless. "I, uh, don't know. I never got around to naming him." I tug on the leash to get him to follow me in the house, but he just sits there staring down the road.

Mama chuckles. "Looks like he needs remedial dog school."

Remedial…the word has a familiarity to it that I can't place. The mutt's ears perk up and he wags his tail. He lumbers to his feet and we follow Mama down the hall to my room. It's warm and inviting. She's even placed a picture of me with Daddy on the bedside table. Over my bed hangs my favorite print from when I was a child. Two children crossing a bridge with an angel behind them. The white wings and female angel somehow don't look right.

"I'm not sure how long you plan to stay." Mama pauses and runs a hand over a non-existent wrinkle in the duvet. "But this is your room, for however long you want to be here."

I hear the longing in her voice. I'm puzzled and shake my head a fraction, taken aback. I thought she'd left Florida to get away from me.

Taking my hand in hers, her face softens. "When I was all alone and afraid I was dying in the ER, all I wanted was to have you there. I needed you, and I realized I let you down when you needed me most. I'm sorry, honey. I hope we can start fresh. All I've ever wanted was for you to be happy."

I place my other hand over hers. "It's okay. I *am* happy, Mama." And I mean it. I feel at peace and as if a burden has been lifted off my shoulders just being here with her. "I know I've had some *issues*, but I'm better. Let's just take this a day at a time, okay? I want to see you get well, first."

She's chewing her lower lip, and I know her concern. I need to set her mind at ease. "I'm off all my medications now, and I'm better. But, if I stay for any length of time, I promise to check in with a therapist if it makes you feel better. I'm sorry for what I've put you through." I suck in a deep breath. I'm unwilling to commit to any long-term plans with our history, but I'm willing to stay at least for a while and try to repair our shaky relationship. She—and apparently, this dog—are all I that I have.

"It's okay. I love you. This is a fresh start, for both of us." Mama smiles and kisses my cheek and I hug her like I haven't in a long time. "Maybe we can manage to get along for a few days without killing one another." Her tone is light and teasing and I grin back at her.

Duchess, our cat, walks by the door hissing at the dog, and we both laugh when the mutt whimpers and hides behind my legs.

I pat him on his head. "You need to get along with Duchess; she rules the house. If you get on her bad side, you'll be a goner." He cocks his head and looks at me with his tongue hanging out of his mouth as if he understands what I've just said. I need to come up with a name for him.

Mama flutters around the room, helping me unpack my things. I don't have much, a few clothes, the locket from Jack, and a ring Daddy gave Mama. My hand brushes something underneath my jeans. Puzzled, I pull out a snow globe. I've always loved snow globes, but I don't remember having one like this. I shake it, and as snow swirls around a black feather, a feeling of joy surrounds me.

"Mama? Does it ever snow here?"

Epilogue

Fifty years later

Cancer has taken its toll on my body making each step painful as I shuffle at a snail's pace. The walker doesn't help, but I use it to make Becky happy. Honestly, it's too heavy to push with my fading strength.

The ravages of my disease are horrendous and I hate looking at myself in the mirror. Brushing a wispy strand of hair out of my face I watch it float to the sink. I should have let Becky shave it when she volunteered. I wash my face, trying not to fret over the dark smudges under my eyes or the hollows in my cheeks. The visible blue veins and wrinkles mark my parchment-thin skin, a roadmap of my life. I pause to catch my breath before brushing my teeth. At least I still have them. Moving at the speed of a turtle, I make my way to bed. I'm tired of the pain of living and long for the sweet relief death will bring.

As part of my nightly ritual, I pick up the old snow globe on my nightstand. A lot of the water has evaporated and the black feather looks worse for wear, but I still love it. I attempt to shake it, but I'm weaker than I realize. It slips and shatters on the floor. The tears that I haven't shed throughout my fight with cancer now fall freely. Too weak to clean up the mess, I manage to crawl in bed and sob into my old, scraggly angel-bear.

It seems ridiculous to cry over an old snow globe. I don't remember where I got it, or who gave it to me, but it has always provided me with a sense of serenity, much like my beloved, stuffed angel-bear. I hold her tight, lamenting the fact she's now wingless from age. Good grief, I've become a crazy old lady.

I look with disgust at the pills Becky has left by my bedside with a glass of water. She's been good to me, taking me to my doctor appointments and to the chemo treatments that haven't been successful this time.

I'm Becky's godmother and I've spoiled her shamelessly throughout the years. My Becky's a smart girl and a hospice nurse. I never dreamed when attending her graduation from nursing school she'd be taking care of *me*.

I close my eyes and smile as my mind wanders back in time. Getting old and dying makes one reminisce, and for the most part, I have happy memories. After I moved here to be with my mother, I loved doing things that some considered risky. I called it taking life by the balls and living. Sky diving, parasailing, cliff diving. Anything that put me in the air made me feel alive and free.

I wasn't always carefree, having made plenty of mistakes. When I was younger, people thought I was crazy. As I got older, I didn't care what people thought. I did see a therapist and worked out some of my co-dependency and guilt issues. My struggle with depression was my greatest challenge, but I've managed to stay off medications. After those bumpy teenage years and disastrous love affair with Jack, I enjoyed a good life. By traveling all over the world, I've seen things some have only dreamed about. I learned to cook and took photography classes. I've had lovers, but not the meaningless relationships of my youth. I sigh. My memories are all I have left. Who'd want a bald, dying old woman who's tired and weak?

Cancer spares no one. Twenty years ago I fought it with a double mastectomy, this time I haven't been so lucky. My darling Becky prays for me to hang on, but it's for her own sake. She'll be fine. She has a lovely husband and three children who will help her through my passing, just as they did when her mother died.

I yawn and close my eyes. As I slip toward sleep, I see the lights of a carnival, hear the sounds of barkers and with wonder watch the beauty of a Ferris wheel…

Warm lips press and tease mine. The constant pain that has been my companion for months seems lighter. I blink and open my eyes.

"Hey, Crazy Girl." Sparkling green eyes crease and his smile lights up the room. He brushes the back of his fingers over my cheek.

"You're here." Memories cascade over me and I can't control the flood of emotions as every minute with Remi flips through my mind like a film in fast motion. He looks the same, young and handsome as sin. Life is so unfair.

"Ah, sweetness, don't cry," he whispers, kissing my tears away. "I told you to trust me." He nuzzles my neck and I'm mortified. I don't want him to see me like this—old, my body ravaged by illness and pain.

"Don't look at me," I croak, attempting to turn away. Pain makes me moan and I hide my face in the ragged stuffed animal he won for me all those years ago.

The bed dips behind me and he spoons my butt. "Why wouldn't I look at my beautiful girl?" He kisses the back of my neck.

I turn and glare at him. "I may wear glasses, but I'm not blind. I know what I look like. I'm seventy-one, I weigh ninety pounds, and I have no hair. *How dare you make fun of me? You're still the worst angel in the history of angels, asshole.*"

He chuckles. "Yeah, there are several back home that agree with you. How dare *you* doubt *me?* I love you." He hovers over me, careful not to crush me, and strokes my cheek. "You're as beautiful as you were when I met you." As if to prove it, he kisses me. I have difficulty catching my breath, and it isn't from pain this time. His kiss still leaves me breathless and curls my toes. I pull away and roll to my side, my back to him. I see the broken snow globe on the floor and another tear slips down my face.

"Please don't cry, Crazy Girl."

"It was you."

"What did I do this time?" He pinches my bottom and I weakly swat his hand away and turn back to face him.

"Is this appropriate behavior for an angel and an old, sick lady?"

"Lady?" He waggles his eyebrows and I roll my eyes. He snickers and winks at me. "When have I ever been appropriate?"

True. "You bought me the snow globe and the bear." I swat his hand away again as he tries to pull me into his arms. "You're incorrigible. Why are you here?"

"It's my weekend off. I just wanted to stop by and let you know I'd see you soon."

I frown. "Is this your not-so-tactful way of saying I'm dying?"

He rolls his eyes. It really is like fifty years ago. "Duh." He frowns at the pills on my bedside. "But remember your promise to me."

I smile despite the effort it's taking to catch my breath. "I won't kill myself."

"Promise?"

"Cross my heart, and hope to die." Sharing the same warped sense of humor, we both smile and I close my eyes. "I'm really tired, Remi."

"I know, sweetness. Go to sleep." He kisses my eyelids, enfolds me in his warm wings, and the pain disappears.

I'm kicked back in my chair, bored out of my mind. Peter's on break and I'm stuck manning the front gate, *again*. Looking around, I don't see anyone that would narc on me if I catch a few z's before the freaking newbie class starts. Propping my legs on the desk, the chair rocks back on two legs. I close my eyes and dream of Ferris wheels, cotton candy, and sweet kisses.

Something wet tickles my neck and I realize I've been caught napping on the job. I struggle to sit up and the chair tips over leaving me flat on my back, my legs up in the air in an undignified position. I shove at the annoying wet nose that's still nuzzling me.

"Does Saint Francis know how you treat poor defenseless animals?"

Twisting around, I grin and stare up into the most beautiful chocolate brown eyes I've ever seen. Evangeline's twisting a long lock of her dark hair around a finger and flipping her feathers flirtatiously. They're red with black tips, and sexy as heck. I'm as smitten as I was when I first saw her naked in her bathtub. I pat Goner on the head. "Where did you find this mangy old dog?"

"He was waiting on me when I got here. Everyone was at my Welcome Party, except *you*. What kind of guardian angel are you?" She starts to tick them off on her fingers. "Let's see, Mama, Daddy, my friend Karen, Jack, and Kayla. Oh, and their cute baby, plus Rafe, Madge, Franco, and the old lady from the bathroom and her sister.

I even met Peter and the Boss. I was a little miffed Jack and Kayla were there, which earned me my first learning lesson on *forgiveness*." She rolls her eyes and wrinkles her nose. "So why weren't you there?"

"I had to work," I protest. "I wanted to be there, but..." Struggling to my feet, I place the chair back upright and face her.

She raises one skeptical brow. "But?" Her eyes narrow and that delectable bottom lip pokes out, temptingly. Her bare foot taps with impatience, as she waits on an explanation.

I shrug and rub the back of my neck as I look at her cute toenails, painted the colors of her wings. "I uh, kinda got in trouble on my last weekend off on earth. I had a date—"

Oomph. Her fist connects with my stomach, and I double over. She still packs a mean punch. "Ouch, what was that for?"

"What was her name?" Flames leap in her blazing eyes, and it's a total turn on.

"You, Crazy Girl. I came to see you. You'd just broken the snow globe I gave you."

Her eyes grow wide and the next thing I know I'm stumbling backward with a hundred and twenty-five pounds of feisty, sexy angel in my arms.

It's a struggle to keep my balance and I can't help but grin as she kisses my face all over. "I love you, I love you, I love you, you horrible angel, you." Her red, black-tipped wings flap like a squawking chicken, although I refrain from mentioning the comparison out loud. No need to get her more riled. She'll learn to control the wings in the newcomers' class.

Capturing her lips with mine, I give her a sound kiss and place her back on her feet. "I love you, too. Now, let's get the official business out of the way."

Out of the desk, I pull out a scroll and dip the feather pen in the ink pot, putting on my official Heaven Greeter persona. "Name?"

"A feather pen?"

I shrug. "Newcomers expect it. Along with the annoying harp music that plays *ad nauseum*." I roll my eyes.

She smirks. "Evangeline Lourdes Salvatore. If you were in charge, Led Zeppelin or Guns N' Roses would be playing."

"You got that right." With a flourish, I write her name on the scroll. This is just for show. The Boss has everything computerized.

"Do I get a halo and a harp?"

"Do you want them?"

"Not really. I never did like hats and have no musical talent whatsoever." She dances around making her wings flap. "But these are the shit."

"Shh," I caution, looking around nervously for the Boss, or worse, that narc Rafe. She's new so she won't be in too much trouble with her profanity slip, but still...

Blushing, she presses her sweet lips together, but her eyes sparkle with merriment. Running a hand through her feathers, she gives me a sexy look over her shoulder. "You like?"

"Very much." The red and black corset dress is a little scandalous for up here, but leave it to Evie to push the boundaries. She's my kind of angel.

"You lied to me, by the way."

I wince. "I'm sorry..."

"Peter says there is too a cloud made of cotton candy." She cocks her head to the side.

"There is?"

"Yup. He said if you ever got off your lazy ass you might find it."

I grin. "Maybe so."

"So now what?"

Peter floats toward us, returning from his break. With a nod of my head, I motion that I'm out of there. Surprisingly, he smiles and waves me to go on.

"Now I welcome you properly and then we'll go look for that cotton candy cloud." I take her hand and lead her to a place where we can be alone to fly.

And I'm not talking about using our wings...

*Personal note
from the author*

This book is a work of fiction. Unfortunately, suicide is all too real. If you or someone you love is struggling with suicidal thoughts, there is help. Please contact The National Suicide Prevention Lifeline:

1-800-273-TALK (8255).
www.suicidepreventionlifeline.org

With help, comes hope.
Nancee Cain

Acknowledgments

Devoted Hubby, I knew the night I met you I wanted to marry you, and yes, it was love at first sight. You will always be my hero and are my happily ever after. Darling Daughter, you are my pride and joy and being your mom is my favorite job of all time. Thank you for putting up with a distracted harried writer for the past year.

I couldn't have done this without the best critique partners in the world, Jill Odom and Carla Swafford. Jill, you taught me how to take my ideas and formulate a story. Both of you have picked me up when I'm down and cheered when I'm up. Your encouragement and sometimes funny, always relevant, red tracker comments keep me grounded.

Thank you to Southern Magic, my RWA group. These talented women shared their vast knowledge and skills to help me grow as a writer. Killarney Sheffield, you patiently went through my first horrific manuscript without laughing too much, and for that I thank you. Jovana Rodolakis, my cohort in NaNoWrimo, Vickie W., and Carrie M. you are the best beta readers, ever. Katherine P., my niece and grammar guru, I no longer fear your red pen and funny squiggle marks. M.V. Freeman, you bore the brunt of my late night rants and tears. I owe you at least a cup of coffee, or a drink. Thanks to Jean T., who named my street team, and the Alabama Maniacs who share my warped sense of humor and love of books. Christine Glover, thank you for generously sharing your knowledge on navigating the scary waters of social media.

Jennifer Haren, Omnific publicist and blogger with The Book Avenue Review, you have the patience of Job. I am forever indebted to you for your help. If I were a Peanuts character, I'd be Linus and you'd be my security blanket. I know I'm an OCD, frantic, anal-retentive writer, but you always calm me down and make everything right. Kelley Jefferson with Smut Book Junkie Book Reviews, your friendship and guidance in this strange, scary world of promotion has been invaluable and your ideas, brilliant. You embody the saying book friends are best friends.

I will always be indebted to Elizabeth Harper and Lisa O'Hara for listening to my first pitch, making me feel comfortable doing so, and then giving me a chance to tell my story. Milli Davis, you're an incredible editor who took a story I love and pushed me to make it even better. Your guidance has been invaluable and taught me a lot about who I am as an author. Micha Stone and Amy Brokaw, my cover is beautiful, thank you for listening to me. It's perfect. Coreen Montagna, you made the interior as pretty as the cover. Last, but not least, Debra Anastasia, through whom I found Omnific Publishing. Your friendship, patience and support have meant the world to me. We share a love of foul-mouthed angels, edgy books and less than perfect heroes. Thank you for not calling the NOLA police on me for stalking you at RT 2014.

About the Author

During the day, Nancee works as a nurse in the field of addiction to support her coffee and reading habit. Nights are spent writing paranormal and contemporary romances with a serrated edge. Authors are her rock stars, and she's been known to stalk a few for an autograph, but not in a scary, Stephen King way. Her husband swears her To-Be-Read list on her e-reader qualifies her as a certifiable book hoarder. Always looking to try something new, she dreams of being an extra in a Bollywood film, or a tattoo artist. (Her lack of rhythm and artistic ability may put a damper on both of these dreams.)

Website: www.nanceecain.com
Blog: nanceecain.wordpress.com
Goodreads: www.goodreads.com/Nancee_Cain
Newsletter: eepurl.com/bhFMtX
Facebook: www.facebook.com/nancee.cain
Twitter: twitter.com/Nancee_Cain
Pinterest: www.pinterest.com/nanceecain

New Adult Romance

Three Daves by Nicki Elson
Streamline by Jennifer Lane
The Shades series: *Shades of Atlantis* & *Shades of Avalon* by Carol Oates
The Heart series: *Beside Your Heart, Disclosure of the Heart* & *Forever Your Heart*
by Mary Whitney
Romancing the Bookworm by Kate Evangelista
Flirting with Chaos by Kenya Wright
The Vice, Virtue & Video series: *Revealed, Captured, Desired* & *Devoted*
by Bianca Giovanni
Granton University series: *Loving Lies* by Linda Kage
Missing Pieces by Meredith Tate

Paranormal & Fantasy Romance

The Light series: *Seers of Light, Whisper of Light* & *Circle of Light* by Jennifer DeLucy
The Hanaford Park series: *Eve of Samhain* & *Pleasures Untold* by Lisa Sanchez
Immortal Awakening by KC Randall
The Seraphim series: *Crushed Seraphim* & *Bittersweet Seraphim* by Debra Anastasia
The Guardian's Wild Child by Feather Stone
Grave Refrain by Sarah M. Glover
The Divinity series: *Divinity* & *Entity* by Patricia Leever
The Blood Vine series: *Blood Vine, Blood Entangled* & *Blood Reunited* by Amber Belldene
Divine Temptation by Nicki Elson
The Dead Rapture series: *Love in the Time of the Dead, Love at the End of Days* &
Love Starts with Z by Tera Shanley
The Hidden Races series: *Incandescent* & *Illumination* by M.V. Freeman
Something Wicked by Carol Oates
Chronicles of Midvalen: *Command the Tides* (book 1) by Wren Handman
Saving Evangeline by Nancee Cain

Romantic Suspense

Whirlwind by Robin DeJarnett
The CONduct series: *With Good Behavior, Bad Behavior* & *On Best Behavior*
by Jennifer Lane
Indivisible by Jessica McQuinn
Between the Lies by Alison Oburia
Blind Man's Bargain by Tracy Winegar

Historical Romance

Cat O' Nine Tails by Patricia Leever
Burning Embers by Hannah Fielding
Seven for a Secret by Rumer Haven
The Counterfeit by Tracy Winegar

←———→Erotic Romance←———→

The Keyhole series: *Becoming sage* (book 1) by Kasi Alexander
The Keyhole series: *Saving sunni* (book 2) by Kasi & Reggie Alexander
The Winemaker's Dinner: *Appetizers & Entrée* by Dr. Ivan Rusilko & Everly Drummond
The Winemaker's Dinner: *Dessert* by Dr. Ivan Rusilko
Client Nº 5 by Joy Fulcher
The Enclave series: *Closer and Closer* (book 1) by Jenna Barton
The Adventures of Clarissa Hardy by Chloe Gillis

←———→Anthologies←———→

A Valentine Anthology including short stories by
Alice Clayton ("With a Double Oven"),
Jennifer DeLucy ("Magnus of Pfelt, Conquering Viking Lord"),
Nicki Elson ("I Don't Do Valentine's Day"),
Jessica McQuinn ("Better Than One Dead Rose and a Monkey Card"),
Victoria Michaels ("Home to Jackson"), and
Alison Oburia ("The Bridge")

Taking Liberties including an introduction by Tiffany Reisz and short stories by
Mina Vaughn ("John Hancock-Blocked"),
Linda Cunningham ("A Boston Marriage"),
Joy Fulcher ("Tea for Two"),
KC Holly ("The British Are Coming!"),
Kimberly Jensen & Scott Stark ("E. Pluribus Threesome"), and
Vivian Rider ("M'Lady's Secret Service")

←———→Sets←———→

The Heart Series Box Set (*Beside Your Heart, Disclosure of the Heart &
Forever Your Heart*) by Mary Whitney
The CONduct Series Box Set (*With Good Behavior, Bad Behavior &
On Best Behavior*) by Jennifer Lane
The Light Series Box Set (*Seers of Light, Whisper of Light, Circle of Light &
Glimpse of Light*) by Jennifer DeLucy
The Blood Vine Series Box Set (*Blood Vine, Blood Entangled, Blood Reunited &
Blood Eternal*) by Amber Belldene

←———→Singles, Novellas & Special Editions←———→

It's Only Kinky the First Time (A Keyhole series single) by Kasi Alexander
Learning the Ropes (A Keyhole series single) by Kasi & Reggie Alexander
The Winemaker's Dinner: RSVP by Dr. Ivan Rusilko
The Winemaker's Dinner: No Reservations by Everly Drummond

Big Guns by Jessica McQuinn
Concessions by Robin DeJarnett
Starstruck by Lisa Sanchez
New Flame by BJ Thornton
Shackled by Debra Anastasia
Swim Recruit by Jennifer Lane
Sway by Nicki Elson
Full Speed Ahead by Susan Kaye Quinn
The Second Sunrise by Hannah Downing
The Summer Prince by Carol Oates
Whatever it Takes by Sarah M. Glover
Clarity (A *Divinity* prequel single) by Patricia Leever
A Christmas Wish (A *Cocktails & Dreams* single) by Autumn Markus
Late Night with Andres by Debra Anastasia
Poughkeepsie (enhanced iPad app collector's edition) by Debra Anastasia
Poughkeepsie (audio book edition) by Debra Anastasia
Blood Eternal (A Blood Vine series single, epilogue to series) by Amber Belldene
Carnaval de Amor (*The Winemaker's Dinner*, Spanish edition)
by Dr. Ivan Rusilko & Everly Drummond

coming soon from
OMNIFIC PUBLISHING

The Ground Rules by Roya Carmen
Twice Upon a Kiss by Jane Susann McCarter
The Keyhole series: *Keyhole Kinklets* (short story anthology)
by Kasi & Reggie Alexander
A Nightingale in Winter by Margart Johnson
True Gold by Kathryn Barrett
Finding Parker by Scott Hildreth
Guardian of the Stone by Amity Grays
The Revenger by Debra Anastasia
Subject X by Emma G. Hunter

CPSIA information can be obtained at www.ICGtesting.com
Printed in the USA
LVOW11s0538100815

449417LV00001B/16/P